"Were yo...
he asked.

She flashed him one of her rare smiles. "Terrified, especially when you left me. I never knew I had so much adrenaline in my body."

...ed her smile and stood. "I'll just get out of here ...n sleep off some of that adrenaline."

She walked with him to the door.

...d to tell her good-night and she stood too close to ...r heady scent surrounded him as he remembered ...her in his arms when they'd danced.

...'t sure if he spoke her name or not, but suddenly ...in his arms and his mouth was on hers. He hadn't ...ermission. He hadn't even consciously made the ...n to kiss her. It had just happened.

...ace in the back of his mind he knew it was a ...thought, and with regret he halted the kiss and ...back from her.

..." he said. "Just chalk it up to lingering adrenaline." ...giving her an opportunity to reply he hurried ...his Jeep.

***

Be sure to check out the next books in this exciting miniseries:
Cowboys of Holiday Ranch—
here sun, earth and hard work turn men into rugged cowboys...and irresistible heroes!

COWBOY OF INTEREST

BY
CARLA CASSIDY

Published in Great Britain 2015
by Mills & Boon, an imprint of Harlequin (UK) Limited,
Eton House, 18-24 Paradise Road, Richmond, Surrey, TW9 1SR

© 2015 Carla Bracale

ISBN: 978-0-263-91542-6

18-0615

Harlequin (UK) Limited's policy is to use papers that are natural, renewable and recyclable products and made from wood grown in sustainable forests. The logging and manufacturing processes conform to the legal environmental regulations of the country of origin.

Printed and bound in Spain
by CPI, Barcelona

Carla Cassidy is a *New York Times* bestselling author who has written more than one hundred books for Mills & Boon. Carla believes the only thing better than curling up with a good book to read is sitting down at the computer with a good story to write. She's looking forward to writing many more books and bringing hours of pleasure to readers.

Chapter 1

Nick Coleman needed to get drunk. Not buzzed, not loopy, but brain-dead, blackout drunk. It was the only respite he might find from the vision burned into his head of seeing Wendy Bailey's dead body stuffed under the floorboards of an old shed on the ranch where Nick worked.

He'd been responsible in his plan to drink himself into oblivion. He'd contacted his good friend Chad Bene from a neighboring ranch to pick him up, bring him here to the Watering Hole and then make sure Nick got back to his bunkhouse on the Holiday Ranch safe and sound.

Chad nursed a soda while Nick motioned to the waitress for a second beer. "You know, getting stupid drunk isn't going to change things, except that tomorrow you're going to wake up and feel as though you've wrestled with the biggest, meanest bull in the entire county," Chad observed.

"But at least maybe tonight I'll sleep without nightmares," Nick replied. It had been three days since Wendy's body had been found, along with six older skeletal remains. It had been three long nights of sleep haunted by the visions of the vivacious black-haired, blue-eyed twenty-three-year-old who had blown into town two months before and instantly attached herself to Nick like an affectionate little sister.

And now she was gone…dead. According to the coroner, she had been stabbed twice in the chest. She had been murdered. If that wasn't horrific enough, Nick knew he was the prime suspect in her murder.

Janis Little, the waitress serving their small two-top table, brought Nick a fresh cold bottle of beer and gave him a quick, sympathetic pat on his shoulder before going back behind the bar to serve other awaiting customers.

At least Janis apparently didn't see him as a murderer, he thought, but that didn't take away any of the heartache and horror he'd lived with for the past couple of days. He couldn't believe that Wendy was dead. She'd had a light too bright to be snuffed out. He couldn't believe that anyone would have wanted to take her life.

"Dillon has the whole ranch basically shut down as a crime scene area," Nick said. He opened the beer, took a deep swallow and then continued. "He's actively working Wendy's case but has called in a forensic anthropologist from Oklahoma City to help with the investigation into the seven skeletal remains. She's supposed to arrive sometime next week."

Chad shook his head. "I still can't believe all those bodies were hidden under the shed. If they're just skeletons, then their murders had to have happened some time ago. I wonder if Cass knew anything about them."

"We'll never know, since Cass is dead." Nick took another drink, and for a few minutes the only sound was the raucous noise of the popular bar on a Friday night.

Thinking about Wendy was almost as painful as thinking about Cass Holiday. Nick had been a sixteen-year-old runaway when he'd been brought by a social worker to Cass Holiday's sprawling ranch to work.

Over the past fourteen years, Cass had been his surrogate mother, his mentor and the best thing that had ever happened to him. Then, a little over two months ago, she'd been killed in a tornado that had ravaged the Oklahoma countryside.

She'd been hit in the head by a tree branch. Her body had been found between her big ranch house and the bunkhouse where her cowboys lived. They all believed she'd been on her way to warn them about the approaching vicious weather when she'd been struck down.

For the dozen cowboys Cass had nurtured from troubled teens to good, responsible ranch hands and upstanding, confident men, nothing had been the same after she was gone.

"Why don't we go shoot a game of pool?" Chad suggested and gestured toward the back room, where three pool tables were located. Two were in use, but one was vacant.

"You're not going to distract me from my mission of drunkenness," Nick replied wryly. "Besides, shooting pool has never been my thing."

"It's a stupid mission, Nick," Chad replied. "If you want a mission, then you should be spending your time helping to find out who killed Wendy."

Nick frowned. "I'm not on the police force. I'm a person of interest in the case."

"There's no way I think that Dillon really believes you had anything to do with Wendy's murder," Chad protested. "He hasn't even brought you in for questioning yet."

"*Yet* being the key word in that sentence. He will. I'm sure I'm at the top of his list. The problem is Wendy and I spent a lot of time together, and as far as anyone can tell, I was probably the last person who saw her alive."

Nick took another drink of his beer and wished he'd never met Wendy Bailey. If he hadn't have met her then he wouldn't be hurting over her loss right now.

"She was missing for almost a month," Chad continued. "From what I've heard, they haven't even been able to pinpoint the exact time of death. Everyone thought she'd just left town. Her motel room was empty and her car was gone."

"I thought she'd left town," Nick agreed. "I was surprised and a little hurt that she hadn't told me goodbye, but she was an impulsive free spirit who I figured just heard the call of a new adventure and went for it. When they found her she was wearing her café work T-shirt, so she was probably killed on Friday night after her shift and after she visited me at the ranch."

"Obviously somebody went to a lot of trouble to make us all believe she'd just moved on. Her car and personal items have never been found." Chad frowned as Nick downed the last of his second beer and motioned to Janis for another.

"Stop giving me dirty looks," Nick said. "I'm only just now starting to get a little bit of a buzz."

"You've always been a lightweight drinker, and the way you're slamming back the beers, I figure within a half an hour or so there will be at least three of us pulling you out from under the table and carrying you to my truck. And just so we're clear, if you throw up in my truck, I'm beating the hell out of you tomorrow when you get sober."

Nick was surprised by the small burst of laughter that escaped his lips. "You and what army?" he replied. Chad was half a foot shorter than Nick's six-two and weighed at least twenty-five pounds less.

Janis arrived with the third beer and the two men once again fell silent. Nick brooded, drank and listened to the ancient jukebox where somebody had paid a quarter to hear an old sad George Jones song.

Nick had no idea why Wendy Bailey had glommed on to him in the initial days of her arrival in Bitterroot. They'd met at the café, where she'd gotten a job as a waitress, and before Nick knew it, they were sharing a pizza or going to a movie together or just sitting under the stars and talking.

Nick had never had siblings and found his role of surrogate big brother to her a surprisingly pleasing one. He'd known if she'd grown more comfortable with some of the younger crowd in town she would have drifted away from him, and that would have been okay, but she'd never gotten the chance.

In the first week of Wendy's disappearance, Daisy, the owner of the café, had printed up posters indicating that Wendy was missing. She was adamant that Wendy wouldn't have just left town without telling Daisy she was going. Even after chief of police Dillon Bowie had checked out Wendy's motel room and found it empty, Daisy had been hard-pressed to believe that the waitress had just up and left town with no notice to anyone.

Daisy had been proved right. Wendy hadn't left town. She'd been murdered. Like Cass's death, Wendy's murder was a tragedy on a hundred different levels, and for Nick it was a personal loss in a stream of losses that had begun in his dysfunctional youth.

"So what did you tell Penny you were doing tonight?" he asked Chad in an effort to stop his mood from plunging to new depths, if that were even possible.

"I told her the truth, that a friend needed me tonight and I'd talk to her sometime tomorrow."

"She's a keeper. You going to marry her?"

Chad grinned. "If she'll have me. I've already bought an engagement ring, but I haven't given it to her yet. I've got to figure out some amazing way to officially propose. Penny won't settle for anything except amazing."

"Then, why is she with you?" Nick replied with a forced lightness.

"Ha-ha," Chad replied. His gaze went over Nick's shoulder at the same time an unfamiliar female voice spoke Nick's name.

"Yes, I'm Nick Coleman," Nick replied.

He half rose from his chair and turned to see a petite woman with long chestnut-colored hair and blue-green eyes.

Before he could say another word, her arm reared back and her small fist connected with his left eye, a perfect center smash that drove him back into his chair.

"What the hel—" he sputtered.

She swung at him again, her eyes swimming with tears as her arms windmilled in an attempt to connect with him.

He jumped up out of his chair, vaguely aware that everyone in the crowded tavern had frozen, their attention on Nick and his pint-size attacker.

Nick had never seen the woman before. He had no idea what her problem was, but there was no way he intended to just stand there and get pummeled in public. Especially by a woman. He already felt the pressure of his eye swelling from the sucker punch she'd managed to land.

He grabbed her and trapped her arms at her sides, but she immediately started to use her feet as weapons. She kicked and thrust her knee upward in an attempt to make dangerous bodily contact with him.

Nick would never hit a woman, but he definitely needed to take control of the situation. He heard the low rumble of male laughter coming from the crowd, laughter that assured Nick he'd be fodder for the gossip mill the next day.

With Wendy's murder, there was already enough gossip swirling around town with his name all over it. Nick drew a deep breath, dodged another knee to his groin, then finally managed to pick her up and throw her over his shoulder like a sack of squirming potatoes.

She smelled like lilacs and vanilla, he thought, even as she kicked and screamed and beat her fists on his back. He carried her through the bar and out the front door. He put her down on the sidewalk and then stepped back a safe distance from her.

"Lady, what in the hell is your problem?" he demanded.

For a long moment, she looked stunned, and tears streamed down her face. "It was you," she finally said. "It was you who murdered my sister."

It was only then that Nick realized the small firecracker standing before him, the pretty woman who had hit him hard enough to swell his eye almost shut, was Adrienne Bailey, Wendy's older sister.

Adrienne stared up at the tall cowboy with his darkening eye and was appalled by her own actions. She'd never hit another person in her entire life. She'd just wanted to get a look at the man she believed had killed her sister, but the moment he'd turned to face her she'd completely lost her mind.

Anger and grief had taken control of her senses,

and she'd reacted with raw, unbridled emotion, something she'd never done before in all of her thirty years.

Although still driven by rage and sorrow, a deep embarrassment now swept over her. She backed away from him and quickly swiped the tears from her eyes.

"I didn't mean to… I'm sorry…" Those were the only words she got out before she turned and ran down the sidewalk.

"Adrienne, wait!" he called after her. "I didn't kill Wendy. Do you hear me? I cared about her and had nothing to do with her death."

Liar.

The derogatory name rang in her head as she headed for her car in the distance, cursing the heels that kept her from running all out. Tears started falling once again, but this time she didn't bother trying to swipe them away, even as they trekked down her cheeks and blurred her vision.

Liar!

She glanced behind her only once to make sure he wasn't following her. Seeing that the sidewalk behind her was empty, she slowed her pace, gulping in deep breaths in an effort to gain control of herself, but it didn't work.

When she reached her car, she threw herself into the driver's seat and locked the doors, then lowered her head to the steering wheel and allowed herself to cry until she couldn't cry any longer.

When chief of police Dillon Bowie had contacted her the day before to tell her about Wendy's death and that a positive identification had been made by Wendy's boss at the café where she'd been working,

Adrienne had gone through the first two stages of grief in the matter of an hour.

She started her car and pulled out of the parking space and headed for the Bitterroot Motel, where she'd checked in just an hour or so before. Wendy had been living at the motel at the time of her disappearance. Adrienne's unit was two doors down from the one that now sported crime scene tape across the front.

Her initial reaction to Chief Bowie's phone call had been immediate denial. Wendy couldn't be dead. Murder happened to other people, but not to Wendy. She was too full of energy, too filled with the joy of life to be dead.

But she'd known that Wendy had been in Bitterroot, Oklahoma, and it had also been a month since she'd heard from her little sister.

Denial had transformed into a grief so all-consuming that she'd barely been able to think or do what needed to get done to leave her home and travel to the small town. It had been only this morning that she'd finally managed to pack up her car and make the drive from her home in Kansas City to Bitterroot.

She'd arrived much later than she had expected. By the time she had checked into her motel room and unloaded her things from the car, her grief had been overwhelmed with growing rage, a rage focused on the man she believed responsible for Wendy's murder—Nick Coleman.

She pulled up in front of her motel unit and parked her car. She wiped at her eyes and grabbed her purse off the seat. As she walked to her door, she consciously kept her gaze away from the unit two doors down.

The sight of the crime scene tape would only make her cry again, and she'd rather feed her outrageous anger than her crippling grief.

Wendy hadn't even been buried yet and Nick Coleman was in a bar having drinks with a friend. How cold could he be? How calculating? But, of course, wasn't that what murderers did? They killed and destroyed lives and then went right back to their normal life as if nothing had happened.

That was how killers were able to hide in plain sight, but Nick Coleman couldn't hide from her. She knew where he worked and where he lived, and she didn't intend to leave this town until he was arrested for Wendy's murder.

Every conversation, each text she'd received from Wendy had contained some little tidbit of information about Nick. It was obvious to Adrienne that the two were close.

Exhausted by the long drive and her overwhelming emotions, she changed out of her clothes and into her cotton, sleeveless nightgown. The motel unit came complete with a kitchenette, a small table and chairs, a television and a love seat. The bathroom was small, the bed was a double, and while everything looked worn and out-of-date, the unit also appeared to be spotlessly clean.

She shut off the light and got into the bed, the springs squeaking slightly beneath her. The only light in the room came from a slit between the curtains at the front windows, allowing in the faint neon red and yellow flashes from the motel sign advertising clean efficiency units.

Rolling over on her side, she squeezed her eyes tightly shut, afraid to sleep and suffer nightmares of Wendy, yet afraid to stay awake and wallow in thoughts of her sister.

Wild and wonderful Wendy. Impulsive and fearless Wendy. Who would have wanted to murder her other than the man she'd talked about in every phone call, in every text?

She must have fallen asleep, for when she opened her eyes again the light seeping into the room through the slight part in the curtains was sunshine.

She immediately jumped out of bed and got into the shower and then dressed in a pair of blue capris and a sleeveless white-and-blue patterned blouse.

She was disappointed when she got to the police station at one end of Main Street only to be told that Chief Dillon Bowie was out on a call and wasn't expected back until afternoon. She left a message for Dillon that she was staying at the motel, and she left her cell phone number so he could call her as soon as he was available.

From the police station she went to the grocery store and filled her basket with everything she would need to make meals for at least a week. Surely it wouldn't take any longer than that to get Nick Coleman behind bars.

She could scarcely believe how she'd reacted the night before at the sight of Nick Coleman.

Adrienne Bailey, control freak and always responsible, a stickler for rules and political correctness, had momentarily gone stark raving mad.

She didn't intend to lose control again, but she had to admit that hitting and kicking Nick Coleman had been more than a little bit cathartic.

And she wasn't done with him yet. Although she planned no further physical attacks on the man, she did intend to haunt him, to shadow his every move until, hopefully, he finally broke down and confessed to what he'd done.

She knew the who, but she needed to know the why. Wendy had been the kind of young woman who never met a stranger, who was curious and friendly about everyone she came into contact with. She'd been adventurous and high spirited, traits that often had the two sisters butting heads, but not traits that got a woman murdered.

Adrienne drank a quick cup of hot tea and then left the motel, this time headed in the direction of the Holiday Ranch. She had no intention of personally engaging Nick again, but she wanted him to know that she was watching him, waiting for him to make a mistake that would ensure him a future behind bars.

She made only one stop at the motel manager's office, where a young man with oversize black-framed glasses and a name tag that read Lawrence gave her directions to the Holiday Ranch.

Early July in Oklahoma wasn't so much different from in Kansas City. The cool of spring was gone, but the heat and humidity of late summer had yet to fully arrive.

She had no idea what to expect from Chief Bowie.

While he'd been kind on the phone when he'd made the notification to her, she didn't know how close-knit Bitterroot might be and if the chief of police would be willing to protect one of his own townspeople against a murder charge.

After all, Wendy had been an outsider who had no ties to the community. How hard would the chief of police work to solve her murder?

If she thought he was shirking his duty, she'd climb up the food chain until she found somebody to do the job right. In the meantime, she planned on being a tick on Nick Coleman's rotten hide.

She slowed as she passed the entrance to what appeared to be a fairly large spread. The wooden entry declared it to be the Humes Ranch.

She drove on, nerves suddenly tingling inside her skin as she thought of seeing Nick Coleman again.

Slowing once again as she saw the entrance to another ranch ahead, she realized she'd made a conscious decision to become a stalker. Wendy's murder had definitely turned her into a woman she scarcely recognized.

She pulled the car to a stop in front of the entrance with the black wrought iron entry that read Holiday Ranch. This was where Nick Coleman worked. This was where he lived. Her stomach twisted with nervous energy.

From her vantage point, she saw a large two-story house and in the far distance lots of outbuildings and men on horseback, but she was too far away for any of the ranch hands to pay attention to a silver sedan parked along the side of the road.

Knowing she was trespassing, she turned into the long driveway and followed the concrete drive and stopped just past the house. She turned off her engine and rolled down her window the rest of the way. She wouldn't move unless somebody asked her to.

Now she could see a bright blue canopy tent in the distance and knew it probably covered the crime scene—the place where Wendy's body had been found, along with six other potential victims.

Chief Bowie had told her that Wendy had been found there, but the skeletal remains of six other human beings had been there, as well. She wanted Wendy's murderer in jail, but wondered what had happened to those other poor souls.

She'd been there only about ten minutes when a cowboy wearing a dusty brown hat walked up to the driver side of her car. "Cassie and Nicolette aren't home right now. Is there something I can help you with?" he asked.

Adrienne had no idea who Cassie and Nicolette were, and in any case, they weren't the reason she was here. "I'm just here to keep an eye on the man who murdered my sister."

The cowboy's sand-colored eyebrows pulled together in a frown. "There are no murderers here," he said. "You've come to the wrong place."

Of course he would say that, she thought. He was probably a good friend of Nick's. "Are you asking me to leave?"

He shrugged broad shoulders. "It's not my place to ask you to go. I don't own the ranch." He turned on the heels of his boots and headed away from the car.

Adrienne narrowed her eyes and tried to discern which of the men in the distance was Nick. She hadn't really gotten a good look at him the night before. She'd just had a quick vision of blue eyes and slightly shaggy dark brown hair.

It was only when she saw the man who'd come to talk to her take off on horseback and approach another man on horseback that she assumed the second man was Nick Coleman.

The two spoke for a moment and then the second man began toward her. His hat was black, his shoulders broad and he rode a huge black horse that would have characterized him as a villain in any respectable Western.

She gripped her hands tightly together in her lap as he drew close enough that she could see the faint darkness of a black eye where she had hit him the night before.

Good.

She'd managed to mark him with her rage, with her grief.

He pulled his horse to a halt right outside her window, forcing her to lean out and look up at a handsome face with cold blue eyes and a mouth set in a grim line. He was an imposing figure.

"What are you doing here?" he asked.

"Protecting all the other young, vulnerable women in town by keeping an eye on you," she replied, pleased that her voice rang with steely determination.

"I did not kill your sister," he said slowly and distinctly, as if speaking to a crazy person.

"I believe you did, and I'm here to make sure that you don't get away with it."

He sighed and pulled his hat off his head. His thick dark brown hair glistened in the sunshine, and he raked his hand through it as if she was a flake of dandruff he could easily dislodge with a sweep of his fingers.

"Look, I'm grieving over Wendy, too. I want her killer to be found, but I'm not him. Maybe instead of playing judge and jury, you and I need to sit down and talk and compare notes."

He placed his hat back on his head. "If you're looking for the truth in Wendy's murder, then meet me at the café at noon and we can have a civilized conversation. If you're looking for an innocent scapegoat, then you can follow me to the ends of the earth and we'll never know who took Wendy's life."

A headache pounded at her temples as she considered his words. At least he'd offered to meet her in a public place where her personal safety would be ensured.

"Okay," she finally said against her better judgment. "I'll meet you at the café at noon."

He nodded, flicked the reins and then took off galloping back to the pasture. She watched him go and realized she'd just agreed to meet a murderer for lunch.

Chapter 2

Nick walked into the Bitterroot Café at ten to twelve and was greeted by owner Daisy Martin, who stood behind the cash register. Normally, when he came here for lunch with fellow ranch hands, they all sat at the counter. In recent months, he had often sat in Wendy's section, but today, he headed for one of the few empty yellow vinyl booths.

He found one toward the back and slid into the side facing the door then placed his hat next to him. He had no idea if Adrienne Bailey would show up or not, despite the fact that she'd said she'd be here.

There was no way to second-guess the actions of a crazy woman, and she'd definitely been crazy last night. He raised a hand to touch his eye, wincing not because it hurt, but because she'd managed to sucker punch him.

He had no idea if he could change Adrienne's mind about him, if he could convince her that the real killer was still out there somewhere, for now flying under the radar. He had no idea if she'd even listen to a word he had to say.

Jenna Lankford approached his booth, wearing the yellow T-shirt that identified her as a waitress. Jenna was an attractive woman about Nick's age, and before Wendy, she had always been one of his go-to waitresses because of her warmth and sense of humor.

"If it isn't one of my favorite cowboys," she said with a bright smile. She eyed him intently. "At least it's not as bad as I imagined when I heard the news."

"What's not as bad?" Nick asked.

"Your face. Rumor is that you got into a bar fight last night and a woman made mincemeat of your handsome mug."

"As you can see, the rumors are vastly exaggerated," Nick replied with a wry grin. "She did manage to hit me once in the eye, but the damage is minimal. In fact, I'm meeting her for lunch. She's Wendy Bailey's sister, Adrienne."

Jenna's smile faltered, and her blue eyes glistened overly bright. "That poor woman. She must be in such pain. I can't believe what happened to Wendy. She was one of the most popular waitresses here and made coming to work such fun." She paused for a moment and then continued, "So you want something to drink while you wait for your guest?"

"I'll take a root beer," he replied. What he probably needed was a good stiff drink before interacting with

Adrienne again. Unfortunately, the café didn't serve booze. Besides, he needed to have his wits about him.

"Coming right up."

He watched Jenna as she walked away from the table, her blond hair caught up in a ponytail that swung side to side with each step she took.

She was also one of the more popular waitresses for plenty of people in town, not only pretty but also friendly and open. As far as Nick knew, she didn't date much and lived on a small ranch just outside town that had been left to her when her parents had died in a car accident a year before.

Thoughts of Jenna immediately left his mind when the front door opened and Adrienne walked in. She hesitated just inside the door, gazing around the café. Her lips pressed together tightly and her eyes narrowed when she spied him.

Even though Nick's nerves tightened up and he knew this meeting would probably be unpleasant at best, he couldn't help but notice that Adrienne was a very attractive woman.

Her reddish-brown hair was in a tidy knot at the nape of her neck, emphasizing her delicate features. Her blue-and-white blouse made her blue-green eyes appear bluer than they had the night before.

He rose as she reached the booth and slid into the seat across from him with an upthrust of her chin.

"Just so that you know, I'm not afraid of you, Nick Coleman," she said firmly.

Nick lowered himself back down to sit. "There's no reason for you to be afraid of me. We're both on the same side."

Once again her eyes narrowed, and he noted her thick, long eyelashes. Adrienne was definitely a looker. She picked up the menu, and he noticed that her fingers trembled, belying her announcement that she wasn't afraid or at least nervous about being in his company.

"Why don't we order first, and then you can tell me exactly how and why you killed my sister," she said.

So much for being on the same side, Nick thought drily. He didn't need to look at a menu. The food at the café hadn't changed much in the past almost fifteen years that he'd been eating here.

Not wanting to stare at her and make her even more uncomfortable, he gazed around the café and wondered who, like Adrienne, believed he'd murdered Wendy.

Certainly, he knew he was a person of interest in the case. He and Wendy had spent far too much time together for him not to be on a list of potential suspects.

It was only when he heard Adrienne's menu hit the table that he once again looked at her. "Ready to order?" he asked.

She gave him a curt nod, as if she begrudged him even asking her the simple question.

He motioned to Jenna, who had just finished serving another table. Jenna gazed at Adrienne and then at Nick with amusement. "She's a little thing to have managed that colorful shiner you're sporting."

Adrienne's cheeks immediately turned pink. "I've already apologized to him," she said. It was obvious to Nick that she wasn't sorry at all.

"Good, then the two of you should have a nice lunch together," Jenna said brightly. "Now, what can I get for you?"

Adrienne ordered a house salad and iced tea, and Nick ordered a bacon cheeseburger and fries. Once Jenna left to fill their orders, an uncomfortable silence settled in and grew to painful proportions.

"I didn't kill Wendy." Nick finally broke the tense silence.

"She talked about you in every text and phone call I received from her. You were the only man she talked about. You were her lover and something went wrong between the two of you and you killed her," Adrienne said with finality.

Nick stared at her in disbelief. "Do you write fiction for a living?"

"Actually, I work as a publicist for authors, but that has nothing to do with what I think happened between you and Wendy."

"You've definitely come up with a story that has nothing to do with reality." Nick stopped talking as Jenna returned with their food.

After Jenna left the booth once again, he continued, "Let me tell you my story, the reality of my relationship with Wendy."

Adrienne jabbed at a piece of carrot, and the force she used made Nick wonder if she were imagining stabbing the fork in his already wounded eye. It didn't matter. Nick intended to tell the truth, and she could either believe him or not.

"I met Wendy here at the café when she got a job

as a waitress. I'm not sure why, but she attached her-self to me like a pesky little sister."

He paused a moment to swallow against the lump that rose in the back of his throat as he thought of the vibrant, happy young woman who had been his friend and now was gone forever.

"She didn't know anyone in town, and for some reason she decided I needed a friend as badly as she did. We spent a lot of time together, but there was absolutely nothing romantic between us. To me, she was just a kid, and she even tried to matchmake for me, insisting I needed a good woman in my life."

A new wave of sorrow swept through Nick.

Adrienne stared at him. Her fork, sporting a small piece of lettuce, halted halfway between her plate and her mouth. "In every text, in every email I got from Wendy when she arrived here in town, you were the only person she ever talked about."

"You already said that, but that doesn't make me her lover, and it definitely doesn't make me the man who murdered her," Nick countered. He picked up a French fry and then dropped it back to his plate, his appetite gone.

"She was like the little sister I never had. I knew she probably wouldn't be in town for long. She told me her plan was to eventually visit all fifty states and work all different kinds of jobs. When she disap-peared, like everyone else, I just figured she'd gotten a wild hair and had moved on. I was devastated when we found her body."

"On the ranch where you work," Adrienne replied flatly. She placed the piece of lettuce into her mouth and chewed it with the expression of somebody tasting something nasty. She swallowed and then leaned forward slightly. "You had means and the opportunity to kill her and hide her body."

"You're missing one important factor. Aside from the fact that I didn't do it, what would have been my motive? Why on earth would I want to kill Wendy?"

"I don't know, but that's what I intend to find out. Maybe it was a lover's quarrel that got out of hand. Maybe you have a bad temper and lost it with her."

Nick sighed and thought of all the things Wendy had told him about her older sister. Stubborn and rigid, Wendy had said about Adrienne. Controlling and a right fighter, Wendy had added and explained that she'd needed to get some distance from Adrienne to figure out who she was away from her sister's firm thumb.

He knew that this little meeting had done nothing to change Adrienne's belief that he'd killed her sister. Adrienne had made up her mind and nothing was going to change it.

"Have you spoken to Chief Bowie yet?" he asked.

"Not yet. I stopped at the station earlier this morning, but he was out on a call. I expect to meet with him sometime this afternoon," she replied.

That would probably only make things worse, Nick thought. He knew he was high on the list of suspects, although they had no evidence tying him to the crime and wouldn't find any because he was innocent.

"The investigation into Wendy's murder has just barely begun," he said. "It would be nice if you had an open mind."

Her shoulders shot back defensively. "I do have an open mind, but I can't ignore my gut instinct, and all of that instinct is pointing directly to you. I don't know you, but I do know that I don't trust you."

"Then, maybe the answer to that is that you get to know me," he replied evenly. "Look, you've already made it clear that you believe I'm guilty and that you intend to keep an eye on me so that no other woman gets hurt or maybe you think I'll somehow give you the evidence you need for me to be arrested. Why not work with me to find the real killer?"

She stared at him as if he'd grown a steer horn in the middle of his forehead. "Why not leave any investigation to the police instead of working with you?" she countered.

"Because Chief Bowie doesn't just have Wendy's murder to occupy his time and attention. I don't know if you heard, but there were six skeletons found in the same area as Wendy's body. There's no question that he'll do the best that he can on Wendy's case, but he's got a lot on his plate right now."

In some place in the back of his mind, Nick knew he was probably crazy to even entertain some sort of partnership with Adrienne. But as he gazed into her lovely eyes and saw the hint of vulnerability that softened her lips, more than anything he wanted her to believe in his innocence.

Dammit, he was innocent.

"I'd be crazy to even consider working with you," she said slowly. "But I've been more than a little crazy since Chief Bowie contacted me about Wendy's death."

Nick reached up and touched his eye. "You were definitely a little crazy last night."

Her cheeks grew pink, only making her prettier. "That wasn't me. I mean, that was completely out of character for me. I don't believe in vigilante justice. I believe in rules and following the law. Before last night, I'd never hit another person in my entire life." She narrowed her gaze, as if blaming him for the way she'd acted.

Nick once again picked up a fry and popped it into his mouth. The ball was now in her court. She could either work with him or against him, but he wasn't going to waste any more of his time or energy trying to talk her into anything.

For the next few minutes, another awkward silence fell, and they each focused on their lunch. He felt the surreptitious glances she threw in his direction, but he kept his gaze on his plate. He had a feeling she was weighing her options.

One thing the conversation had done for Nick was make him decide that he was going to actively try to find Wendy's killer, with or without Adrienne.

What he'd said about Chief Bowie was true. The man had a lot on his plate right now and a small force to deal with everything. Dillon was a good man, a good investigator, and he had good men on the police force, but Nick wanted his own name cleared sooner rather than later.

She finished her salad before he'd finished his burger. She shoved her dish aside, grabbed her purse and clutched it to her chest in a defensive manner.

"Okay," she said.

He raised an eyebrow, unsure what exactly she was okaying.

"Okay, I'll work with you," she said. "Although I feel like I'm making a deal with the devil."

Nick frowned. "Trust me, the devil is still out there somewhere. Why don't we plan on meeting here first thing in the morning and we can figure out where we'll go from there."

She slid out of the booth. "Nine o'clock?"

"Sounds good," he replied.

With a curt nod of her head, she turned and walked away. Nick watched her go, unable to help but notice that she had a nice butt. In fact, she had a slim but slamming body.

His frown deepened. There was no question that he was perversely physically attracted to Adrienne Bailey as he hadn't been attracted to a woman in a very long time. She was definitely a hot little number.

But she didn't like him. She believed he'd killed her sister, and he knew she'd do whatever possible to prove that fact. It made him wonder who, of the two of them, had really just made an agreement with the devil.

Adrienne had just gotten into her car to leave the café when her cell phone rang. She opened her purse to retrieve her phone, which was nestled next to the Colt .380 Mustang pistol that she had carried with her for the past nine years, since she was twenty-one and living on the wrong side of town with fourteen-year-old Wendy. It had been shot only on the firing range, and she kept her conceal-and-carry permit up-to-date.

The phone call was from Chief Dillon Bowie, who told her he was in his office and available to speak to her anytime.

She backed out of the parking space in front of the café and thought about the meeting she'd just had with Nick. She hadn't expected him to be so handsome. During her fight with him the night before, she'd been too out of her mind to really look at him.

She'd definitely gotten a good look at him today, and what she'd seen had attracted her. She'd also been surprised by the fact that he appeared to be about her age, not Wendy's age. Her belief that he and Wendy had been lovers wavered slightly. Wendy had never been into older men.

The sun drifting in through the window had glinted on his dark brown hair. His eyes were the dark blue of approaching storm clouds, and his features were lean and sharply defined.

Of course, women had found Ted Bundy to be quite attractive, she reminded herself. Murderers came in all shapes and sizes, including handsome cowboys who talked a smooth game.

She'd work with Nick Coleman for now. It was a matter of keeping your friends close and your enemies even closer. Besides, it wasn't as if she intended to allow Nick to get her alone in the dark, and she had her gun and wouldn't hesitate to use it if necessary for her own protection.

She arrived at the police station and was led to a private office where Chief Dillon Bowie greeted her and led her to the chair across from his desk.

"I'm so sorry to meet you under these difficult circumstances," he said.

Chief Bowie was a handsome man with dark neatly cut hair and soft gray eyes. He looked tired, as if he hadn't slept for days. There was a file folder on his desk, and Adrienne knew it held everything that had been done since the discovery of her sister's body.

She repressed a shudder as she thought of the crime scene photos the folder probably held.

"Daisy, the owner of the diner where your sister worked, made an initial identification due to the fact that the woman discovered was wearing the diner T-shirt that all the waitresses wear. I'm afraid that the decomposition was such that it was impossible to identify her by facial features, although the body had long black hair."

His words sent a shaft of pain through her.

The body. My sister.

She felt as if she were having an out-of-body experience, and for a moment was so light-headed she thought she might be sick or pass out.

"Are you all right, Ms. Bailey?"

She sat up straighter and nodded. "I'm okay, and please make it Adrienne."

"Now that you're here, I'll order DNA testing to be done so that there's no question that the woman is your sister. In the meantime…" He reached into his top desk drawer and retrieved a brown envelope. He opened it and poured out the contents. "These were on the body when she was found."

A watch with a brown band decorated with happy faces slid out of the envelope, along with a gold

necklace with an angel charm holding a tiny opal—
Wendy's birthstone. The sight of the items punched
Adrienne in her stomach and stole away any doubt
she might have had.

"Those belonged to my sister," she said. She had
been with Wendy when she'd bought the watch, and
the necklace had been a gift from Adrienne to Wendy
when Wendy had turned twenty-one.

"There's no question that these are Wendy's." She
fought against her hot tears. There had really been no
question in her mind when Chief Bowie had initially
called her to tell her that the young woman found
murdered and buried was probably Wendy.

Chief Bowie pulled out a notepad and pen. "I need
to ask you some questions. Are you okay to do that
now?" She nodded, and he continued, "When was
the last time you spoke to Wendy?"

For the next half an hour, he asked her questions
about Wendy and about their communications while
she'd been in Bitterroot.

"Do you have any suspects in mind?" she asked.

"At this point, every man in town is a potential suspect," Chief Bowie replied. "We've only just started
the investigation."

"What about Nick Coleman?" Even saying his
name out loud knotted a ball of tension in the pit of
her stomach.

Chief Bowie grimaced. "All of the ranch hands
at the Holiday Ranch are persons of interest because
Wendy's body was found on the property. But I have
to tell you, I've known those cowboys for years and I
find it hard to see any one of them as a killer."

"But Nick seemed to be particularly close to Wendy," she said.

He nodded. "I'm aware of the relationship between your sister and Nick. Unfortunately, we can't be sure exactly when Wendy was murdered. All we know for sure is that she was last seen out on the Holiday Ranch on a Friday night and then didn't show up for her morning shift at the diner the following Monday."

"But if she was found in her diner shirt, then she must have been killed that Friday night," Adrienne said.

"That's the potential assumption we're working from," Chief Bowie agreed.

"So as far as you know, Nick was the last person to see her alive," Adrienne said flatly.

"Not necessarily. It appears as if your sister packed her things and made a decision to leave town at some point during that Friday night. She might have left the Holiday Ranch and been carjacked or picked up a dangerous hitchhiker on her way out of town."

"Then, why bury her body on the Holiday Ranch?"

Chief Bowie sighed and leaned back in his chair. "I don't have the answers yet." His eyes narrowed to steel-colored slits. "But I'll get them eventually. I've put out bulletins for every law-enforcement entity in a four-state area to be on the lookout for her car. I don't even have a crime scene to examine for evidence. This is not going to be an easy open-and-shut case. It's going to take some time."

"I understand. I intend to stay in town until you have all the answers," Adrienne replied. "I'm staying at the Bitterroot Motel in room 105."

Chief Bowie leaned forward. "I'll warn you, you might be here a long time."

"I'll be here as long as it takes. I noticed there was crime scene tape on the motel unit where Wendy was staying."

"We did a cursory search of the room, but it was obvious it was not the place of her murder. I planned on pulling down the tape today and releasing the room."

"Do you mind if I'm there when you do that? I'd like to see the room." Adrienne wasn't sure why, but she wanted to see the last place her sister had been before her murder.

"That's fine with me." He stood. "If you have time, we can head over there right now."

"I have nothing but time," she replied, and also stood. "I'll follow you to the motel."

Before they left, a female officer swabbed the inside of Adrienne's mouth for the DNA test that would positively confirm Wendy's identity, but to Adrienne it was a moot point. She already knew that it was Wendy.

Minutes later, she followed the patrol car and wondered if the motel room still held the hint of Wendy's scent, that exotic patchouli-based perfume that she'd practically bathed in.

If Adrienne smelled a trace of her sister, it would be a bittersweet heartbreak all over again. She and Wendy had had so many issues between them, and Adrienne had always thought there would be time to resolve them.

She hadn't mentioned to Chief Bowie her tentative partnership with Nick Coleman. She had a feeling the lawman wouldn't approve and would warn her to leave the investigation to the authorities, and she simply wasn't willing to do that.

She couldn't help but remember what Nick had said about six other skeletons. It had been only three days, and already Chief Bowie looked exhausted. There was no way she intended to leave the investigation to an overworked chief of police and his small band of men.

Although she was sorry for the other people found with Wendy's body, finding Wendy's killer was her sole concern. And she couldn't believe that those skeletons had anything to do with Wendy's murder. Whatever had happened to those people had to have happened years ago for the remains to be skeletal. Surely the only connection to those dead souls and Wendy was the coincidence of their burial site. Still... she supposed she had to consider that there might be a possible link.

They reached the motel, and Adrienne parked in front of her unit. The lawman stopped in the office, probably to get a key, and then pulled his car in front of the door that had the horrifying black-and-yellow crime scene tape across it.

Adrienne got out of her car, her feet suddenly dragging as she walked toward the unit where her sister had lived for the two months she had been in Bitterroot.

Dillon ripped the crime scene tape off, balled it up into a wad and then used a key to unlock the door. He opened it and gestured for Adrienne to go inside.

Her heart beat a frantic rhythm, and a deep dread overwhelmed her as she stepped over the threshold. She wasn't sure what she expected, but what she found was a neat and clean motel room exactly like the one she had checked into the night before.

There was no sign of a struggle, no blood spattering the walls, and her heart found a more normal beat. There was also no scent of Wendy lingering in the air.

She walked into the bathroom, although she knew the chief and his men had probably already looked there. There was nothing to find, nothing left of Wendy and no hint that anything untold had happened here.

She left the bathroom and noticed the hand-size glass bluebird figurine on the windowsill in front of the small table. Her blood froze, and for a long moment, she couldn't make herself move.

"Ms. Bailey?" Dillon's voice seemed to come from very far away as she continued to stare at the bluebird. "Ms. Bailey? Adrienne, are you all right?"

He took a step toward her and broke the trance of horror she had momentarily stumbled into. She gazed at him, his face shimmering beneath the tears that had sprung into her eyes.

"No, I'm not okay." She pointed to the glass bird on the sill. "That belongs to Wendy. It was her most prized possession. Our mother gave it to her just before she died. Wendy would have never left it behind. It would have been the first thing she packed to leave here."

Dillon frowned. "You don't think it's possible she just forgot and accidentally left it behind?"

"Never," she replied adamantly. "That bluebird went everywhere with her."

Dillon's frown deepened. "Then, it's possible your sister didn't pack her own things before she left. Somebody else did it for her, somebody who didn't know the bluebird belonged to her or at least how important it was to her."

"That's exactly what I'm saying." Adrienne looked around the room that had now taken on an ominous aura. "This is where the crime began," she said softly. "Whatever happened to Wendy started here."

"I'll get some men out here to do a more thorough examination," Dillon said, his eyes appearing even more tired. "Maybe we can pick up some fingerprints or forensic evidence that can be used to find the killer."

"Can I take the bluebird with me?" she asked.

"I'm sorry, not right now. If what you believe is true, then it is part of the crime scene. I'll see to it that you get it back when we're finished processing everything."

After a promise to stay in touch, Dillon got on his cell phone and Adrienne walked to her own unit, unlocked the door and then sat on the edge of the bed.

Her mind whirled with images of Wendy in her room, being forced to pack her belongings and drive to whatever location to meet her death. Had Wendy purposely left the bluebird behind as a clue that she'd been forced to leave under duress?

Had Nick Coleman been in the room, forcing Wendy to gather her things and load them into her car? Or had it been a nameless stranger who had seen Wendy as a vulnerable target?

Adrienne knew that if she sat and allowed her mind to work over what little she'd learned so far, she'd drive herself crazy, so she decided to spend a couple of hours doing real work.

She'd set up her computer last night on the small dining table, along with several folders of active clients who depended on her expertise.

She'd struggled for years as a freelance book publicist, augmenting her finances by cleaning houses and working fast food during the hours when Wendy was in school. She'd been willing to do whatever it took to keep a roof over her and her sister's head, utilities functioning and food on the table.

It was only in the past couple of years and the birth of self-publishing authors that her business had exploded and become more successful than she'd ever dreamed possible.

As always, it didn't take her long to lose herself in the work of making authors visible to readers and to get good books the kind of publicity they deserved.

The rumbling of her stomach finally pulled her from the work, and she was surprised to realize twilight had fallen and the room had grown dim.

She closed the curtains at the window and then turned on the lamp next to the bed and the small overhead light in the kitchenette area.

She had arrived in Bitterroot certain that Nick and Wendy had been lovers and that he was responsible for her murder. Yet when he had spoken about Wendy this morning, it had been with real affection, without any hint of any romantic love. He'd confused her. The fact that Chief Bowie had said that he found it difficult to believe that any of the men who worked the Holiday ranch was a killer confused her even more.

Was Nick just that good at hiding an evil inside him? Or was he truly as innocent as he proclaimed?

Chapter 3

Nick was in a foul mood. He'd had trouble sleeping the night before, and when he had fallen asleep he'd suffered wild dreams. He'd awakened before dawn after a particularly disturbing dream.

He now stabled his horse, Raven. It was eight o'clock and he headed back to his bunk to clean up for the morning meeting with Adrienne.

He'd been up and out in the pasture early, chased out of bed not by nightmares of Wendy, but rather by inappropriate erotic dreams of Adrienne.

He'd thought the early-morning air and the sight of a beautiful sunrise would erase the unacceptable visions his unconscious mind had conjured up during sleep, but it hadn't worked.

As he showered and dressed in clean jeans and a navy T-shirt, he dreaded his own suggestion that he and Adrienne work together to figure out who might have killed Wendy.

He might have suffered hot dreams of her, but he had a feeling by the time he'd spent an hour in her company, he'd be pulling his hair out in frustration. Still, as much as she wanted to keep an eye on him, he wanted to keep an eye on her. He didn't want her somehow interfering or tainting the investigation, an investigation he hoped would quickly exonerate him. He had too much to lose if she screwed something up.

At eight-thirty, he stepped out of his bunk and nearly ran into Dusty Crawford, a fellow ranch hand. "I thought I'd see if maybe you want me to go with you this morning," Dusty said, his dimples flashing with his smile.

"And why would I want you to tag along?"

Dusty's smile widened. "She beat you up once. I just thought you might need the services of a personal bodyguard."

"You aren't kidding me with your stupid offer to be my bodyguard. The only reason you'd want to go with me is to get a chance to talk to Trisha," Nick replied.

Trisha Cahill worked as a waitress at the café, and it was no secret that Dusty had a major crush on the blonde, who had a four-year-old son.

Dusty's smile faded. "I've never had a woman give me so many mixed signals. One minute I think she's about to agree to go out with me and the next she acts as though she doesn't even want to talk to me."

Nick clapped the younger man on his back. "If getting a date with Trisha is the biggest problem you have in your life, then consider yourself lucky." He

checked his watch. "And now I've got to get going…
without a bodyguard at my side."

Dusty laughed and, with a tip of his hat, headed
toward the stables while Nick walked to the oversize
shed that served as a garage where the ranch hands
parked their personal rides.

A variety of black pickups filled the garage, the
favorite mode of transportation for most of the men
who worked at the ranch. Nick's ride was a gray Jeep.
He pulled out of the garage and a knot of tension
formed in his stomach at the thought of meeting with
the woman who had occupied so many of his dreams.

He wished he had another suspect to throw out to
her, but he had no idea who Wendy had spent time
with when she wasn't with him. She'd never mentioned anyone else.

He wasn't surprised to see Adrienne's silver sedan
already parked in front of the café when he arrived.
He found her seated in the same booth they'd occupied the day before, although this time she was facing the door.

She was clad in a sea foam–green blouse today.
Her eyes were more green than blue, although there
was no more warmth in them today than there had
been yesterday. Not that he'd expected any welcome.

Sunday mornings, the café was relatively quiet.
Things would pick up after church services when
families would start to arrive for the afternoon meal.

He slid into the seat across from Adrienne and
placed his hat next to him. Before they'd even had a
chance to speak, Jenna was by the booth. "Adrienne

has already ordered," she said. "What can I get for you, Nick?"

"Just a cup of coffee," he replied. He'd eaten breakfast hours earlier in the ranch hand dining room.

"Coming right up," Jenna said.

"Good morning," he greeted Adrienne the minute Jenna was gone.

"It won't be a good morning until my sister's murderer is behind bars," she replied.

"Nothing like cutting to the chase," Nick said drily.

She didn't blink an eye. "There's some new information about the case that you probably haven't heard yet, unless, of course, you're responsible."

He sat up straighter. "And what's that?"

Jenna returned to their table with Nick's coffee and an order of toast and a cup of hot tea for Adrienne. "Anything else I can do for you two?"

"This should do it," Nick replied, eager for her to leave and Adrienne to tell him what new information she possessed.

"Let me know if you need anything else," Jenna said, and once she was gone, Nick focused his attention on the woman across from him.

"Chief Bowie and I believe Wendy didn't pack up her things and leave her motel room under her own volition," she said. "Did Wendy ever tell you about her blackbird figurine?"

He frowned at her. "I don't know anything about a blackbird, but she did show me a bluebird that was given to her by her mother before she died. It was very important to her."

"It was still in the room where she stayed."

Nick raised an eyebrow. "She wouldn't have left it behind." He leaned forward slightly. "A blackbird? Was that some sort of test to see if I knew about the bluebird or not? Did I pass?"

"Yes," she replied succinctly.

"Are there going to be more tests?"

"Maybe...I don't know. I'm just being careful about trusting you."

"You can trust me, Adrienne," he replied.

"Anyway, when I left the motel this morning, there were several deputies inside her room. I assume they were fingerprinting and collecting anything that might point to the guilty." She took a sip of her tea, her gaze never leaving his. She placed her cup back down in the saucer. "Are they going to find your prints in that room?"

"Probably," Nick replied honestly. "There was an evening not long before she disappeared that we ate take-out pizza in her room." He frowned and stared into his coffee cup. "I don't know what to say to convince you that Wendy and I were just friends. I didn't kill her. I didn't pack up her belongings in that motel room. I had nothing to do with any of this."

He looked up at Adrienne. "She'd just moved to a new town, and I think she was lonely. I think she sensed a loneliness inside me. Other than my fellow ranch hands, I only have a couple of friends. I tend to be a loner, but Wendy was like a force of nature. Once she'd made up her mind that we were going to be friends, I was helpless."

For the first time since he'd met Adrienne, a small smile curved her lips. The beauty of it nearly stole his breath away. "She *was* like a force of nature, fierce and fearless. She was like a windstorm that only stopped when it finally blew itself out." Her smile faltered.

"Wendy and I saw each other once or twice a week while she was here," he said. "What we need to find out is who she might have been seeing, what she might have been doing during the time she wasn't with me."

"And how do we go about finding those answers?" she asked.

"We start right here, where she worked." He slid out of the booth. "Wait here and I'll be right back. If that toast is your breakfast, then I suggest you eat it because it might be a long day."

He went in search of Daisy, the owner of the café. If anyone would know the people Wendy interacted with both at work and outside of work, it would be Daisy. She thrived on the café business and gossip. He had no idea if Chief Bowie had already talked to Daisy, but it didn't matter if he had. Nick wanted to hear from the woman himself. He found the plump woman in the kitchen seated at a small table sipping a glass of tomato juice that matched the color of her hair.

"Hey, Nick," she greeted him. "What are you doing back here in my kitchen? Is Jenna not doing her job right?"

"No, Jenna is just fine. I was wondering if you'd have a few minutes to come out and sit with me and Wendy's sister, Adrienne, and answer some questions for us."

"Even if I didn't have time, I'd make time." She set her glass down and stood. "That poor woman. I can't imagine what she's going through. I know how much I miss Wendy, and I only knew her for a couple of months."

She followed Nick out of the kitchen and to the booth, where Nick noticed that Adrienne had nibbled down half a piece of toast. Nick picked up his hat and placed it on his lap so that Daisy could scoot in next to him.

She instantly reached across the table and clasped Adrienne's small hands in her meaty ones. "Honey, I'm so sorry for your loss. For the brief time she was here, Wendy was like a breath of fresh air, a new member of my family."

She released Adrienne's hands and leaned back in the booth. "So Nick said you two have some questions for me." She looked from Adrienne to Nick.

"I know Wendy was a popular waitress, but we were wondering if you could think of anyone in particular who showed an unusual interest in her," Nick said.

"She wasn't just a pretty girl and something new and shiny in town. She was also friendly and a bit of a tease," Daisy said. "When she worked, her section was always full. She drew everyone to her. The cowboys especially. Her section was almost always full of single ranch hands vying for her attention."

"Did she make anyone mad or upset?" Adrienne asked. "Did she have problems with any of her co-workers? I know Wendy could be wonderful and charming, but I also know she had a bit of a temper and could be a brat." Adrienne's face paled, as if she was sickened by speaking anything ill about her sister.

Daisy frowned thoughtfully. "I think she might have had some choice words with Zeke Osmond. He sat in her section one day, and I think he got a bit vulgar with her. She called him a filthy pig and refused to finish serving him. After that, he always sat at the counter with his lowlife friends."

"Zeke Osmond?" Adrienne looked at Nick curiously.

"He works on the Humes Ranch," Nick replied.

"The one next to where you work," Adrienne said.

Nick nodded thoughtfully. Zeke Osmond was another piece of nasty in a group of nasty that worked for Raymond Humes. There was no question that there was bad blood between the two ranches. Was it possible Zeke had murdered Wendy and then had buried her on the Holiday Ranch to implicate one of the Holiday ranch hands?

He focused his attention back to Daisy, who had continued talking. "Of course, Greg Albertson is Zeke's shadow and was with Zeke when Wendy and Zeke had words. Then there's Perry Wright, who seemed to take a real shine to Wendy. He's so shy, I don't know whether he ever asked her out or not, but it was obvious he was crazy about her whenever he came in to eat."

"Have you told Dillon all this?" Nick asked.

Daisy shook her head. "I haven't talked to Dillon since I made the initial identification. I told him what I knew about Wendy's interactions here in the café then." She kept her gaze away from Adrienne.

"And you can't think of anyone else that Wendy might have had problems with?" Adrienne asked.

"Not while she was working here. Now, what happened on her own time I really don't know about." She looked at Nick. "I know she followed you around like a lost little puppy, but I don't know who else she spent her downtime with. If she was seeing another cowboy or any other man, I didn't hear about it."

Adrienne's eyes narrowed once again as she looked at Nick. Daisy caught her look and laughed. "Honey, if you think Nick had anything to do with your sister's death, you're barking up the wrong tree." Daisy placed a hand on Nick's forearm. "I've known this man since he was a teenager. There isn't a bad bone in his entire body."

"Thanks for the vote of confidence, Daisy," he said.

She rose from the booth. "You don't have to convince me of your innocence." She jerked a thumb in Adrienne's direction. "She's the one who has suspicion in her eyes."

"So what happens now?" Adrienne asked after Daisy left.

"We find Dillon and give him the three names that Daisy just gave us," he replied. He was particularly interested in Dillon following up on the potential Zeke Osmond and Greg Albertson connection.

Last month one of Humes's men, Lloyd Green, had been suspected of terrorizing the new owner of Holiday Ranch, Cassie, and her friend Nicolette at the

Holiday Ranch. He was eventually cleared, but Nick wouldn't put anything past any of the ranch hands who worked for Raymond Humes.

They were suspected in all kinds of mischief that had happened at the Holiday Ranch...missing cattle and broken fence line and dozens of other issues.

It seemed as if Raymond Humes had gone out of his way to staff his ranch with rough and mean ranch hands, men who had no moral compasses and who thrived on stirring up trouble. As far as Nick was concerned, it was very possible there could be a murderer among the bunch.

"Let's go see Chief Bowie," Adrienne said, pulling him from his thoughts.

Minutes later, they pulled up side by side at the police station only to discover that Dillon was out at the crime scene at the ranch.

Adrienne followed Nick to the ranch, her car like a shining star behind his Jeep in the midmorning sunshine. How did people prove their innocence when there was no evidence to prove their guilt?

It was obvious he'd made little to no headway in making Adrienne believe in his innocence, and what bothered him was how badly he wanted her to believe him.

There had been few people in Nick's life he'd wanted to please. Certainly not the woman who had given birth to him and then had abandoned him at the zoo when he was eight, leaving him to a foster care system that had, at times, been brutal.

When he'd been brought to the Holiday Ranch, he'd desperately wanted to please Cass Holiday, who had given him real-life lessons and a sense of worth and had taught him how to be a good, self-respecting man.

He'd also wanted to earn the respect and friendship of all the men he worked with at the ranch. He'd managed to do that, and considered each and every cowboy on the Holiday Ranch as a brother.

What he didn't understand was why it was so important that he somehow prove himself to a woman he barely knew, a woman with chameleon eyes and an unexpected smile that had lit up something inside him.

Adrienne followed behind Nick's Jeep, her thoughts in turmoil. She'd come to town wanting to hate Nick Coleman and firm in her belief that he'd killed Wendy. She'd come to town expecting a monster.

What she'd found was a hot, sexy cowboy who seemed as determined as she was to find the real killer. Jenna, the woman who had waited on them the day before, had certainly shown no fear or trepidation around Nick, and Daisy had practically laughed at the very idea of Nick being involved in any way in Wendy's murder.

So who exactly was Nick Coleman? Was he a cold-blooded killer or simply an innocent man who had struck up a friendship with a young, vibrant and lonely newcomer to town?

There was no question that something about him drew her despite her wish to the contrary. She'd never been a woman particularly attracted to eye candy, although there was no question that Nick was easy on the eyes.

There was definitely some emotion in the depths of his blue eyes that tugged at her, a haunting sadness that occasionally shone through otherwise fathomless waters.

At thirty years old, there had been few men in her life. In fact, there had been only one. At the time, when most young women had begun to date to find their lifelong mate, she'd been busy raising Wendy.

A little over two years ago when Wendy had taken off on her own, Adrienne had done little to improve her love life. Wendy had often told Adrienne she was too rigid, too uptight to ever find a man who'd want to spend his life with her.

Even though Wendy had usually said those words in the heat of an argument, Adrienne realized some of them had taken purchase in her heart, making her leery of even seeking any personal relationship with any man. The one time she'd made an attempt, Wendy's prediction had proved true.

She followed Nick's Jeep beneath the wrought iron entrance to the Holiday Ranch, her thoughts focused solely on meeting up with Chief Bowie and hopefully furthering the investigation into Wendy's death.

Nick parked next to the house, and she pulled in just behind him. In the distance, she could see men on horseback and a huge herd of cattle. She could also see the bright blue tentlike canopy that covered the remains of an old shed where Wendy's body had been discovered, along with the skeletons.

She swallowed against any emotion that might

sneak up on her and fell into step next to a silent Nick. She had to take two steps to his one in order to keep up with his long-legged pace.

They walked about halfway between where they had parked and the blue canopy-topped tent when an officer appeared and approached them.

His name tag identified him as Officer Juan Ramirez. He nodded to Adrienne. "Ma'am," he said and then turned his focus to Nick. "Nick, you know you shouldn't be anywhere around the crime scene."

"We have no intention of getting any closer," Nick replied. "But we heard Chief Bowie is out here and we'd like to talk to him."

"I'll go see if he's available." Juan turned on his heels and walked back to the tent and disappeared inside.

A moment later, Dillon appeared and headed in their direction, his features appearing haggard and his uniform dusted with the rusty color of the Oklahoma dirt.

"I can't do anything with the skeletal remains until our expert gets here," he said as if somebody had asked him a question. "But we've been digging around the area where Wendy was found to make sure we haven't missed anything related to her murder."

"And have you found anything?" Adrienne asked, eager to hear something positive.

His tired eyes held frustration as he shook his head. "Not yet. So Juan said you two needed to speak to me."

Adrienne remained silent as Nick told Dillon

about the conversation they'd shared with Daisy over breakfast.

"Zeke Osmond, Greg Albertson and Perry Wright," Dillon repeated. "I'll add them to the list. Right now I've got a couple of my men interviewing all the men who work here at the ranch."

Adrienne sensed the tension that filled Nick, making him stand a little taller. "None of those men are capable of murder, and nobody has questioned me yet," he said.

"We're taking this slow," Dillon said. "Trust me, Nick, you will be thoroughly questioned, but we only figured out yesterday, thanks to Adrienne, that the crime probably began in the motel room."

"I saw your men there this morning. Were they able to come up with anything?" Adrienne asked.

Dillon frowned. "No. In fact, they couldn't pull a single fingerprint from any place in the room."

"So whoever packed her things also took the time to completely wipe down the room," Nick said.

"It would appear so," Dillon replied.

Had Wendy been tied up on the bed while the killer had packed her things and cleaned the room? Or had she already been dead and buried and the killer had come back to her room alone in the dead of night to tie up loose ends?

Adrienne's knees weakened, and she stumbled against Nick's side as horrendous visions played and replayed in her mind. His arm immediately went around her shoulder, anchoring her to his strong body. She knew she should step away, but she lingered for just a moment, feeding off his strength, oddly comforted by his warmth.

She quickly locked her knees, banished the horrific visions from her brain and stepped away from Nick, appalled that she'd found any modicum of comfort in his nearness.

"If that's all you want with me, then I need to get back to work," Dillon said. "Nick, I'll have that interview with you sometime later this afternoon. Adrienne, I'll try to keep you up to date with anything we learn."

Adrienne and Nick headed back toward their vehicles, but before they reached them, a pretty, petite blonde stepped out of the house and onto the back porch.

"Nick, why don't you two come in for something cold to drink," she said.

"Who is that?" Adrienne asked softly.

"Cassie Peterson, my boss," he replied. He waved to her. "We might as well go inside. You can meet her and the others who live here."

Nick introduced Adrienne to Cassie, who greeted her warmly, her blue eyes filled with the compassion Adrienne had come to expect from the people in Bitterroot who knew about her sister.

Cassie led them through a small formal parlor area and into a great room where a lovely dark-haired woman and a young boy sat on the sofa thumbing through a catalog. The woman stood and the boy ran to Nick.

"Hi, Cowboy Nick. Whatcha doing?" He looked at Adrienne. "Hi, I'm Sammy and that's my mom,

Nicolette, and we just bought a house with Cowboy Lucas, who is going to be my new dad as soon as they get married."

"Sammy." His mother smiled apologetically and moved closer to Nick and Adrienne. "I apologize for my little chatterbox."

"No apology necessary," Adrienne replied and then introduced herself.

Nicolette took her hand and squeezed it tightly. "I'm so sorry for your loss. Unfortunately, Cassie and I arrived in town after your sister had gone missing, so we never got an opportunity to meet her. I've heard she was a wonderful young woman." She released Adrienne's hand and motioned both her and Nick to the sofa. "Sammy, why don't you take the catalog and go upstairs to your room. You can use a crayon and mark what you like."

Adrienne was disappointed that they hadn't known her sister, but before she could scarcely blink an eye, she was on the sofa next to Nick with a glass of iced tea in her hand.

It didn't take long for Cassie to explain that the ranch had belonged to her aunt Cass, who had died almost two months ago in a tornado. Cass had left the ranch to Cassie, who had left her art and clothing boutique in New York City and had brought her best friend and her son with her to check out her inheritance.

"It was when the men were pulling down an old shed that had been damaged in the tornado that we discovered the bodies," Cassie said, her blue eyes darkening.

"On that note, I'd like to ask you for some time off," Nick said. "You know I'm a person of interest in Wendy's murder, and Adrienne and I are doing a little investigation of our own in an attempt to find the real killer."

"You can take as much time off as you need," Cassie replied easily. "I know your fellow cowboys will fill in for you."

"And you know that you have our one hundred percent support," Nicolette added as she looked at Nick. "More than once over the past two months I left my son's safety in your hands. I wouldn't have done that if I didn't trust what kind of man you are, and you aren't a killer."

The obvious respect and support the two women showed Nick only managed to confuse Adrienne more. Was he so good that he had managed to fool everyone around him? Or was he really innocent and didn't warrant her suspicions at all?

By the time they left the house, it was well past noon.

"By the way, who is Perry Wright?" she asked before they got into their vehicles.

"He's a shy, quiet young guy who works in medical billing at the hospital. I don't know him very well. He lives in an apartment in town and pretty much keeps to himself."

She nodded. She'd find out more about these men in the next couple of days. "What now?"

He frowned thoughtfully. "I think the best thing

for me to do right now is hang around here and wait for Dillon to contact me about that interview."

"Then, I think I'll just wander around town a bit and ask some questions," she replied.

"I'd rather you not do that alone," he said. "For the most part, Bitterroot is filled with good people, but there are also some rough characters. Besides, you're a stranger, and folks around here can be pretty close-mouthed with outsiders."

"Are you afraid for my safety or about something I might learn about you?" she asked.

His sensual lips thinned to a grim line before he replied, "I thought we were partners working together on this."

"Is that what you are? My partner, or are you managing me, making sure I only talk to people who believe you're innocent?"

"Wendy told me you could be impossible," he said, his eyes flashing with obvious annoyance. "Go talk to whoever you want to, and far be it for me to worry about your safety."

He didn't give her an opportunity to reply. He got into his Jeep, started the engine and headed to a large structure in the distance.

Adrienne got into her car with the sting of his words in her heart. Of course Wendy had told him she was impossible. Adrienne could only wonder what other negative things her sister had said about her. She'd been tough on Wendy, but at the time she'd felt she had to be. Now she lived with the regret of second-guessing every decision she'd made during Wendy's growing years.

She pulled away from the Holiday Ranch and headed back toward town. She consciously willed away thoughts of her sister's hurtful words and instead focused on what she intended to do when she got back to Bitterroot.

If Nick thought she was just going to return to her motel room and cool her heels for the rest of the day, then he was sadly mistaken.

She had a gun in her purse and knew how to keep out of dangerous situations. Somebody in town knew something about Wendy that would lead to the identification of her killer, and she intended to ferret out that information, with or without Nick's presence.

With this plan in mind, she found a parking space smack-dab in the center of Main Street and decided she would begin at one end of town and work her way to the other. There were plenty of stores that Wendy would have frequented, and people in those stores who would have interacted with her.

She not only wanted to find out what she could about Wendy's interactions in town, but she also wanted to dig up what she could about the three men Daisy had mentioned. And if she happened to learn more about Nick, she'd consider that a bonus.

She figured she'd work the streets and stores until it grew dark and then she'd head back to her motel room for dinner and to work a couple of hours on her personal business until bedtime.

It didn't take her long to realize that, unlike Nick's

comment about outsiders and closed mouths, some of the people in Bitterroot liked to talk…a lot.

The first person she spoke to was the owner of the small grocery store that served the town. Sharon Watson was an older woman with salt-and-pepper hair who spent much of her time as not only the owner but also the head cashier.

"I was always riding your sister when she'd come in here for groceries," Sharon said. "She'd buy frozen burritos and cheap pizzas, chips and dip and all kinds of cookies. I told her she needed to be buying some fruits and vegetables, maybe cook herself a roast or some juicy pork chops, but she just laughed at me and said she liked her junk food diet."

Adrienne's heart squeezed tight. Yes, that sounded like Wendy. Getting her to eat a healthy meal had always been a challenge.

By the time she left the store, she knew the eating habits of half the inhabitants of Bitterroot. She'd also learned that Sharon thought Zeke Osmond was a punk, that Greg Albertson was Zeke's tagalong and that Perry Wright was a sweet, soft-spoken man who had helped Sharon with her insurance claims when she'd had her gallbladder out the year before.

She had no intention of interacting with any of the three men by herself, and she had a feeling her "partnership" with Nick was finished. He'd been angry with her when they'd parted ways earlier. She'd have to depend on Chief Bowie to do his job when it came to those men.

It was almost eight o'clock when she finally returned to her motel room. She parked in front of her unit but remained in the car for several long minutes, discouragement weighing heavily on her shoulders.

She'd managed to talk to people in only four different places of business and hadn't learned any more than she'd initially gotten from Sharon at the grocery store.

She'd found most of the men she tried to talk to closemouthed about the case and the three men she'd asked about. The women were chattier, but had no real information to offer her.

Remembering that moment of leaning against Nick, of feeling his strong arm around her, she realized that was what she'd like at the moment—a strong arm around her and somebody comforting her.

She straightened and drew a deep, fortifying breath. She hadn't needed a strong shoulder to lean on when she'd been ten years old and their father had walked out on them, never to be heard from again. She hadn't needed anyone when she was eighteen and her mother had died, leaving an eleven-year-old Wendy to raise.

She'd never needed anyone, and she didn't now. All she wanted was dinner, a little work at her computer and a good night's sleep. Tomorrow was another day, and she would continue to walk the streets and talk to strangers in an effort to gain answers to who had murdered her sister and why.

Finally, she dug the motel room key from her purse and got out of her car. She was just about to unlock her door when she noticed a folded piece of paper shoved in a crack between the door and the doorjamb.

She grabbed the paper, unlocked her door and went inside. She immediately turned on lights to ward off the darkness of deep twilight that had fallen. Then she set her purse on the table and opened the paper.

Printed in bold, black letters with a felt-tipped marker were the words, "BE CAREFUL WHO YOU TRUST."

Chapter 4

The morning sun was bright as Nick sat in his Jeep, parked at the motel entrance, unsure what he should do next...what he wanted to do next. There was a part of him that wanted to run as far and as fast as possible from the woman who believed him guilty, a headstrong, rather combative female he certainly didn't want or need in his life.

Yet there was another part of him that remembered the unexpected fall of her softness against him, the slightly dizzying scent of lilacs and vanilla that emanated from her. That part of him recognized that she was a grieving woman whose eyes occasionally expressed a fragile vulnerability and a loneliness and grief that called to something deep inside him.

The interview the afternoon before with Dillon had gone the way Nick had expected. Dillon had asked tough questions about Nick's relationship with Wendy and Nick had answered honestly.

A far as the timeline of Wendy's disappearance, Nick surmised that he had been the last person to see her alive other than her killer.

He remembered that Wendy had come to the bunk-house after work on that Friday night and they had carried lawn chairs down by the pond and had star-gazed and argued over the reality of space aliens.

The last things Nick had seen that night were the taillights of her car when she'd left around eleven.

Once the interview with Dillon was over Nick had eaten dinner with the rest of the cowboys, and then he'd gone to his bunk with memories of Wendy min-gling with thoughts of Adrienne.

He and Adrienne hadn't exactly parted on pleasant terms the day before. In fact, he'd hit a bit below the belt by repeating one of the things Wendy had said about her older sister.

He knew Adrienne was in her unit because her car was parked in front. It was after nine o'clock, so he assumed she was probably up and around.

They both wanted the same thing, for the killer to be caught. But maybe it was best if he left her to her own devices and just stayed out of her way.

"Oh, hell," he muttered, and turned into the motel parking lot. He parked next to her car and got out of his Jeep. The worst that could happen would be she'd slam her door in his face.

He barely knocked when she opened the door. Her hair fell in loose waves below her shoulders, and her yellow blouse and crisp white capris gave her an impression of freshness that her slightly tired-looking eyes belied.

She opened the door to allow him inside, and before he was completely in, she sat at the table with her purse at her side. "I didn't expect to see you here this morning."

"I didn't expect to be here until I was here," he replied honestly. "May I?" He gestured to the chair across from hers. When she nodded, he sat. She looked at him expectantly above the screen of a laptop. At least she hadn't narrowed her eyes yet, a sure sign of her displeasure.

"I didn't know if after yesterday you still wanted to work with me or not," he said.

He couldn't help but notice the computer equipment that sat on most of the tabletop. Not only was there the computer, but also a printer that looked as if it could do everything but vacuum the floor. He didn't know a lot about technology. He knew horses and cattle and the scent of sweetgrass and rich earth.

She powered off the laptop that was between them and closed it, giving him an unimpeded view of her. "How did your interview with Chief Bowie go?"

"I'm not in jail, so I guess it went okay," he replied with a hint of humor. He'd love to see her smile again, but knew he had nothing to make her smile.

"I spent the rest of yesterday afternoon walking in and out of stores on Main Street and talking to people about Wendy and the three men Daisy mentioned to us."

Nick frowned. He didn't like the idea of her asking questions and potentially stirring things up all alone, but there wasn't much he could do about how she chose to spend her time. He'd probably feel more comfortable about her if she was locked up in the jail, where she couldn't mess things up.

"What did you learn?" he asked.

"The popular cakes that Sally Smith brings to town functions come from a box although she pretends they are homemade, that Albert Faulkner is addicted to Corn Nuts and that Judy Vitters only buys green apples, never red."

Nick couldn't help the small burst of laughter that escaped him. "You must have talked to Sharon at the grocery store."

A hint of a smile lifted one corner of her mouth. "I didn't think I was going to get out of there until she'd told me what every person in town put in their shopping carts. Unfortunately, she didn't tell me anything really useful."

"Who else did you speak to?" he asked, oddly pleased to realize she had a sense of humor.

"A man working in the post office who didn't know Wendy and a woman clerk in the Western Wear shop who also didn't know Wendy, but told me Zeke Osmond and Greg Albertson were both jerks and Perry Wright was a nice man who occasionally came into the shop with his older brother."

She pulled a folded piece of paper from the edge of the bottom of her laptop and worried it between her fingers. "By that time, it was getting late, so I came back here and found this on my door." She hesitated a moment and then handed the note to him.

Nick unfolded the paper, read the note and then

looked back at her. "There's two ways of looking at it," he said. "Of course, the first is that somebody thought they were doing you a favor and wants to warn you about trusting me. It's also possible somebody doesn't like the fact that we're working together to find the killer and so they're attempting to stop us by creating even more mistrust than you already have for me."

He stared at her expressionless face and in the back of his mind wondered what her hair might feel like. Was it really as silky as it looked? Where exactly on her body did that heady scent of lilac and vanilla come from? Would her eyes be more blue or green when she made love?

The inappropriate thoughts forced him to break eye contact with her, and instead he looked out the nearby window.

"What do you think about it?" he asked.

She sighed. "To be honest, I tossed and turned all night trying to figure out what to think about the note." Nick looked back at her as she continued, "I mean, it doesn't specifically tell me not to trust Nick Coleman. It might just mean for me to be wary of anyone I talk to about Wendy's case."

"So where do we stand?" he asked. "Do we part ways now and I go back to the ranch and my job, or are we still partnering up to continue to investigate?"

She hesitated a moment. "We still investigate."

Nick hadn't realized how much he'd wanted them to continue together until now. But he wanted to set some ground rules. "If we're going to work together, then I don't want you talking to anyone unless I'm with you."

He leaned back in his chair and continued, "And I'm not trying to 'manage' you. But whoever killed Wendy was cunning and methodical. It seems so far as if he didn't make any mistakes. I don't want you at risk. It would also be helpful if you could put as much passion into looking at other people as suspects as you put into looking at me as a suspect."

She stared out the nearby window for a moment and worried her hand through her hair, the movement causing the sunlight from the window to dance through the rich reddish-brown strands.

She looked at him once again. Her gaze held a faint hint of vulnerability as she dropped her hand from her hair and instead clasped her hands together in her lap. "I'm trying, but I'm not quite there yet, Nick."

"Fair enough. I appreciate your honesty," he said, although slightly disappointed that he hadn't managed to earn her complete trust. He reminded himself that she'd really known him for only a couple of days. He was expecting too much. It would take time for her to trust him completely.

"Then, what should we put on our agenda for the day?" he asked.

"I'd like to do a little more of what I did yesterday, just walk the streets and talk to people who might have known my sister." She frowned thoughtfully.

"Initially, I didn't think I wanted to have any personal contact with any of the men Daisy had mentioned, but sometime during the middle of my sleepless night, I changed my mind. I want to talk to them. I want to look them in the eye."

Nick frowned thoughtfully. "Talking to Perry Wright should be easy enough. He'll be at work at the hospital. Our best chance to talk to Zeke and Greg would probably be sometime tonight at the Watering Hole, the local bar. They hit the bar on most nights."

He smiled at her. "How well can you hold your liquor and dance?"

She raised her chin and cast him a smile that was positively breathtaking. "Don't you worry about me, cowboy. I can drink and dance anyone under the table, especially if it means getting closer to the man who killed my sister."

It was just before eight when Adrienne looked in the mirror at her reflection. Within minutes, Nick would arrive to pick her up to go to the Watering Hole for an evening of hopefully getting close to anyone who might have had something to do with Wendy's death.

This was the first time since Wendy's death that she'd gone to any trouble with her clothes and makeup. She wore a pair of skinny black jeans and had paired them with a royal blue blouse with a dipping neckline that was sexy but not slutty.

She'd left her hair loose and had swiped mascara on her eyelashes and a touch of blush on her cheeks. She had decided the best approach for the night was to be friendly rather than adversarial. Catch more bees with honey than with vinegar, her mother used to say.

She did a final spritz of her favorite perfume and

then left the bathroom and sat on the edge of the bed to wait for Nick. On the nightstand were Wendy's watch and her opal necklace—the two items of jewelry Chief Bowie had given her.

Looking at them brought grief, but it also brought strength, the strength and resolve to see this through, no matter how long it took or how difficult things became. Closure for herself and justice for Wendy, that was all that was important to her.

The day had brought no real surprises, other than knowing she'd pleased Nick by agreeing to ride with him in his Jeep when they'd left the motel earlier in the day. It was a sign to him that she was starting to trust him. Besides, her gun went with her everywhere.

Now Adrienne was eager to see Zeke Osmond and Greg Albertson up close and in person. She'd heard nothing good about the two cowboys from the few people who had answered her questions about them.

She jumped up off the bed after a knock fell on her door. Before answering, she grabbed her purse and opened it, reassured by the silver gleam of her little Colt Mustang.

Never leave home without it, she thought.

She closed her purse. "Who is it?" she called. When she heard Nick's voice she opened the door. Even though she'd spent most of the day with him, she hadn't been prepared for the sight of him dressed for a night out at the town's popular bar.

His jeans fit his slim waist and long legs just right, and he wore a light blue, short-sleeved button-down shirt that lightened the hue of his eyes and displayed an amazing set of biceps.

He smelled of a sexy, spicy cologne she hadn't noticed before, and his smile of pleasure at the sight of her shot a ridiculous warmth through her.

"I'd ask you if you're ready, but it's obvious you're ready to break every cowboy's heart in town," he said, his voice deep and slightly husky.

"I don't care about breaking hearts, but I'd like to break the guilty into a confession," she replied.

They stepped out of her cool motel room and into the warm night air. "You don't really think that's going to happen, do you?"

"Probably not, but if I play nice, I might learn something new that will help." She picked up his hat that sat in the passenger seat and then slid into his Jeep.

He got in behind the steering wheel and turned to her with a look of amusement. "Can you do that? Can you really play nice? Because I haven't seen much of that side of you." He took his hat from her and put it on his head.

"I can be very pleasant when I want. I just haven't exactly been motivated to play nice with you."

He started the engine. "Still don't trust me?"

"Let's just say I'm more open-minded about you than I was when I first arrived in town."

He flashed her another one of his devastating smiles that stirred a pool of warmth in the pit of her stomach. It should be against the law for Nick Coleman to smile, especially at her. "At least I'm making some progress."

"Maybe a little," she conceded.

He pulled out of the motel parking lot and headed

in the direction of the Watering Hole on the other side of town. His words whirled around in her head.

Yes, he was making progress, but in areas she hadn't expected. He professed himself to be a loner, but as they'd walked the streets that day she'd noticed how many people had greeted him with friendliness and respect.

The first place they had gone that morning was to the small hospital/clinic that served the town. They'd met with Perry Wright, a clean-cut, respectful man. He was like the kind of man Adrienne would hand-pick for her sister to date, which also meant Wendy would have had no interest in him.

Perry had openly admitted to having a crush on Wendy, and his grief over her death had appeared genuine. He'd extolled her virtues until Adrienne and Nick had ended the conversation.

Nick. She cast him a quick glance and then looked back out the passenger window. She hadn't expected her physical attraction to him. It was almost impossible to believe that she liked him despite not quite trusting him.

Unwilling to entertain any more thoughts about her complicated feelings toward Nick, she mentally shifted gears.

"When you dropped me off earlier, I got a call from Chief Bowie. They're releasing Wendy's body tomorrow. I called and made arrangements with Radley's Funeral Home to have her buried the day after tomorrow in the Bitterroot Cemetery."

To her surprise, he reached over and covered her hand with his. "I'm sorry this has happened, and I'm sorry you had to deal with that." He pulled his hand away from hers. "Are you sure you want her final resting place to be here instead of in Kansas City?"

She again looked out the passenger window, her hand still warmed by his unexpected gentle touch. "I thought long and hard about it, and I think Wendy would want to be here. She loved Bitterroot, and I'm not sure she ever would have left here. This is where she belongs."

The heartache that was ever-present when she thought about her sister threatened to overwhelm her. She clenched her hands into fists in her lap and managed to maintain control.

There was nothing she could do about Wendy's murder. It had happened. Wendy was gone, but she could seek justice, and that was exactly what she intended to do. She was willing to stay in Bitterroot until her sister's killer was behind bars. She owed it to Wendy to see this through.

Nick pulled into an empty parking space about a block from the Watering Hole. Although Adrienne had been inside the night she'd first arrived in town and had punched Nick, she had no memory of what the place looked like.

She had suffered complete tunnel vision that night and had focused only on finding the man she'd believed had killed her sister.

They walked down the sidewalk, and as they got closer, the sound of the jukebox playing a rousing country song drifted out of the open front door. Several men stood around the entrance smoking cigarettes that created a fog she and Nick had to walk through to get inside.

On the right side were tables and chairs, on the left wall was a long bar with stools and in the center was a dance floor where a single couple was dancing to a country song that Adrienne didn't recognize.

Nick led her to one of the empty tables next to the dance floor. "We're a little early for the main crowd to show up," he said. A waitress appeared at their table. "A beer for me," he said and then looked at Adrienne.

"Make that two," she said. She would have preferred a nice glass of white wine, but when in cowboyland, drink like a cowboy, she thought.

Within minutes, she and Nick had been served and Nick was telling her about the other people present. "The couple on the dance floor is Art and Helen Olson. They've been married six or seven years, and every night after dinner they come in here for a couple of drinks and to dance together."

"That's sweet," she replied.

He continued to fill her in, pointing out cowhands and telling her what ranch they worked on and naming people who worked at a variety of the businesses in town.

As time passed, more people arrived, some hitting the dance floor while others headed to the stools at the bar or the last remaining open tables. One group headed for the pool tables in the back room, and before long, they were hooting and hollering to the clack of colored and striped balls.

She was so out of her comfort zone. She couldn't

remember the last time she'd been in a bar before coming to Bitterroot.

It was almost ten o'clock when Nick sat up straighter in his chair. Adrienne followed his gaze to the door, where a tall, well-built man walked in. He had his hat pulled down low and looked as if he'd always worn a frown.

"Who is that?" she asked.

"Lloyd Green from the Humes Ranch. I imagine it won't be long now before Zeke and Greg show up."

Her heart fluttered slightly as she thought about coming face-to-face with the two men she knew had interacted with Wendy in a negative way before her death.

Lloyd sat on one of the bar stools and said something to the younger men on each side of him. Both of them got up and moved, presumably leaving the stools empty for his friends, who hadn't yet arrived.

"He's a bully," Adrienne observed.

"Among other things," Nick replied, raising his voice to be heard amid the raucous laughter, the rocking jukebox and the cheers coming from the back room, where the pool tables were located.

"He looks mean." She stared at Lloyd.

"He's like a rattlesnake that has been poked one too many times with a stick. He's all coiled up and ready to spring at any moment," Nick replied.

"Are they all like that on the Humes Ranch?"

"Mostly." Nick nodded toward the door. "And there are your targets. The shorter one is Zeke."

Her heart stutter-stepped as she eyed the two men who had just come inside. Zeke Osmond's black hair was slicked back by some kind of gel, emphasizing his ferret-like features. He wasn't a big man, but his T-shirt displayed lean, wiry muscles. He worked a toothpick in his mouth from one side to the other as he made his way toward one of the empty stools next to Lloyd.

Greg Albertson was taller and bigger with less swagger than Zeke, and he had a more pleasant-looking face. He waved to several people on the dance floor before sitting next to Lloyd.

"Now that I see them, I'm not sure what to do next," she admitted. "I don't think I have the nerve to just belly up to the bar next to them."

Nick stood and reached for her hand. "Come on, let's dance. If we get close enough one of them will say something crappy to me."

Adrienne barely had time to process his words before she was in his arms. The song playing on the jukebox was slow and Nick held her tight as he spun her toward the center of the dance floor.

It would have been easy to forget the reason she was here. It would be far too easy to get lost in the experience of being held so closely in Nick's arms and in the scent of his heady cologne.

The physical attraction she'd felt for him nudged upward into the unknown territory of lust. She looked up and met his gaze, and in the depths of his blue eyes she recognized desire.

She quickly broke the eye contact and instead looked toward Zeke and his buddies. Nick danced her closer to where the three sat, each of them turned in their stools to face the dance floor.

"New victim, Nick?" Lloyd asked when they were within hearing distance. "At least this one looks to be more your own age."

The other men snickered.

Every muscle in Nick's body tensed. Adrienne patted him on the shoulder, stepped away from him and then shooed him away with her hand. "I'm nobody's victim. Nick is nothing more than just a drink and a dance to me."

Nick remained just behind her, and she turned and gave him a look to scram. Reluctantly, he headed back to their table, and Adrienne turned her attention back to the three men on the bar stools. "Looks as though now I'm without a beer or a dance," she said with a flirtatious lilt in her voice.

"I think we can remedy that." Zeke slid off his stool. "Joe, get the lady a beer on my tab," he said to the man behind the bar.

Thankfully, the music now playing was upbeat, and as Zeke pulled her to the dance floor, she managed to keep some distance between their bodies and fought against revulsion at his touch.

"I know who you are," he said with a sly look. "You're Wendy's sister."

"Don't remind me. I'll get all sad and weepy," she replied. "I still can't believe something so awful happened to her." She felt like an undercover agent trying to hide her true motivations.

"Yeah, such a shame," he said, but his voice held no remorse, no real feelings. He pulled her a little closer, his gaze going to the dipping neckline of her blouse and then back to her face. "You've been asking questions about me and some of my buddies."

"That's true," she replied. "I've been asking a lot of questions about a lot of people."

"Are you a cop of something?" He pulled her a little bit closer still, and she fought the urge to cringe away from his scent of stale smoke and body odor. He grinned, as if he knew his closeness made her uncomfortable.

"No, I'm just a sister looking for answers," she replied. "I heard you didn't think much of my sister."

His mouth twisted into a smirk. "When I first saw her, I thought she was a little hottie. She had all that black hair and those big blue eyes and a slamming body." He whistled below his breath. "She definitely revved my motor."

"Did you date her?" Adrienne asked innocently and fought against wanting to slap him for talking so disrespectfully about her sister.

"I tried to charm her a bit, but after talking to her for a few minutes, I realized she was just a bitch with an attitude."

Adrienne stepped away from him, stunned by his obvious vitriol in his voice. "Did you kill her?" The question fell out of her mouth without her realizing she intended to ask it.

He laughed, an ugly sound coupled with the narrowing of his flat, black eyes. "I wouldn't waste my time. In fact, if your sister had been on fire I wouldn't have even worked up my energy to spit on her. You think I'm stupid? That I don't know you're working with Nick? It was fun for a minute, you playing all nice with me."

She spun away from him and hurried toward the table where Nick awaited, Zeke's nasty laughter following after her.

"Are you okay?" Nick asked in obvious concern.

"I'm fine. I just feel as though I need a long, hot shower." She sat and took a sip of her warm beer and fought back a shiver of revulsion. "He's a creep, and he definitely hated Wendy. He didn't even try to pretend otherwise."

"But is he a killer?" Nick asked.

She looked over to where the three men had risen from their stools and appeared to be leaving. "I don't know." As the three men disappeared out of the bar, she released a sigh. "It was stupid of me to think that just by looking at him, by talking to him, I would know if he was guilty or innocent. I asked him if he killed Wendy as if I expected him to answer truthfully."

"Why don't we get a fresh beer and take another turn on the dance floor?" Nick asked.

Adrienne knew it would be best to just call it a night, but she'd rather leave here with the scent of Nick in her head, with the feel of his arms around her instead of the smell of Zeke's sweat and his clammy hands on her.

"Why don't we just skip the beer, have a dance and then I'm ready to call it a night."

"Sounds like a plan to me," he agreed.

Thankfully the jukebox was once again playing a slow song, and as Nick took her into his arms, she fought the desire to melt against his muscled, broad chest. Instantly, any presence of Zeke fled her mind as Nick filled all of her senses.

Was she dancing in the arms of her sister's killer? Certainly, as they'd walked the streets earlier in the day, there was no question that Nick had a lot of supporters, but there had also been more than a handful who had made it clear they believed he was probably guilty.

As far as she was concerned, the verdict on Nick was still out, although she was leaning toward innocence. Maybe she just wanted him to be innocent because she was attracted to him. As she thought of the touch of his hand when she'd told him about Wendy's funeral arrangements, as she remembered how comforting he had been, it was definitely hard to believe he was capable of murder.

After talking to Zeke, she found herself wondering how many other Zekes might be out there.

How many lonesome, swaggering cowboys had tried to pick up beautiful Wendy only to be rejected by her? Was there some man out there not even on their radar who had hated Wendy so much he'd killed her?

By the time the music stopped, she was exhausted and oddly disappointed when Nick dropped his arms from around her. He stopped at the bar to pay the tab, and then, together, they stepped out into the night to head back to his Jeep.

They had walked only a few steps when what sounded like a big firecracker popped and a sharp ping struck the car next to them.

Before she could think, before she could even begin to process what had made the strange noises, Nick grabbed her by the arm and yanked her behind the rear bumper of the nearest car.

"Somebody just shot at us," Nick said with surprise. To Adrienne's shock, he pulled a gun from his boot.

"You have a gun," she said inanely.

"Never leave home without it." Tension rode his voice.

Adrienne opened her purse and withdrew her weapon.

He glanced at her and then back up the street. "You have a gun."

"Never leave home without it," she said, echoing his words.

Nick leaned out around the bumper, and instantly there was another explosion and ping as a bullet slammed into the rearview mirror of the car they hid behind.

At that moment, the reality of the situation set in, and her heartbeat quickened with fear. Somebody was trying to kill one or both of them.

Chapter 5

Nick's adrenaline spiked as he tried to figure out exactly where the shots were coming from. At that point, he didn't give a damn who the shooter might be. He was more interested in locating the attacker's position so he could protect Adrienne from danger.

The buildings on each side of the street made a perfect echo chamber so that the sound of the gun seemed to be coming from all directions.

He'd felt animosity emanating from some of the men in town, men he assumed believed he'd killed an innocent young woman. He hadn't thought about one of them seeking any form of vigilante justice, but there was no way to mistake this as anything but what it was: an attack.

With his heart pumping fast and furious, he glanced toward Adrienne. Her eyes were wide, and the hand holding the small gun shook like a ranch dog after a bath. She may have a gun, but he didn't consider that an asset. He doubted that she'd have the nerve to pull the trigger.

"I can't tell where the shooter is. I've got to get closer," he whispered to her. "You stay here and call Dillon. Tell him we're pinned down between cars by gunfire."

She dropped her gun into her purse and withdrew her cell phone, her eyes simmering with fear. At the same time, Nick moved to the side of the bumper that was closest to the sidewalk, hopefully making it more difficult for the shooter as he moved forward car by car.

The minute he left the cover and moved along the side of the car, more shots resounded, bullets slamming into the street and into the buildings behind him.

He muttered a curse as he reached the back bumper of the car ahead. It sounded as if the shooter was using a rifle, and he was shocked that the sound of the blasts hadn't pulled people out on the street, which was deserted. He supposed he should be grateful that nobody else was at risk for being hit by a stray bullet, but the shooter was bold and determined to take him down.

Parked about five vehicles ahead of him was a van, and he suspected the shooter was hidden behind it. He wanted to neutralize the danger and identify who was behind that gun. He had yet to fire a single bullet and wouldn't until he had a definite target.

As long as Adrienne remained where she was, she

should be safe, and in any case, he didn't believe this was about her. He knew there were plenty of people who thought not only that he and Wendy had been lovers, but that he was responsible for her murder.

Wendy had been popular at the café, especially among most of the cowboys who ate there. Nick wouldn't be surprised if one of them had decided it was time to avenge Wendy's death.

The heat of the night closed in around him as he remained in place, waiting to see what might happen next. Would the shooter advance? Or was he being patient, waiting for Nick to make another move?

Seconds ticked by and then minutes. A trickle of sweat worked its way down the center of his back, and he wiped his sweaty gun hand on his jeans then regripped his gun.

"Nick?" Adrienne's voice cried out. He didn't answer her. He didn't want to give away his position. The silence continued.

Maybe it was over. Maybe the shooter had already left the area. He decided to attempt to move up to the back of the next car, closer to where he presumed the shooter hid. He drew a deep breath and then left his cover.

He ran in a crouched position, his movement drawing four quick shots. He slid into the space between the next two cars, eternally grateful that whoever was doing the shooting didn't have a sniper's good aim.

Resting his back against the bumper, he tried to slow the frantic beat of his heart. One wrong move on his part would put him at deadly risk.

Hell, he was already at risk for death.

He needed another plan. Leapfrogging from vehicle to vehicle was risky—too risky. Even if the shooter's aim had been off so far, it would take only one lucky shot for one of those bullets to hit him…to potentially kill him.

Before he could come up with a new plan, a siren pierced the air, letting Nick know reinforcements were on the way. He scooted over and peeked out to see Dillon's patrol car slowly making its way down Main Street.

A bright beam of light from the vehicle's driver side flashed back and forth, sweeping the areas on both sides of the street.

The light finally reached Nick, momentarily blinding him as the patrol car pulled to a halt. Dillon got out, his gun drawn and his features taut with tension. "Are you okay?" he asked as he faced the street he'd just driven down. "I didn't see anyone. I've got a couple of officers parked at the end of Main Street and checking things out on foot."

Nick slowly rose to his feet, grateful when there was no answering gunfire. He had a feeling the shooter was long gone. He'd probably run the moment he heard the siren. "Adrienne is hiding a couple of cars back," he said.

Dillon followed Nick as he returned to the back of the car where Adrienne was still crouched down, her gun once again in her hand.

"Whoa, put that away," Dillon exclaimed. "Do you have a permit for that?"

"Of course I do," she said as she placed the gun back in her purse and then stood. Her gaze lingered on Nick for a moment, simmering with emotion. "I didn't know what was happening. I didn't know if you'd been shot." Her voice broke slightly.

"I'm fine," Nick replied. He smiled in an attempt to take the fear from her eyes. "Faster than a speeding bullet and all that."

"Come on, superhero, why don't you and Adrienne take a ride with me to the station, where I can get a full statement from both of you. My men will continue to canvass the area, and when I'm finished talking to you, I'll bring you back to your car."

"I think I can safely say that I was the target," Nick said minutes later when they were all seated in Dillon's office. "Thank God whoever was pulling the trigger wasn't a crack shot. Otherwise, I'd probably be dead."

"I was afraid of something like this happening," Dillon said with a frown.

"Afraid of what?" Adrienne asked.

Dillon leaned back in his chair, his frown deepening. "Most folks in town knew that Nick and Wendy were spending a lot of time together, and some of those people believe he murdered her. I was hoping there wouldn't be any kind of vigilante issues to deal with, but I think that's what might have happened tonight."

"So you're telling me I need to watch my back," Nick replied.

"Obviously," Dillon replied drily.

"What about Zeke and Greg and that Lloyd man?" Adrienne asked. "They left the bar right before we did. I had a nasty encounter with Zeke."

As she explained her dance with Zeke, Nick remembered the surprising sharp jealousy that had whipped through him when he had seen the man's hands on her.

"That doesn't explain why Zeke would take potshots at Nick," Dillon replied.

"Maybe he's ticked because we've been asking a lot of questions around town," Nick said. "Maybe he killed Wendy and our questions are making him uncomfortable. Maybe it was the real killer taking those shots at me."

Dillon leaned forward, a look of frustration usurping his deep frown. "We're in the middle of the investigation into Wendy's death. We have a lot of investigation left to do. Gunfire in the streets of my town is unacceptable. Right now, what I want to do is get that shooter behind bars."

"I wouldn't mind that happening, either. Maybe your men will find some shell casings or some other evidence that will point to the identity of the shooter. It was definitely a rifle firing those bullets, and you should be able to pull bullets from any number of places," Nick replied. "There were at least nine or ten bullets that missed me but hit cars or buildings."

"So I'm probably going to have some ticked-off people in here due to car damage," Dillon said in disgust.

"And on that note, I'm taking Adrienne home now."

She appeared exhausted, her eyes dulled with what he suspected was a touch of shock. He imagined it wasn't a normal occurrence for her to be a participant in a shoot-out.

She needed to get back to her motel room, and he needed to rethink this whole partnership deal. If there was a target on his back, he didn't want her to somehow end up as collateral damage.

Dillon took them back to Nick's Jeep. The streets were deserted other than the officers Dillon had walking the area. Nearly all of the cars that Nick had used as cover were gone. Hopefully the officers working the area had managed to pull bullets and casings from the cars before the owners had gone home.

It was almost twelve-thirty. The Watering Hole closed at midnight on weekdays and at two on weekends. The drinkers and dancers had all gone home, and someplace out there was a person who had just tried to kill Nick.

"I'll be in touch," Dillon said as Nick and Adrienne got out of his patrol car.

They were silent on the drive to the motel, as if everything they had to say had been said to Dillon in their formal police statements.

"Will you come in for just a little while?" she asked when he parked his car in front of her motel unit. The request both surprised him and indicated to him that she was still shaken up by what had happened. Hell, he was still more than a little shook up.

"Yeah, I will. Besides, we need to talk."

She looked at him questioningly before getting out of the Jeep. Once inside, they sat at the small table, and she spoke first.

"You want something to drink?" she asked.

"No, I'm good."

"You seem to have taken this all in stride. Weren't you afraid out there?"

"The last time I was truly afraid was when I was eight years old. Fear is an emotion I really haven't felt since then." It was true. He hadn't been afraid out there with the shooter. He'd been frustrated and angry, but not particularly afraid.

"What happened when you were eight?" she asked.

"That's not important right now. What's important is that we now know I have a target on my back, and I think the best thing for you to do is to stay as far away as possible from me."

"You mean you want to stop investigating?"

"No, I intend to keep snooping around, but I don't think we should be partners anymore, and I don't think you should be asking any more questions to anyone."

She raised her chin and narrowed her beautiful eyes. "Well, I don't agree with you. What happened tonight changes nothing as far as I'm concerned. It only proves to me that we might be on the right track in flushing out the killer."

"And that's why I think it's best for you to keep your distance from me," he countered. "And keep out of the investigation altogether."

She crossed her arms over her chest and shook her head in obvious disagreement. "I should be the one to make the decision on this. We're a team, and we work on this together. I accept the risks involved. I'm just really starting to trust you, Nick. You can't walk away from me now. Now isn't the time for us to stop."

Her blue-green eyes held myriad emotions, the easiest ones to discern strength and determination. The others he didn't even try to figure out. He leaned back in the chair and released a deep sigh.

"Okay," he relented against his better judgment. "For now, we'll continue together, but if anything else happens that places you in any kind of danger at all, then I'm out of this partnership for good. And it's time we exchange cell phone numbers so that we can stay in touch when we aren't physically together."

She uncrossed her arms and relaxed back into the chair. "Thank you. I know Wendy better than anyone else, and you know the people in this town. We make a good team, and we both have the same goal in common."

She offered him her cell phone, where he added his name and number to her contacts while she did the same on his phone.

Wendy had told him that her sister was strong and tenacious, and Adrienne was showing those very characteristics now. He couldn't help but admire her. Most women would bury their dead and boot scoot it out of town after what had just happened.

"Were you afraid tonight?" he asked.

She flashed him one of her rare smiles. "I was absolutely terrified, especially when you left me. I was afraid I'd get shot. I was equally afraid that you'd be shot. I never knew I had so much adrenaline in my body."

He returned her smile and stood. "I'll just get out of here now so you can sleep off some of that extra adrenaline. Why don't you call me tomorrow when you're up and around and we can go from there?"

"Okay." She walked with him to the door.

He turned to tell her good-night, and she stood too close to him. Her heady scent surrounded him, and he remembered holding her in his arms when they'd danced. She'd been so soft against him, and they had fit so well together.

He wasn't sure if he spoke her name or not, but suddenly she was in his arms and his mouth was on hers. He hadn't asked permission; he hadn't even consciously made the decision to kiss her. It had just happened.

She didn't fight him. She raised her arms around his neck and melted against him as their tongues swirled together. He raked his fingers through her hair, loving the feel of the silky strands. In turn, her fingers played in the hair at the nape of his neck.

He was acutely aware of every point of body contact. Her soft breasts pressed against his chest, and there was nothing he wanted more than to back her up in the room and to the bed.

Someplace in the back of his mind, he knew it was a foolish thought, and with regret, he halted the kiss and pulled back from her. She appeared stunned, and he wondered if she was already regretting her easy acquiescence.

"Sorry," he said. "I didn't mean for that to happen. It shouldn't have happened. Just chalk it up to that lingering adrenaline. I'll talk to you tomorrow." Without giving her an opportunity to reply, he hurried toward his Jeep.

He drove away from the motel and cursed himself for kissing her. Now all he could think about was his desire to kiss her again...and again.

He didn't want a romantic relationship with any woman. From what he'd heard from Wendy about her big sister, Adrienne definitely wasn't a one-night stand kind of woman. She wouldn't be satisfied with what little he could offer her.

He didn't know who had tried to shoot him, but he did know for sure that the worst thing he could do was develop any meaningful feelings for Adrienne. Because if there was one thing he'd learned early in life, it was that when things got tough, women walked away.

Two mornings later, Adrienne awoke with a sense of dread that made her reluctant to get out of bed. Today she would be saying her last goodbye to Wendy.

She rolled over on her back and stared up at the ceiling, where sunbeams slipping through the crack between the curtains danced and played.

At least it appeared it was going to be a beautiful sunny day. Wendy deserved that. Adrienne had arranged with a local preacher to do a short gravesite service at two o'clock that afternoon.

She didn't expect a lot of people to show up. Wendy had been in town less than two months. She imagined a few of Wendy's coworkers might show up and that would be it.

The day before, Nick had picked her up and they'd had a late breakfast at the café. After that, they'd walked the streets, talking to people and asking questions, trying to find somebody, anybody, who might have a smidgen of information about who else Wendy might have been seeing before her death.

They'd ended the day with a late dinner at the café, and by the time nightfall had come, she'd been back in her room alone. She'd worked on her computer until almost midnight, trying to clear her mind both of her dead sister and the kiss she'd shared with Nick.

She now reached up and touched her lips, thinking about the fire of his mouth against hers, the fierce desire that had roared through her as he'd held her so tightly against him.

She wished he'd been a sloppy kisser. She wished he would have been the world's most awful kisser. It would have made things so much easier. Instead, she found his kiss dizzying and wonderful, no matter how often she replayed it in her mind.

It was after ten when she finally dragged herself out of bed, sick of her own thoughts. She took a long, hot shower and then pulled on a robe. She made up her bed and pulled from the tiny closet a sleeveless black dress she'd specifically packed for the somber occasion. She carefully placed it on the bed and then made coffee.

As she sat at the table drinking the fresh brew, she thought of the night of the shooting. Yesterday, when Nick had picked her up, she'd noticed that he wore his gun in a holster at his waist. It had reminded her that not everyone in town believed in Nick's innocence, that he did have a target on his back.

The shooting hadn't completely taken Nick off her person-of-interest list in Wendy's murder. A sneaky little voice in the back of her head whispered that it was possible the whole thing had been a setup, that one of Nick's buddies had taken potshots at him to take the heat off him.

The more rational side of her brain told her the thought was crazy. Besides, spending time with him and rereading Wendy's emails, remembering their phone conversations, had nudged him closer to falling off her suspect list.

While Wendy had talked a lot about Nick, she'd never given any indication that there was anything between them except friendship. Adrienne had simply jumped to the conclusion that they'd been lovers.

All too soon, it was time for Nick to pick her up for Wendy's burial. He arrived at her door clad in a pair of neatly tailored black slacks, a white short-sleeved shirt and his black cowboy hat. The holster and the gun hanging from his black belt made him look like a dashing gunslinger.

"Are you okay?" he asked once they were in his Jeep and headed for the small cemetery.

"I always thought we'd have more time. Wendy and I had some issues between us, and I always believed we'd eventually get to a place and time to resolve them." She sighed and stared out the passenger window, a deep sorrow filling her soul.

"Wendy told me you were only eighteen when your mother died and you petitioned the court to allow you to have custody of her," Nick said. "That was a selfless thing for you to do, to take on the raising of an eleven-year-old when you yourself were so young."

She looked at him, his profile a study of handsome angles and planes. Thankfully his eye no longer held any hint of the punch she'd delivered to him. "It wasn't selfless, it was what family does. She was my sister. I couldn't let her go into the foster care system. I wanted her with me."

"Not everyone would make the same choice," he replied.

"It was the only choice for me."

They remained silent for the rest of the short ride to the cemetery. When they pulled through the iron gates, it was easy to see where the ceremony would take place. A large white canopy rippled in the faint warm breeze. It would provide welcome relief from the hot sun to anyone who attended.

Nick and Adrienne got out of his Jeep and walked toward the canopy. When they got close enough, she saw a man she assumed to be Pastor Jim Baldwin already there.

The pastor introduced himself and held Adrienne's hand as he expressed sorrow for her loss. After that, he and Nick stepped aside, giving Adrienne an opportunity to spend some quiet time in front of the plain white coffin, covered by a spray of pink roses.

Pink roses. They had been Wendy's favorite flower. When she was twelve, she had taken scissors and stripped a neighbor's rosebush of every pink rose and had proudly presented the bouquet to Adrienne.

Adrienne had been appalled and had punished Wendy by grounding her for a week and making her do lawn work for the neighbor for a month.

Adrienne had thought she'd shed all the tears

within her already, but as she stared at the pink roses and the coffin, a wealth of emotion rose up inside her.

There would be no time to enjoy her sister adult to adult, as friend to friend. She'd wanted them to just enjoy being sisters rather than the roles they had been cast in when Adrienne had been forced to become the parent figure.

She'd wanted them to go to lunch together, to shop for sales and to take walks arm in arm, laughing in retrospect about the terrible days of the past.

"I'm sorry, Wendy," she whispered softly through her tears.

She was sorry for all the times she'd been too rigid, too controlling. She was sorry for being so strict and intractable with her high-spirited sister, but Adrienne had been so afraid of getting it wrong, of not being good enough to keep Wendy safe, not just from others, but also from herself and her own impulses.

She heard the approach of vehicles and quickly swiped away her tears to see who was arriving. Two cars had pulled up. Daisy and the waitress Jenna got out of one car, and four cowboys she'd never seen before got out of the other.

She stepped close to Nick's side. "Who are those men?" she asked.

"They're from my ranch," he replied.

"Did they know Wendy?" she asked.

"Not really."

"Then, why are they here?"

"To pay their respects to Wendy and you and to support me," he replied. "I imagine everyone from the Holiday Ranch will show up."

To her shock and surprise, he was right. By the start of the service Adrienne was amazed by the number of people who had shown up to pay their respects. Cassie and Nicolette were there, along with ten of Cassie's cowboys. Nick explained that one of the men had stayed at home with little Sammy.

There were also a handful of people from the café, Chief Bowie and three of his officers and several men, including Zeke, Greg and Lloyd from the Humes Ranch. Thankfully the Humes ranch hands stayed some distance away and didn't interact with anyone else.

Adrienne could only assume they were there in an attempt to spoil what was already a rotten day. She refused to look at any of them and only wished they'd never shown up.

Perry Wright was also in attendance, looking devastated as he stared at the coffin. At one point, he appeared to be openly weeping.

When the ceremony was finally over, Cassie approached her. "Before we left the ranch, I instructed Cookie to set up a spread of food for you and anyone else who would like to join us. Nick can take you home afterward. Please come."

Adrienne was touched by the gesture, and Cassie didn't need to ask twice. Adrienne wasn't ready to go back to her motel room alone. She needed company, but she also knew that being alone with Nick in her vulnerable state would be dangerous.

She'd want him to hold her. She'd want to succumb to him. She'd need him to make love to her to take away the aura of sad finality and death that the day had brought.

"I'd love to come," she said, and looked at Nick to make sure he was on board. He nodded.

"Whenever you're finished up here, just come on out to the ranch. Nick will show you where the cowboys' dining room is, and that's where we'll all be," Cassie said.

Adrienne wanted to weep again, this time because of the kindness that surrounded her. There had been very little kindness in her life after her mother's death. There had only been struggles and strife.

She and Nick remained at the gravesite until the last person had left. Then Adrienne said her final goodbye to the little sister she had loved. Afterward, they got into his Jeep to head to the Holiday Ranch.

"Did you know Cassie had this planned?" she asked.

"She told me about it last night. She figured since you didn't have any family around here it would be nice for you to be surrounded by friendly faces after the service."

"No wonder Wendy liked it here," Adrienne replied.

They were silent for the rest of the drive to the ranch. Once there, Nick pulled into a large garage and parked his Jeep. They stepped out of the garage and Nick pointed to a long building that looked like a motel.

"When Cassie's aunt first started hiring new help after her husband died, she built the bunkhouse where each of us could have our own private space. The back of the building is a combination dining and recreation room," he explained as they walked.

"All the men who work here also live here?"

"That's right. A cowhand named Cookie provides us three meals a day, and we're all like one big family."

"How many cowboys work here?" she asked.

"If I don't count Cookie, we're an even dozen, although we're about to lose one."

"Lucas," she said, remembering her conversation with Cassie and Nicolette when she'd first met them. "Nicolette said that she and Lucas had bought a place, and I assume that means Lucas won't be working here anymore."

"That's true," Nick agreed. "We've all been together for the past fourteen years or so. It will be strange not to have him around anymore."

At least Lucas would still be in town, Adrienne thought. Nick would be able to meet him for drinks or share a meal with him. She'd never get the opportunity to have any kind of interaction with Wendy again.

She shoved this sad thought away as they rounded the bunkhouse and walked into the common room. It was a huge area, with picnic tables lined up for the men to sit and eat and a smaller nook-like space that held a television and several sofas and chairs.

Long tables along one wall held a variety of food, but before she could process what exactly had been prepared, she found herself being greeted by cowboy after cowboy expressing sorrow for her loss.

The cowboys weren't the only people there. Daisy

and Jenna and several other waitresses from the café were there, as well. For a long moment, Adrienne was overwhelmed, but Nick stepped to her side and took her hand, instantly creating a sense of calmness inside her.

It shouldn't have. Of all the people in the world, it shouldn't be Nick Coleman, a person of interest in her sister's murder, who made her feel so calm and secure.

By the time they sat down to eat, her head spun as she tried to put faces and names to the cowboys who were obviously close to Nick.

There was Forest, a big man with a gentle smile. Then there was Dusty, who was blond and had charming dimples and was the youngest of the men, and Adam, who was the ranch foreman. The others all blurred together in her mind.

As they ate, Nick played the game of name that cowboy with her, teasing her into laughter when she got them all confused. She felt guilty laughing on this day, and yet knew in her heart that Wendy would be glad that Nick had made her laugh. Wendy would want food and laughter and joy even while they mourned her absence from the earth.

After most of the people had eaten, one of the cowboys, Mac, picked up a guitar and began to strum some music into the room. Adrienne sank down on one of the sofas, and Nick sat next to her.

The songs Mac played were slow, not particularly sad but rather with a spiritual tone appropriate for the situation. Adrienne fought the impulse to lean against

Nick's side, to feel his body warmth infusing her and the solidness of him intimately against her.

Jenna sat down on the other side of Adrienne. "I just wanted to tell you again how sorry I am for your loss. Wendy was so special."

"Thank you," Adrienne replied.

"So will you be heading out of town now that she's been laid to rest?" Jenna asked.

"No, I don't intend to leave until her killer is arrested," Adrienne replied.

Jenna touched the back of Adrienne's hand and smiled sympathetically. "I'd feel the same way if I was in your shoes, and it looks as though you have a devoted partner in Nick."

"Nick wants to clear his name as much as I want to find the real killer."

"I hope you both get what you want," Jenna said. "I've told you everything I know, but if you think of any other way I can be helpful, please don't hesitate to ask."

"Thanks, Jenna," Adrienne replied, pleased by the obvious show of support.

Late afternoon turned into late evening, and by eight-thirty the food had been packed away, all of the people who didn't belong on the ranch had left and the cowboys had begun to drift away to their individual bunks.

"I don't know how to thank you for everything," Adrienne said to Cassie as Adrienne and Nick prepared to leave.

"Food, friends and music can't fix a broken heart, but hopefully they helped a little bit," Cassie replied.

Adrienne hugged Cassie, and minutes later, she and Nick were on their way back to her motel. "Wendy would have liked having everyone together on her behalf," Adrienne said.

"She would have wanted male strippers," Nick replied.

Adrienne laughed. "You're absolutely right. Hopefully, there are dancing male strippers in heaven."

"She loved you, you know."

Nick's unexpected words pierced through her. "Thank you," she replied softly, her heart squeezing tight. "I needed to hear that, especially today."

By that time, he'd parked in front of her motel unit. "No need for you to get out," she said as she opened the passenger door.

"You'll be all right?"

"I'm tired, I'm sad, but I'll be fine. Thank you for being there for me all day, Nick. I appreciate your support. You'll call me in the morning?" she asked.

"You know I will. Good night, Adrienne."

She stood in front of her motel room door and watched until his taillights disappeared from view. It would have been far too easy to invite him in. It would have been far too tempting to seek his comfort, to lose herself in his arms.

She turned with her key in hand to unlock the motel door, and a creepy-crawly sensation tickled at the back of her neck. It was that odd feeling that somebody was watching her, that somebody was near.

She unlocked her door and then twirled around to survey the surroundings. The only other car parked in front of the motel unit was on the other side of the office.

A large trash dumpster stood on the right side of the parking lot, and a little distance away, several trees grouped above a picnic table and a rusty barbecue grill.

There was nobody whom she could see, nobody hiding near the dumpster and nobody around the picnic table area. Still, as she entered her motel room and closed and locked the door behind her, she couldn't shake the feeling that somebody was out there in the dark, watching her…and waiting.

Chapter 6

The knock on the motel room door pulled Adrienne from her sleep. Groggy, she glanced at the illuminated clock on her nightstand. It was just after one in the morning. She blinked sleepily and wondered if the knock had been part of a dream she'd been having.

She'd gone to bed unusually tired after all the emotional roller coaster of the funeral yesterday and then pounding the pavements with Nick all day today.

She now closed her eyes and had almost fallen back asleep when the knocking came again, three sharp, unmistakable bangs on her door.

"Wait a minute," she yelled as she reached for the short emerald-green robe at the end of her bed.

She pulled it around her and wondered who on earth would be at her door at this time of night.

Nick?

Chief Bowie?

As she approached the door, the pounding came again. It sounded angry, aggressive, and a wary caution filled her. There was no way the person on the other side of the door was either man. They would have called out to her by now.

She peeked out the peephole in the door but saw nothing except the darkness of night. Whoever was at the door didn't want to be seen.

"Who is it? Who's there?" she cried as her heart began to bang frantically.

The doorknob began to jiggle back and forth and back and forth as if in an effort to spring the lock and get the door open. The lock was so flimsy Adrienne expected it to pop free at any moment.

"What do you want? Who are you?" she cried out again, and gasped in horror as the lock clicked and the door opened a couple of inches. The only thing keeping the person out of the room was the rusty brown chain lock.

Adrienne shoved against the door and felt pressure from the other side. She didn't try to peek out to see who was there. All her focus was on pushing her weight against the door to keep the intruder out.

She didn't expend any energy on asking any more questions. She felt a malevolence thick in the air and knew that if the intruder got inside she was in big trouble.

Anybody showing up at her door at this time of

night and hiding in the darkness could mean nothing but something bad. She was in big trouble now. There was no way she could leave the door to grab her purse that sat on the table. The gun she carried for protection was of no use to her now. With the sheer strength of terror, she managed to shove hard enough to get the door closed again.

She fumbled to relock the doorknob lock only to realize it was definitely broken. The rusty safety chain was her last defense. Once it was broken, the intruder would be inside, and Adrienne didn't trust that she would have time to leave the door, fumble in her purse and grab her gun before she'd be attacked.

There was no way she believed this was some kind of robbery attempt. Whoever was on the other side of the door wanted to hurt or kill her. She felt it in her bones, the evil that emanated from the other side of the door.

The door banged open again. The chain pulled taut, and Adrienne screamed.

Why was this happening? Who was outside her door?

She screamed again as she threw her weight forward, giving the chain a little bit of slack. She didn't expect her screams to be heard. There was nobody in the units next to hers, nobody to hear that she was in trouble and needed help.

Sweat beaded her brow. Her heart beat so fast she was breathless. But she couldn't give up. Danger was at her door, and she couldn't let it inside.

She got the door closed again only to have it spring open an inch. She turned so that her back was at the door, and she used the strength of her legs to dig into the carpeting to aid her.

It was like stepping into somebody else's nightmare.

Go away. Leave me alone.

She screamed and screamed again in hope that somehow, some way, somebody would hear her.

She waited for the next assault.

Nothing happened.

Adrienne gulped in deep breaths of air and rebraced her legs against the floor. But instead of a new push to open the door, the knocking started again.

Hard, angry pounds hit the door in rapid succession, ringing in Adrienne's ears and making her feel half crazed with terror.

Suddenly...silence.

An ominous silence.

Adrienne steeled herself for what might come next. She glanced at the nearby window, worried that the next attack might come from there.

She sensed an absence of energy but was afraid to trust in it. Maybe the silence was simply a ruse to make her let down her guard.

Tears of fear raced down her cheeks, but she didn't dare take a hand off the door to wipe them away. The anticipation of another attack was almost as horrible as the attack itself.

She heard the roar of a car engine just outside her unit, and instinctively she knew it was the potential intruder making an escape.

She hadn't been able to see the face or form of the person trying to break in, but maybe she could get a glimpse of his vehicle. Taking a calculated risk, she left the door and ran to the window. She yanked the curtain aside in time to see the car that revved its engine and tore out of the motel parking lot.

Her brain went numb. Impossible, and yet her eyes didn't lie. She stumbled to the table and grabbed both her cell phone and her gun. The first thing she did was dial Nick. She fought against a rising hysteria, the cell phone trembling uncontrollably against her ear.

He answered on the second ring. "Adrienne?"

"Can you come to the motel? Wendy's killer just paid me a visit."

"On my way." He clicked off.

She dropped the cell phone back in her purse and grabbed her gun. She walked over to the door and unlatched the chain lock, her mind slowly focusing and leaving the momentary brain freeze behind.

She walked to the bed and sat in the center, her body trembling but her gun focused on the door to see who might appear.

Nick?

Or the return of the killer?

Nick drove like a bat out of hell. It was one-thirty, and there was no other traffic on the road. He broke the speed limit and flew through red lights and stop signs. What would normally take him fifteen to twenty minutes to reach the motel tonight took only ten.

He pulled up next to Adrienne's car, his heart beating faster than he ever remembered. *Wendy's killer just paid me a visit.* Adrienne's words had chilled his very soul.

He had no idea what had happened, but was just grateful that she'd been in a condition to call him. Her motel room door was open a crack, and he shoved it open and stepped inside to see her seated on the bed, her gun pointed directly at him.

"Adrienne," he said softly. "Put the gun down. I'm here now and you're safe."

Her face was paper white and her eyes the hue of the green robe she wore. He saw no wounds, except in those eyes of hers, which held a stark terror he could barely stand to see.

"Honey, it's okay. Just put the gun down." He took a step toward her.

Still, she remained as she was, with the gun in her hands and terror screaming from her eyes.

"You don't want to shoot me, Adrienne," he said in a soothing voice. "You're safe now, and it's time to put the gun down."

Her hands trembled as she slowly placed the gun on the bed next to her. With a small cry, she catapulted herself from the bed and into his arms, weeping like a terrified child. He embraced her tightly, whispering soothing words in her ear.

As he tried to calm her, he gazed around the room, seeing no sign of a struggle, no indication of anything amiss. But it was obvious by her violent trembling, by the sound of her cries, that something or someone had absolutely terrified her.

When her sobs finally began to subside, he led her back to the bed, where he sat her down and then grabbed her gun and placed it on the nightstand.

He pulled his own gun from its holster and

checked the bathroom. Nobody was there and nothing appeared out of place. "What happened, Adrienne?" he asked softly as he stood between her and the front door.

She looked so fragile as she visibly fought for composure. Her lower lip trembled, and tears still pooled in her eyes, but she straightened her shoulders. He couldn't help but notice her slender, shapely legs beneath the short green robe.

"He was here," she finally said, her voice a mere whisper. "The killer was here, and he tried to get inside my room."

He frowned and wondered if maybe she'd just had a nightmare that had seemed unusually real. If a man wanted to come through the motel room door, it would have been a fairly easy task. The doors were simple hollow-core ones, and the locks were equally as flimsy.

"At first, he just knocked on the door," she continued. "I asked who was there, and he wouldn't answer, he just kept knocking. Then he jiggled the doorknob so hard he sprung the lock." Her voice trembled with each word that escaped her.

Nick walked over to the door and checked the lock, a chill whispering through him as he realized it was, indeed, broken. He turned back to look at her. "And then what?"

"The chain lock was in place, and he tried to get in, and I used every ounce of strength I had to keep him out. We went back and forth, and if it had gone on any longer, I think the chain would have pulled out of the wood or broken in two and he would have gotten to me."

Once again, Nick looked at the door, this time focusing on the chain. She was right. The end attached to the doorjamb was nearly pulled out, showing the stress of the battle she'd described. This had been no nightmare. It had been very real.

"And then he started knocking again, and finally he stopped, and there was nothing." She shivered, her eyes still holding the horror of her experience.

"Did you see him at all?"

She shook her head. "No, but there's no question in my mind that it was Wendy's killer."

"How can you know that?" he asked. He sat on the edge of the bed, wishing he could take away the fear in her eyes, wishing he'd been here when some creep had tried to break in.

"I heard the start of a car engine right outside, and I knew it was him leaving. I ran to the window and looked out." She moved closer to him on the bed and grabbed his forearm, her fingernails biting into his bare flesh.

"It was Wendy's car, Nick. The person was driving Wendy's car," she exclaimed. "It had to be her killer."

His blood grew even colder. "Are you sure?"

Her eyes blazed brightly. "Positive. It was Wendy's red Mustang. I know it was hers because she had a big dent in the rear quarter panel and she'd put a bumper sticker on it that read 'Ouch.' I saw it, Nick. I saw the car. I saw the bumper sticker. Nobody would be driving her car except the man who killed her."

"We need to get Dillon over here. Maybe his men

can pull some prints off the door." Nick's stomach churned. She was right. There was only one person who could be in possession of Wendy's car, and that was the man who had killed her.

He stood and pulled his cell phone out of his pocket and made the call to Dillon. When he was finished, he sat back on the bed and pulled her into his arms in an attempt to further calm the shivers that still suffused her.

"You're so brave," he said. "Wendy always said you were tough."

"I'm not feeling so tough right now," she replied and cuddled closer against his side. She looked up at him, her now green eyes simmering with emotion. "The only good thing that came out of this is that I think I just cleared your name. You couldn't have been here terrorizing me and then drive off in Wendy's car and gotten back here as fast as you did."

"It's good to know my partner finally believes in me," he replied. "All it took was a black eye, a shoot-out in the street and now this attempted break-in to convince you that I'm really on your side."

"I'm not apologizing for the black eye again," she said and then buried her face against his side as he tightened his arms around her.

Certainly, Nick felt protective over his fellow cowboys on the ranch, and when Cass had been alive, he'd felt the same way about her. But never had he felt the surge of desire to protect a woman as he did now. It filled him heart and soul, the absolute need to keep her safe at any cost.

They remained seated on the bed, Adrienne cuddled in Nick's embrace, until Dillon arrived with two of his officers and then Adrienne moved to sit at the table. As Adrienne retold Dillon what she'd told Nick, he saw the new tremors that filled her body, and he wanted to press her tightly against him.

Officers Michael Goodall and Aaron Kelly pulled on gloves and set to work dusting the door and the doorknob for prints. "I've told Fred a million times that these doors should have dead bolts," Dillon said in obvious frustration.

"At least we now know Wendy's car is still in the area someplace," Nick said. "The killer must be keeping it under wraps, in a garage or a shed somewhere."

"It could take months to search every barn or shed or garage in the town and on the surrounding ranches," Dillon replied. "With the skeletal remains still being guarded day and night by my men, I'm already shorthanded, but I suppose I could assign a couple officers to start a search for the car."

"At least that's something," Adrienne said. "And I hope the first place they start is the Humes Ranch. I just have a bad feeling about that creep Zeke Osmond."

"Most women in town have a bad feeling about Zeke," Dillon said drily. He focused on Nick. "I guess this lets you off the hook."

"I told you all along that I would have never done anything to hurt Wendy," he replied. He looked at Adrienne. "I cared about that girl, and to me she was a funny, bright and lonely kid. She was a friend who didn't deserve to die."

"Nothing on the doorknob or on the door," Officer Kelly said from the doorway. "It looks as though the whole door was wiped clean and the perp must have worn gloves."

Nick wanted to cuss. Damn, but they couldn't seem to get a break. "This creep is so damned smart and so organized."

Was Zeke Osmond capable of being so meticulous in covering his tracks? The thought was a fleeting one. Nick definitely knew Zeke was capable of terrorizing a woman alone in a motel room.

"I do have one bit of information for you," Dillon said. "You were right about the shooter the other night using a rifle. The bullets were .30-30 Winchesters, which accounts for the damage they caused when they hit the buildings and cars."

"Big enough to take down a deer or a bear," Nick said thoughtfully. "So you might be looking for somebody who likes to hunt, although they aren't very good at it since they didn't hit me."

"What in the heck is going on here?" Fred Ferguson, the owner of the motel and the father of Lawrence, who often worked the desk, walked into the room. His bald head shone in the artificial lights overhead. "Lawrence called me and said that the law was here and there was all kinds of activity going on."

"Somebody tried to break in," Nick said. "Thank God Adrienne managed to keep him from getting inside."

Dillon frowned at Fred. "I want dead bolts put in all of the units within a week. I've been telling you for years that you need better security for your guests.

If I had my way, I'd have you replace all these cheap doors, as well."

"We definitely need a new lock on this door for the night," Nick said. "Adrienne is going to pack an overnight bag and come with me. I want to make sure the rest of her things are secure for the night, and then we'll come back tomorrow to get everything and check her out of here."

He felt Adrienne's surprised gaze on him and half expected her to protest, to tell him that she was fine staying here as long as she had her gun and a new lock. But her gun hadn't helped her tonight. He had a feeling that the gun was more an accessory that gave her a false sense of safety than a weapon she would have the guts to use if necessary.

"Where are you taking her?" Dillon asked.

"She can stay at the ranch for now," Nick replied. Nick kept his gaze away from her, knowing she would hate decisions being made without her opinion.

But this was a matter of life and death. The killer knew she was in this room. There was no way he intended to allow her to stay here. She was out of options other than the one he intended for her.

"There's not much else we can do here," Dillon said, deep lines of weariness radiating out from the corners of his eyes. "I'll get a couple of men started on searching for the car, and I'll check out Zeke Osmond's whereabouts during the time in question. That's the best I can do for tonight."

Nick nodded and gazed at Adrienne. "Pack an overnight bag," he said.

"And I'll go get a new lock for the door," Fred

said. He turned on his feet and disappeared back into the night.

Within minutes, everyone was gone except Nick and Adrienne. While she packed a bag, Nick made a phone call to Lucas Taylor, who had moved into the big house at the ranch when he'd hooked up with Nicolette, Cassie's friend.

It took only a minute to explain the situation to Lucas, who assured him Adrienne would have a room at the ranch for as long as she needed one.

By that time, Adrienne had changed in the bathroom from her robe and nightgown to a pair of jeans and a navy T-shirt. All she was missing were boots and a hat to be a cowboy's pinup queen.

He frowned, irritated by his thoughts, especially given the fact that she had just gone through what he considered to be a life-or-death situation. He was a weasel to be thinking about how sexy she looked at that particular moment.

It didn't take long before she had an overnight bag packed and was ready to leave. Fred had returned with a new doorknob and assured her that her things would be safe that night, even if he had to sit in front of the unit with a shotgun.

"I'm sure Lucas was thrilled to be awakened at two in the morning to be asked if a virtual stranger could stay at the house," she said once they were in Nick's Jeep.

"Lucas assured me you were welcome, and Cassie and Nicolette will feel the same way when they hear what happened. You need a safe place to stay for the rest of the night, and you'll definitely be safe there."

"And what about tomorrow?"

Nick hesitated a moment before replying, "Maybe it's time for you to consider heading back home to Kansas City."

"Why would I want to do that now? We've just flushed out the killer." The tremor in her voice that had been apparent since he'd arrived at the motel was gone, and the strength was back.

"And tonight could have ended tragically," he replied. His fingers tightened around the steering wheel as he imagined finding her dead body in the motel room the next morning instead of finding her alive and well.

"If he'd managed to get through that door, you wouldn't have had a chance. You really should consider going home, getting back to your life, and leave the investigation to Dillon and his men."

"I don't think he wanted to kill me tonight," she said slowly...thoughtfully.

He shot her a quick look of surprise. "What makes you think that?"

"Let's be honest. I'm not a big woman with lots of muscles and physical strength. If he really wanted to get through that door, he could have easily overpowered me at any time and gotten in."

"Then, what was his goal?" Nick turned into the entrance of the ranch.

"I think he wanted to terrorize me. I think he wanted to force me to make the decision you just suggested. He wants me to get out of town and stop asking questions."

Nick pulled up to the back porch, where the light

was on. Lucas stood in the doorway. She opened the passenger door. "He scared me tonight, but I'm not leaving, Nick. I'm going to keep pushing and prodding and questioning until Wendy's murderer is behind bars."

She got out of the Jeep, slammed the door and then opened the back door to retrieve her bag. "You've been cleared of the crime. I understand if you want to quit and get back to your own life. Now is the time to tell me if you're in or out of continuing on with me."

"I'm still in," he replied, albeit reluctantly. He couldn't help but worry about her safety after the most recent events. There was no way he could walk away from the situation—from her—now.

"Good. Then, I'll talk to you in the morning." She grabbed her bag, closed the door and then walked to the porch, where Lucas let her into the house.

Nick drove his Jeep into the garage, parked and then got out to walk to his bunk. He'd had no choice but to tell her he was still in.

He had no idea what the killer had intended tonight. Had he simply wanted to scare Adrienne right out of town? Or had he been scared off by a passing car or the fear that somebody might eventually hear Adrienne's screams?

He didn't know if Adrienne had truly processed how close danger had come to her tonight. All he knew for sure was that before tonight he'd known he had a target on his back. He wasn't sure she understood that there was also a large target on her back, as well.

Chapter 7

Cassie Peterson awoke before dawn, as always a sense of frustration gnawing at her. Each morning that she awakened in this bed, her aunt Cass's bed, instead of her own in her apartment in New York City, she was frustrated.

She didn't want to be in Nowhere, Oklahoma. She wanted to be back at her apartment, working her shop in the Soho district and far away from the red dust and lack of civilized amenities of this place.

She hated the brown plaid bedspread, the brown curtains at the windows and the overall depressing decor of the bedroom where she'd awakened for the past couple of months. This might have suited her aunt, but it definitely didn't suit her.

When her aunt Cass had been killed in a tornado a little over two months ago, Cassie had been shocked to learn that she was the beneficiary to this large, thriving ranch.

She, her best friend, Nicolette, and Nicolette's young son had traveled here to check things out. The storm damage had been everywhere, in the fallen trees, the damaged roofs and the shed that had been completely destroyed.

Her plan had been to get the damage fixed as quickly as possible, sell the sprawling, financially successful place and return to her real life in the city.

She hadn't told any of the cowboys working the ranch that she intended to sell, afraid that they'd cut and run to find new jobs before the work here was done.

She felt guilty each time she sat up in bed and faced the wall opposite, where pictures of her aunt Cass and each of her dozen cowboys were framed and hanging.

She'd felt guilty each time foreman Adam Benson had taken time to teach her about the ranch's work-ings, about the bookkeeping and everything she'd need to know to continue on as the owner of the prof-itable ranch. He'd spent a lot of his time attempting to get her up to speed on things.

But her plan to sell had never changed.

For the most part, her plan had worked. Fallen trees were cut and stacked as winter firewood both next to the ranch house and the cowboys' dining room. Roofs were fixed, storm damage was cleaned up and fenc-ing was mended. She'd been so sure her return to the city was simply a week or two away.

Then they'd started the teardown of the damaged

shed, and all hell had broken loose. First, the horrifying discovery of Wendy Bailey's body and then the shocking finding of six skeletal remains, which turned the ranch into a crime scene and ruined her plans to sell out.

Every day she stayed, she got to know the men who worked for her better, understood that they were not just solitary cowboys, but rather brothers bonded by experiences she couldn't begin to understand.

They had loved her aunt Cass, but had made it clear they were withholding judgment where she was concerned. They were Cass's cowboys, and Cassie didn't plan on sticking around long enough for them to consider themselves her cowboys.

She squeezed her eyes closed and tried not to think about what their futures might be when she was finally allowed to sell the ranch.

Right now, she didn't have to think about it. Who knew how long it would be before the crime scene was completely cleaned up and the land released.

They were still awaiting the arrival of the bone specialist, the forensic whatever expert who would work to identify the skeletal remains. That could take weeks or months.

In the meantime, she was trying to make the best of things, but why did all those bodies have to be found on her land? It was as if fate was forcing her to stay despite her desire to leave.

She squeezed her eyes more tightly closed, wishing for another couple of hours of sleep before she had to get up and face another day in this godforsaken country.

* * *

Adrienne opened her eyes to the unfamiliar room Lucas had led her to in the middle of the night. She hadn't paid attention to much of anything except changing into her nightgown and climbing into the queen-size bed. She'd immediately fallen asleep, her mind and body unable to function for another minute.

Sunshine drifted through white lace curtains, and she plumped the pillow beneath her head and looked around the room. It was a pleasant room with a white-and-mint-green bedspread. The nightstands and the long dresser were pinewood with white pulls on the drawers.

There was an adjoining bathroom with white and green tiles and matching striped towels. She knew she should get up and take a shower, get ready to face another day, but she remained unmoving beneath the clean, wind-scented sheets.

Her mind replayed the events of the night before. If only she had looked out the crack between the chain and the door. If only she'd gotten a glimpse of who was trying to get to her, then this would all be over and she'd be on her way back to Kansas City knowing that justice for Wendy had been achieved.

However, she hadn't seen a face or a form that would have allowed her to identify the killer. That meant another day of asking questions and pushing Chief Bowie for answers. At least Nick had agreed to continue to help her.

Nick. She knew virtually nothing about him except that he had been her sister's friend, and yet she trusted him as she'd never trusted a man before. If she was honest with herself, she would acknowledge that she'd never lusted after a man as she did Nick.

Why hadn't he married? Why hadn't some woman scooped him up and lawfully bound him to her? Maybe if she knew more about him she'd learn the reasons why. Not that it mattered to her.

She knew she wasn't marriage material. She wasn't even relationship material. What she didn't know was if she could be a one-night stand kind of woman. When she was around Nick, she thought it might be possible just to take her pleasure with him, satisfy her lust for him for as long as she was in town and then return to her life in Kansas City satisfied with only sweet, passionate memories.

These thoughts pulled her out of bed and into an unusually cool morning shower. She had to stay focused on the reason she had come to Bitterroot, and that reason had nothing to do with making love to Nick Coleman.

She felt unaccountably shy after she showered and dressed and made her way downstairs toward the kitchen, where voices could be heard.

She entered the kitchen to see Nicolette and her son, Sammy, seated at the table. "Good morning," Nicolette greeted her warmly. "Coffee is on the counter. Help yourself to a cup and come join us."

Adrienne poured her coffee and took a seat at the table, where paint samples were scattered between Nicolette and Sammy. "We're picking out colors for our new house," Sammy explained. "I've already picked out the color for my bedroom."

"What color did you pick?" Adrienne asked.

"Blue like the sky. Cowboys like blue skies," he replied.

"And I know a cowboy who hasn't made his bed yet," Nicolette said. "Why don't you head upstairs and get it done and let me visit a bit with Adrienne."

"Okay," Sammy agreed. He got up from the table and disappeared from the room.

Nicolette gathered the paint samples into a neat pile. "Lucas told me what happened last night. How are you feeling this morning?" Her pretty features radiated sympathy.

"I was terrified last night, but it only made me more determined to stick around and find the killer. I'll have Nick take me someplace today where I can rent a room. Surely there's a bed-and-breakfast or something like that in town."

"Nonsense, you'll do no such thing," Nicolette replied firmly. "Cassie left a little while ago with Adam, the foreman. They headed into town to get some supplies, but before she left she told me to tell you that the room upstairs is yours for as long as you need it. We have plenty of room here, and there's no reason for you to go anyplace else."

"I don't know what to say. You've all already been so kind to me." Adrienne wrapped her fingers around her warm coffee cup. "You all don't even really know me."

"But we know Nick, and we know you're important to him, and that's good enough for us," Nicolette replied.

Adrienne took a sip of her coffee. She was important to Nick only because she had boldly insinuated herself into his life, making them both a target of some unknown killer.

"Are you hungry?" Nicolette asked. "I'd be glad to whip something up for you."

"No, thanks, I'm fine with just coffee. Have you heard from Nick this morning?"

"He came in earlier and told me to tell you to call him when you're ready to head back to the motel and get your things."

Adrienne nodded and tried not to think about the crazy thoughts she'd entertained about Nick that had pulled her out of bed. She'd call him after she drank her coffee and chatted a bit more with Nicolette.

Nicolette told her about her own harrowing experience just weeks before when her ex-husband had first tried to kidnap Sammy, and then had attempted to kill Nicolette. Thankfully, Lucas had come to her rescue, Nicolette's ex was now under arrest and Lucas and Nicolette were planning the rest of their lives together.

"We're planning a simple wedding ceremony in about a month," Nicolette said, her eyes shining with a happiness that Adrienne envied. "But the house we bought should be ready for move-in within the next couple of weeks."

Adrienne drank a second cup of coffee, and they talked about the plans for Nicolette's wedding. By that time, it was nearly ten o'clock and time to get to the motel to get checked out.

She called Nick, who appeared within minutes in his Jeep just outside the back door. With a goodbye to Nicolette, Adrienne left the house and slid into the passenger seat of the Jeep.

"Good morning," she said and wondered if there would ever come a time that she'd ever stop wanting to look at him. His face was all intriguing angles and planes that showed both strength and character.

"Good morning to you," he replied, and put the vehicle in gear. "Did you sleep well?"

"I almost hate to admit that despite the trauma of the night I slept like a log. What about you?"

"I tossed and turned and tried to figure out a way to force you to go back to Kansas City." They left the ranch, and he turned on the road that would take them into Bitterroot.

"There's nothing you can say or do to force me to leave here until my business is done," she replied with a hint of coolness in her tone.

"I figured that out, and that's when I finally fell asleep." He cast her a quick glance of amusement. "And you don't need to take that cool princess tone with me."

"I'm just sorry you wasted a minute of sleep thinking about me," she replied.

He shot her another sideways glance, his eyes a midnight blue. "Last night wasn't the first time I lost sleep thinking about you, especially since we shared that kiss."

Her heart nearly stopped beating. "You've thought about that kiss?"

"Daily," he replied. "What about you?"

"Several times a day," she confessed and felt her cheeks warm with a blush. "So what are we going to do about it?"

"Nothing," he replied, and his jaw bunched with a

small knot of tension. "Absolutely nothing. It wouldn't be fair to you to take it any further. I have no desire to form a romantic relationship."

"Pretty egotistical of you to just assume that if we kissed again or did anything else together I would want or expect a romantic relationship with you," she countered. "I don't know anything about you except that you like your eggs over easy and your burgers well-done and with bacon."

Of course, she did know more than that about him. She knew the feeling of safety whenever he embraced her, the warmth of his most simple touch. She knew he had a wry sense of humor and the ability to make her feel as if she was the most important woman on the face of the earth.

"All you need to know about me is that I want Wendy's killer caught as much as you do," he said.

By that time, they had reached the motel. Nick went into the office to get the key for the new lock that Fred had put on the door the night before, and then he parked in front of her unit.

Adrienne stared at the door, and memories of the intruder flashed through her mind. The tormenting knocking, the push against the door to keep the killer out and finally the horrifying view of Wendy's car pulling away. The memories were still so fresh.

"If I'd just been able to grab my purse, I would have shot him," she said as Nick unlocked the door.

Nick looked at her dubiously. "You don't strike me as the type of woman to shoot a person. Why do you even have the gun?"

They stepped into the room. "I got it when I was

twenty-one and living in a bad area of town with Wendy." She began to pack up her computer. "The neighborhood was bad, and I never felt safe there. I thought having a gun was a smart thing."

"Let me do that and you can pack up your clothes," Nick said. He took over the computer equipment while she pulled a large suitcase from the closet and began to pack her clothing.

They worked in silence, and it didn't take long before they had all her belongings loaded into the back of the Jeep. "Why don't we stop in at the café for an early lunch before heading back," he suggested.

"That sounds good to me," she readily agreed. "I skipped breakfast this morning."

When they arrived at the café, they were greeted by Daisy, who led them to a table for two. "Trisha will be right with you." Trisha was the pretty blond waitress that Dusty had a crush on. She and Jenna often alternated sections of the café.

"What are our plans for today?" Adrienne asked while they waited.

"Let's eat and then talk plans," Nick replied.

"Hey, you two." Jenna approached their table, her eyes lit with concern as she looked at Adrienne. "I heard you had a scary night. Thank God you're okay."

"As usual, the grapevine is alive and well," Nick said drily.

Jenna smiled. "Fred was in early this morning and told us all about it. I just stopped by to say that I'm glad to see you well." She touched Nick's shoulder. "And you might want to know that Daisy whipped up a batch of those cinnamon apple dumplings you love."

"Thanks, Jenna. I might have to indulge myself," Nick said and gave her a friendly smile.

Trisha arrived to take their orders, and Jenna hurried back to her own section to take care of her own patrons.

While they ate, Adrienne tried to focus on the food, but her brain worked to figure out what she and Nick should do next in an effort to further the investigation.

She gazed around the room, wondering if one of the men seated at the counter or at one of the booths had killed her sister and come after her.

Last night had been a nightmare, but it had also proved to her that they had touched the killer's nerves, forced him out of hiding and into the open.

They were getting closer, and now it was just a matter of whether they'd find the killer's name before he silenced them forever.

Nick could see the wheels whirling in Adrienne's head as she ate her breakfast. Her gaze darted around the café often, and she was far too quiet.

Whatever plan she intended for after their breakfast, he was going to shut it down. Things had gotten too gnarly the night before.

Each time he thought of her fighting to keep the motel room door closed, of the terror she'd gone through all alone, a knot of fear and tension balled up tight in his stomach.

They were too hot. Danger had come far too close. He owed it to Wendy to ensure her sister's safety. At least at the ranch she should be safe. She'd not only have his eyes on her, but also his fellow cowboys' eyes, as well. No one would dare try anything against the Holiday cowboys.

It was over apple dumplings and coffee that she asked again about their plans. "First, we'll head back to the ranch and get your things unloaded and let you get settled in there. After that, I think we'll see if we can get you on the back of a horse. Have you ever ridden before?"

She stared at him in confusion. "No, and how is getting me on the back of a horse going to help us find Wendy's killer?"

"It's not," he admitted. "But I think we need to cool things down a bit, give Dillon a chance to get us some answers." He could see the mutiny building in her eyes, but he continued, "Adrienne, you got lucky last night. If any number of things had happened differently, then you'd have been another victim and I'd be planning on burying you next to your sister. I can't let that happen. I couldn't live with myself."

He took a sip of his coffee, leaned back and prepared himself for a fight. She stared down at her plate, and when she gazed up at him again, the mutiny in her eyes was gone.

"Okay," she said, surprising him. "We'll take the day off, but that's all I'm willing to agree to right now. One day off."

It was enough for him. He'd worry about tomorrow when the time came. Before they left the café, Perry Wright came in. He hesitated at the sight of them, and then, to Nick's surprise, approached their table.

He nodded to Nick and then offered Adrienne a

shy, sad smile. "I just wanted to let you know that every time I come in here for a meal, I miss seeing Wendy." He shifted from one foot to the other, obviously uncomfortable. "She was such a ray of sunshine and always made me laugh. I miss seeing her pretty smile. I miss everything about her."

He turned abruptly and walked away, sliding into a booth on the other side of the room.

"He's kind of an odd duck," Adrienne said as they left the café.

"His older brother is just the opposite of him. Larry owns a car dealership on the south side of town. He's a loudmouthed, opinionated, egotistical man who probably never let Perry get a word in edgewise when they were growing up."

"Perry just doesn't strike me as the type who could kill a woman, bury her under a shed and then terrorize me last night," she replied thoughtfully. "My bet is still on Zeke Osmond or one of his nasty friends. I want to call Dillon when we get back to the ranch and see if he checked out Zeke's alibi for last night."

"One phone call," Nick said. "And then for the rest of the day you can focus on being a cowgirl instead of catching a murderer. You need a break away from all this. I need a break."

It was true. Nick needed a break from the case, from the constant tension of being on guard. But as he remembered the conversation they'd had earlier about their kiss, he wondered what would be easier: forgetting for a day about murder or forgetting for a day his ever-present and growing desire to take Adrienne to bed.

Chapter 8

It was just after three when Adrienne had her belongings unpacked in the bedroom where she'd slept the
night before. Cassie had been kind enough to let her
set up her computer equipment at the built-in desk in
a corner of the kitchen.

A phone call to Dillon had yielded nothing. Zeke
was alibied for the night before by half a dozen of the
Humes ranch hands who swore they were all involved
in a poker game that had gone on well into the wee
hours of the morning.

Adrienne hung up the phone half fuming and fully
frustrated. Zeke Osmond and his merry men would
alibi each other no matter what the truth might be.
Unless one of them broke ranks, there was no way to
prove the alibi false.

After making the call, she met Nick in the great

room, where he was waiting to take her out to the stables. "I just talked to Dillon. He had nothing, just like he's had nothing since I got to town." She flopped down on the sofa and heaved an angry sigh.

Nick sat on the opposite side of the sofa and leaned toward her. "Give the man a break. He's doing the best he can considering there is no forensic evidence to tie anyone to Wendy's murder. His men are searching for the car, and they're questioning people just like we were. Sooner or later, something is going to break, and the killer will be caught. You should calm down."

She glared at him. "For any future dealings you might have with a woman, never, ever tell her to calm down when she's angry," she exclaimed. "I'll calm down when I'm good and ready to and not because you tell me to."

Nick raised his hands as if in surrender. "Sorry, I just can't take you out to meet the horses when you're obviously upset. They're very sensitive to people's moods."

Emotion pressed tight against her chest. It wasn't anger. Rather, it was a bittersweet regret and sorrow that she'd allowed anger to overtake her. "No, I'm sorry, and you're right, I need to give Dillon a break. This isn't like a crime drama on television where everything is solved easily in an hour. It's just that I need to do something for Wendy to make up for all the things I did and didn't do when I was raising her."

"The last thing Wendy would want is you putting your life on the line for her," Nick said. He stood and held out his hand to her. "Come on, let's go for a walk."

She got up, took his hand, and together they left the house by the back door. The mid-July heat beat down on her shoulders as Nick led her toward the stables.

Just inside the building hay bales were stacked in an otherwise empty horse stall. He pulled her into the stall and gestured for her to sit on one bale of hay while he sat on another one next to her.

"Let's talk about Wendy," he said.

She started to protest, but then realized she wanted—she needed—to talk about her sister and the complicated relationship they had shared. "I'm sure she told you I was mean and hateful when she was growing up, and maybe I was." She drew in a deep breath, calmed by the scent of horse and leather, of hay and Nick.

"I could only afford an apartment in a bad neighborhood with gangs and drugs and crime. I was so afraid of getting it wrong with Wendy. I had nightmares about her joining a gang or losing her to the world of drugs, and so I was tough and rigid and kept her on a very tight rein."

Nick laughed softly. "Knowing your sister, that wasn't a small task."

She offered him a small smile that lasted only a moment. "She fought me every step of the way. She called me a wicked witch who didn't want her to have a life. I didn't want her to have a life. I was too afraid of what she would do with it." She picked up a piece of hay and worried it between her fingers.

"I promised my mother on her deathbed that I

would keep Wendy safe. Mom knew that Wendy could be a wild child, that she was emotional and impulsive and might find trouble. Even after I managed to get us out of the bad neighborhood, I was still too strict. I was too rigid, and when she finally got the chance to be out from under my thumb, she left town. That was almost two years ago."

"But you two kept in communication," Nick said.

She nodded. "She'd call maybe once a month or so. Mostly we texted each other, but our contact was sporadic. I mostly left the contact up to her. I didn't want to intrude in her new life away from me. I don't think she ever really forgave me for being so tough on her when she was young."

Nick relaxed back against the hay, looking like a pinup for a hot cowboy calendar. "She not only forgave you, she admired you," he said.

He pulled his hat off his head and placed it next to him. "Yes, she said you were tough, but she also said it was your toughness that kept her out of trouble. She told me you were uncompromising, overbearing and that there were times growing up that she resented you, but she also told me that if you hadn't been all those things she probably would have wound up dead on the streets."

His words found the perpetual ache that had been inside her soul and gently soothed it. A pressure that had been inside her for a very long time began to release. Wendy had understood why she'd been so tough on her.

"You were her hero, Adrienne," he continued. "She knew the sacrifices you made to keep her out of foster care, to keep her safe and secure. She knew you sacrificed your own youth for her. She not only left you to seek her own freedom, she wanted you to have yours, as well. She hoped you'd finally have a chance to stop worrying about her and start living for yourself."

Adrienne's eyes misted with tears. "She really told you all that, or are you just making it up to make me feel better?"

Nick laughed. "I don't make things up."

"Tell me about you and Wendy. I know she thought a lot of you because she talked about you in her texts to me. That's why I just assumed…" She allowed her voice to trail off.

"That we were lovers." He finished her sentence. "Nothing could be further from the truth. In fact, she often teased me by calling me her favorite uncle Nick." He sat up, a thoughtful expression on his handsome features.

"I don't know why Wendy chose me to latch on to. I do know that she was new to town and hadn't really connected with people her own age yet, and so we just started hanging out together. It was usually in the evenings when she'd finished her shift at the café."

"What did you two do? What did you talk about?" Adrienne asked, hungry to know anything and everything there was to know about the last days or weeks of her sister's life.

He shrugged. "We talked about life. She wanted to know everything there was about working on the ranch. She told me she was still trying to figure out what she wanted to do with her life. She told me she'd gotten a degree in business, but she loved traveling around and meeting new people, experiencing different kinds of work, but hadn't settled on exactly what she wanted to do for the rest of her life."

A small smile curved his lips upward. "She was obsessed with the idea of matchmaking for me. I told her I wasn't interested in a relationship, but she insisted all I needed to make my life complete was the right woman. I think she was using me as a stand-in for you."

Adrienne gazed at him curiously. "What do you mean by that?"

Nick shrugged. "She felt bad that you were so busy raising her you never dated, that you never had any relationships with any men. Your sister was a romantic at heart. She wanted everyone she cared about to be happy and in love."

"I guess she wasn't very successful in her matchmaking attempt for you," Adrienne said.

"No, she wasn't. I don't invest my emotions in other people." He said the words firmly as his gaze held hers, and she didn't know if he was merely sharing something with her or warning her that he might want her, but it would never go any deeper than that.

He abruptly stood. "Now, how about we see if we can get you comfortable in the saddle?"

As he helped her up, she wondered what forces had played out in his life that had made him a confirmed solitary man.

"I heard the forensic anthropologist is supposed to arrive sometime tomorrow," Forest said to Nick as they shared a table at dinnertime.

"Dillon has been saying that for the past couple of days," Nick replied, "but he hasn't shown up yet. Hopefully, he'll arrive soon and get the bones identified quickly and get them off the property."

The tent that protected the crime scene where the old shed had stood was a haunting daily reminder not only of Wendy's death, but also of something evil that had once happened on the ranch. There was no telling when that evil had occurred until the professional arrived to age the bones and the approximate time that the people had died.

"Actually, it's a she. Dr. Patience Forbes," Forest replied. Forest Stevens was a big man, the go-to cowboy when something heavy had to be lifted or moved. But his true talent was in working with the horses. He had the gift of gentling the wildest horse and earning the animal's trust.

"Dillon looks as though he's aged ten more years every time I see him," Dusty Crawford said. At twenty-six, Dusty was the youngest of the cowboys working at the ranch and was usually the most teased of the bunch.

"He's got a lot on his plate right now," Nick replied.

"I wonder if he'll have to call in the FBI." Forest scooted over on the bench to allow Adam to join them.

Adam grinned at Nick. "I saw you managed to get Adrienne riding this afternoon."

Nick nodded. "It was my effort to try to get her mind off everything that's happened since she arrived in town. If she had her way, she'd stand in the middle of Main Street and taunt the killer to come after her again."

"What are the odds of that happening anyway?" Forest asked. "The killer trying to get to her again?"

Nick frowned thoughtfully. "I don't know. What happened at the motel scared the hell out of me. I can't bet on the killer not coming for her again, especially as long as she stays here in town and keeps digging for answers."

"So what's your plan?" Forest asked.

"If I can keep her here for a while, out of town and not stirring up things, then she should be okay. But the biggest problem for me is going to be keeping her here at the ranch. She's stubborn and she wants justice."

"Nothing worse than a stubborn woman," Dusty said and released a deep sigh. Everyone knew that Dusty had a crush on Trisha Cahill, one of the waitresses at the café, but so far she wasn't biting on what he was selling.

Forest smiled. "Don't worry, Dusty. You're young enough that you'll eventually learn that all women have more than a little streak of stubbornness in them. You just need to learn how to gentle them."

"And you've figured that out? I don't even remember the last time you had a date," Dusty retorted.

Forest gave him a rueful smile. "Horses I understand. I have yet to master the art of charming a woman."

After dinner, Nick sat in his bunk and thought of Adrienne's tunnel-vision stubbornness when it came to her desire to catch the killer.

He'd hoped that in talking to her today about her sister and how much Wendy had loved her, he'd ease the driving need she had to catch the killer. He'd hoped to give her enough peace that she might decide to go home and pick up the pieces of her life away from here. But that hadn't happened.

Somehow, he needed to keep her occupied at the ranch for a while. He didn't want her putting herself at risk again. The less she was seen in town asking questions, the better for everyone.

Maybe tomorrow he'd sneak in a word with Nicolette and Cassie and see if they could help him keep Adrienne busy here, where she would remain safe.

Adrienne had proved to be all in when it came to riding a horse. She'd tackled it just as he suspected she tackled everything in life—with determination and steely strength. She'd climbed on the back of the horse and within an hour had learned the tools to control and ride without issues.

He couldn't deny that each moment he spent with her only shot his desire to make love with her higher. There was no way to pretend that the sexual tension between them wasn't intense.

But he was confident that he had a handle on it, that nothing would come of it. He could want her and not act on that desire. He was confident of his self-control.

He was also vaguely surprised to realize that despite the fact that she'd punched him in the eye when she first met him, in spite of her stubborn strength and bullheadedness, he liked her. She had the ability to make him laugh, and when she looked at him, she made him feel as if he wanted to be a better man, wanted to be whatever she needed at the moment.

It was twilight when Nick made his way from the bunkhouse to the big house, the first step in keeping Adrienne on the ranch the foremost thought on his mind.

Lucas answered the back door, appearing unsurprised by Nick's appearance. "I'm assuming you're here for Adrienne."

"No, I just missed seeing your ugly mug and decided to come by," Nick replied. Of all the cowboys working the ranch, Nick had always felt closest to Lucas.

"Yeah, right," Lucas said drily as he opened the screen door to allow Nick inside.

Nick heard the murmur of voices coming from the great room, and before Lucas could take him there, Nick grabbed Lucas's arm. "I'm planning on taking Adrienne down by the pond for a little stargazing. I want to keep her out late enough that hopefully she'll sleep late in the morning."

He quickly explained his desire to keep Adrienne busy at the ranch for a while and away from town. Lucas readily agreed to enlist Nicolette and Cassie's help in the plan.

Assured by Lucas, the two men headed for the great room, where Cassie and young Sammy were playing a video game on the television and Nicolette and Adrienne were on the sofa cheering them on.

Adrienne looked up at him as he entered the room, and warmth filled her eyes and lifted the corners of her mouth into a bright smile. "Nick, I didn't expect to see you again today."

He hated the way the warmth of her gaze burrowed into him, and suddenly he thought his idea for the night was a bad one. But it was too late now.

"I thought maybe you'd like to join me down by the pond and do a little stargazing," he said.

"Ah, be careful, Adrienne, it was stargazing that turned me from a New York woman into an Oklahoma one," Nicolette said, and exchanged a loving glance with Lucas.

Adrienne got up from the sofa. "I'll take my chances," she said.

"Let me get you a spare key to the back door," Lucas said. "Just in case you come in after we've all gone to bed." He walked over to the bookcase and opened a black-and-gold trinket box. He withdrew a key and handed it to Adrienne, who shoved it into the front pocket of her capris.

"Ready?" Nick asked.

"Sure, let's go."

They left by the back door in the kitchen. Twilight was just barely hanging on, and the air smelled of earth and grass and a whisper of Adrienne's heady perfume.

"This is a surprise," she said as he led her in the direction of the bunkhouse.

"Your sister used to like sitting by the pond at night, so I thought you might enjoy it, too," he replied. "We just need to stop by the dining room and grab a couple of lawn chairs and a flashlight."

"Sounds like a plan," she replied.

They retrieved the lawn chairs and flashlight from a large closet in the cowboys' dining room. Nick grabbed a small duffel, placed a couple of beers inside and then they set off walking to the pond in the far distance.

From the pond, the crime scene tent couldn't be seen, nor could many of the ranch outbuildings. The only other structures were half a dozen silos that rose up from the ground, looking like huge beer cans decorating the landscape.

At this time of night, the cattle grouped in an area some distance away from the pond, although they greeted the two humans with low moos.

"They're so big," Adrienne said as they set up their lawn chairs on a small wooden dock. "Will they come any closer?" There was a touch of concern in her voice.

"No, they won't bother us." Nick set up the chairs on a small wooden dock that extended out a bit over the pond water. He set the flashlight next to his chair and then pulled a beer from the bag, unscrewed the top and handed her the bottle. He then got himself a beer and settled back in the chair.

"What's inside the silos?" she asked.

"Corn. Cass dabbled in a little bit of everything. We don't use the corn here on the ranch, but she sold it to locals who use it for feed."

"Sounds as if she was a smart businesswoman."

"She was," he agreed. "Time will tell if Cassie is as ranch business savvy as her namesake."

Adrienne relaxed back into the chair. "It's been a

nice day," she said. "I can't believe how nice everyone is, and Sammy is a little cutie."

"Don't let him hear you call him that. He's a cowboy and that's all he wants to be."

"Is that what you wanted to be when you were a little boy?" she asked and took a sip of the cold beer.

"No, I didn't realize I wanted to be a cowboy until I was sixteen and started working here. Before that, I didn't know for sure what my future held." A familiar knot of tension grew hard in his chest. It was familiar in that it always appeared when he thought about his life before coming to the Holiday Ranch.

"Looks as if the moon is showing off for you tonight," he said and pointed to the full moon shining down.

"It is beautiful," she replied. "It looks close enough that you could just reach up and wrap your arms around it." She turned and smiled at him, her pretty features lit with the silvery lunar light.

You're beautiful. The words were on the tip of his tongue, but he swallowed them away and instead stared at the shimmering shine of the moon on the pond water.

For a few minutes, the sound of insects, the throaty croak of a frog and the occasional splash of a fish were the only noise. For Nick it was a pleasant kind of white noise that brought relaxation and a peace he rarely found anyplace else.

"All of you men who work here, you seem very close," she said, finally breaking the silence.

"We are. We all came to the ranch around the same time as teenagers and grew up together, and we're all like brothers," he replied. "I always know they have my back, and they know I have theirs."

"It sounds as though you're going to miss Lucas when he and Nicolette move into their new place."

"Lucas will still be around and a part of my life," he said with confidence.

"Cassie said there were twelve of you. Will she hire somebody else on to take Lucas's place?"

"Probably eventually, but with everything that's going on at the ranch right now, I doubt if she does anything anytime soon."

"It's definitely creepy, the discovery of all those skeletons. Has anyone said anything about how they got there?"

"Nobody at the ranch has any knowledge about it. For all we know, they were there long before we came here, maybe even before Cass and her husband bought the ranch."

"I guess you'll get some answers soon. Cassie told me at dinner that they were expecting the bone expert to arrive tomorrow."

"That's what I heard, but she's been held up a couple of times already. Besides, we aren't out here to talk about murders or skeletons. Surely we can find something more pleasant to talk about." He gazed at her once again, wishing she didn't look so stunning in the moonlight.

"You're right," she replied with a smile. "It's been much too pleasant a day to end it with such talk. Look, there's the Big Dipper."

Nick followed her gaze upward and then began to point out other constellations in the star-studded sky.

They cracked open another beer and talked about the possibility of life on another planet, what those aliens might look like and if they believed there were aliens walking and living on earth.

It was a ridiculous conversation that resulted in shared laughter. It was the first time he'd heard her really laugh, and he definitely liked the sound of it. Her laughter did something physical to him…unlocked pieces of him that made him feel more relaxed, more comfortable with her.

"Do you cook?" she asked after they talked about their favorite kinds of food.

"No way. If it wasn't for Cookie and the café, I'd probably starve to death. I'll bet you're a good cook."

She smiled. "Initially, Wendy and I lived on a lot of frozen pizzas and boxed macaroni and cheese, but as I started making more money with my business, I also developed an interest in real cooking. Wendy got the worst of fast food and boxed meals and some of the best cuisine I could possibly whip up in her years with me."

"You know, they say food is the way to a man's heart," Nick said, surprised at a small flutter of jealousy as he thought of her cooking something wonderful for some special man.

"That's not true. At least it wasn't true for me in my brief foray into the dating world. About a year ago, I met a man and we started dating. I pulled out all the stops, cooked him gourmet meals, tried to be as accommodating as possible, and I thought we were moving along in the relationship nicely."

She paused and stared at the pond. She didn't look

sad or bitter. Rather, she looked resigned. "Anyway, it didn't work out, and it just confirmed to me that I'm better off alone."

Whoever the guy was, he must have done a number on her for her to come to that conclusion after only one attempt at finding love.

"What happened to end it?" he asked, knowing he was prying but also wanting the answer.

"He told me I was too set in my ways. I had no spontaneity and liked to control things. Enough about me," she said and turned to gaze at him. "Tell me about you, Nick. Are you originally from around here?"

"Oklahoma City," he replied, the knot of tension once again balling up in the center of his chest.

"Do you still have family there?"

"I haven't had family since I was eight years old." The knot of tension tightened. He didn't talk about his past. The only people who knew his story had been Cass, the social worker who had brought him to the ranch and the other ranch hands, who had their own sordid stories of hellish youths to tell.

"What happened when you were eight?" she asked, her voice a soft caress that urged him to share.

He realized he wanted to share, not because the story was sad and she'd feel bad for him, but because it would make her understand why he had no desire to emotionally invest in anyone ever again.

"When I was eight, my mother took me to the zoo," he began, and the knot in his chest felt as if it might cut off his breath. "It was a special day because she didn't often go out of her way to pay much attention to me. She spent most of her time when I was young trying to find a husband while I spent a lot of time with babysitters.

"Anyway, we saw the monkeys and the seals, the giraffes and elephants, and then we came to the lion display. She sat me on a bench and said she was going to get us ice-cream cones."

He finished his second beer, dropped the empty bottle in the duffel bag and then stared out at the pond, unable to look at Adrienne while he accessed the old memories that, surprisingly, still had the power to haunt him.

"I watched her walk away and couldn't wait for her to come back. It was late afternoon, and I'd never been so happy in my life," he continued. "A day with my mom and ice cream to boot. It was a stellar day for me."

"What about your father?" Adrienne asked. "Did he have any part in your life?"

"Never knew him. I'm not sure my mother knew who my father was, but in any case, I never knew his name, and he certainly wasn't a presence in my life."

"I don't know what's worse, never knowing your father or having him in your life for almost ten years and then have him walk away from the family and never look back. Mine left when Mom was pregnant with Wendy. Wendy was an oops baby, and my father had no interest in raising another kid." Adrienne sighed. "Anyway, back to the ice-cream cone and the zoo."

"Like I said, it was late afternoon when she left me, and I waited and waited for her to come back with the ice cream. As time passed, I started to get scared. I started thinking about all kinds of terrible things. She'd fallen into the lion's den or maybe somebody had kidnapped her. It finally got to be closing time, and a zoo worker found me on the bench and called the police. Two officers came and discovered that my mother's car was gone from the parking lot."

Once again, he stared off in the distance, where a faint light winked in the distance from the isolated cottage where Cookie lived alone. "I went into child protective services, and the police began an investigation."

"Did they ever find out what happened to her?" Adrienne's voice held a wealth of emotion, emotion he didn't want to feel or tap into in any way.

"Yeah, they finally found her two months later in Phoenix, Arizona. She'd married and was living a nice life. She signed away any parental rights to me, and for the next seven years, I bounced from foster home to foster home. I was an angry, confused and hurt child who couldn't quite grasp the idea that my mother didn't want me."

"Oh, Nick, I'm so sorry."

"Don't be," he replied quickly. "It happened a long time ago. When I was fifteen, I ran away from the system and took to the streets. When I was sixteen, a social worker who unofficially worked with the runaways asked me if I wanted something better than sleeping under bridges and eating out of trash cans. She's the one who brought me here to Cass, and I found a home here with other damaged kids Cass had brought here to turn into cowboys and work her ranch."

He finally turned to look at Adrienne, and in the moonlight, he saw tears trekking down her cheeks. "Don't cry for me," he said. "Coming here was the best thing that ever happened to me."

"I'm not crying for the man you've become. I'm crying for the little boy who waited for his mother to come back and she never did." She swiped at her tears.

"That little boy is long gone," he said. "But that's why I don't invest too much in people. I loved my mother, and she walked away from me. I loved Cass, and she died in the tornado.

"When I was twenty-two, I fancied myself in love with a woman named Michelle. When I asked her to marry me, she told me she was looking for more than a foster-kid cowboy, and I watched her walk away from me. I'm not giving anyone else a chance to get into my heart again."

He said the last words as a warning to her. He was capable of helping her find her sister's killer. He was also more than capable of taking her to bed and giving her as much pleasure as possible.

But his heart was locked up tight and would never again be accessed by anyone. He couldn't stand the idea of watching somebody he loved walk away from him one more time. He refused to allow himself to love somebody who could be taken from him.

Chapter 9

It was just after eleven when Adrienne finally made her way downstairs the next morning. She was appalled by how late she had slept. Of course, it had been after two when Nick finally walked her back to the house the night before, and it had been after three before she'd finally fallen asleep.

She'd been in Bitterroot only a week and a day, and yet it felt as if she'd been here for months, given everything that had happened in such a short time.

She walked to the kitchen, where she found Cassie, Nicolette and Sammy preparing food for lunch.

"There's the sleepyhead," Cassie said with a grin.

"I can't believe I slept so long," Adrienne replied. "Between Nick keeping me out so late last night and everything else that has gone on in the past week, I guess I just finally crashed out."

"You must have needed the extra sleep," Nicolette replied. She stood at the counter, cutting up a head of cabbage for what Adrienne assumed would be cole-slaw. Cassie was at the oven, where the scent of a cooking ham filled the air, and Sammy was busy setting the table.

"Is there anything I can do to help?" Adrienne asked.

"Pour yourself a cup of coffee and relax. We've got this covered," Cassie replied.

"Are you Cowboy Nick's girlfriend?" Sammy asked.

"Sammy!" Nicolette exclaimed, and Adrienne couldn't help but laugh.

"No, I'm not Cowboy Nick's girlfriend. I'm just a friend who he is helping out right now." Adrienne poured a cup of coffee and then sat at the table.

"You're pretty enough to be a girlfriend," Sammy said and gave her a bright smile.

"And you're quite the charmer this morning," Adrienne replied.

"He must have been bitten by the charm bug over-night," Nicolette replied lightly.

Sammy giggled, and Adrienne found herself re-laxing into the domestic scene and the interaction between mother and child. She also envied the obvi-ous close friendship between Cassie and Nicolette.

Adrienne didn't have any close female friends. When she'd been raising Wendy there had been no time for friendships, no time for clubbing or doing lunch with anyone.

After Wendy had left Kansas City, Adrienne's work was at home, and she rarely went anywhere to make friends. She'd always hoped that eventually she'd have that kind of relationship with her sister. She'd always hoped that Wendy would be her built-in best friend.

She shoved away thoughts of Wendy and what might have been and instead promised herself that when she got back home she'd find a book club or join a gym…do something and go somewhere in an effort to make new friends.

"Has anyone seen Nick this morning?" she asked.

"He stopped in earlier and said to tell you he had a few things to take care of and would see you some-time after lunch," Cassie replied.

"About this afternoon, Cassie and I have a big favor to ask you," Nicolette said.

"We know it's a big imposition, but Nicolette and I have an appointment with a lawyer this afternoon for some business, and we were wondering if maybe you wouldn't mind watching Sammy," Cassie said. "It shouldn't take us more than an hour or two."

Although Adrienne wanted to get back on the street and continue their investigation, she definitely couldn't refuse to do a favor for the people who had taken her in and provided her safety.

"Of course I wouldn't mind," she replied and smiled at Sammy. "Maybe you can teach me to play some of your games on my computer."

"Sure, I'll teach you how to play 'Zombie Cow-boys.' It's one of my favorites," Sammy said.

"That sounds scary. It won't give me nightmares, will it?" she asked.

"Nah, it's more funny than scary. The zombies are

really dorky and dumb, and the cowboys always win the battles," Sammy explained.

It was exactly noon when Lucas came through the back door. At the same time, Cassie added a platter of sliced ham to the other food items on the table and pronounced that lunch was served.

While they ate, Nicolette and Lucas talked about the work they were finishing up on the house he had bought for them, their plans for a wedding within the next month and Sammy's intention to get a puppy the minute they got settled.

Adrienne listened to the talk of weddings and new beginnings and an unexpected yearning whispered through her. She'd once thought she could have a special man, a happily-ever-after with a person whom she loved and who loved her.

But life events had stolen that dream from her. She was damaged goods...like Nick. Her years of raising Wendy had turned her into a woman no man would ever want forever.

Her heart squeezed as she thought of what Nick had endured as a child. Abandoned by his mother and eventually preferring life on the streets to foster care, it was no wonder he didn't trust his emotions to anyone anymore. He'd had so much loss in his life.

After lunch, Lucas went back outside to work and Cassie and Nicolette left for their appointment with the lawyer. Sammy and Adrienne were playing on her computer in the kitchen when Nick came in the back door.

"What's up, short stuff?" He ruffled Sammy's hair and smiled at Adrienne.

"I'm teaching Adrienne how to play 'Zombie Cowboys,'" Sammy replied.

Adrienne smiled up at Nick, who looked totally sexy in his worn jeans, a white T-shirt and his black cowboy hat on his head. "So far, I stink," she said. "The zombies keep kicking my butt."

Nick laughed. "Maybe it's time to step away from the game. I have some hay to move from the barn to the stables, and I was wondering if anyone would be up for a short hayride." Nick's eyes held none of the darkness they had the night before when he'd shared his memories, his past with her.

"I'm up for a hayride." Sammy jumped out of his chair like a piece of popped corn.

"Thank goodness, saved from the killer zombies," Adrienne said with a laugh as she also stood.

"I've got a wagon hooked to the tractor just outside the back door," Nick replied. Before the words were out of Nick's mouth, Sammy grabbed his cowboy hat off a hook in the kitchen and ran out the back door.

Nick laughed and shook his head. "For a former city boy, Sammy has definitely embraced the country life."

"I'm just grateful not to have to face another zombie," she replied. "They just kept coming, and I wasn't fast enough at the controls to stop them from turning me into a zombie."

They stepped out the back door, where Sammy was already in the back of an empty wood-sided wagon hooked up to a tractor. "Come on, Adrienne," he said. "You have to get in here and hang on while Nick takes us to the barn."

Adrienne climbed up into the wagon and walked toward the front, where Sammy clung to the thick plywood siding that was tall enough to hit her midchest.

"All set?" Nick asked.

"Ready, set, go!" Sammy cried.

Nick climbed onto the tractor seat and started the engine. Sammy whooped his excitement and reminded Adrienne to hang on tight. Then they were off across the uneven terrain toward the barn in the distance.

Each time they hit a bump Sammy giggled, his laughter riding the light breeze that was warm, but not unpleasantly so.

"Faster, Cowboy Nick," Sammy yelled.

Nick raised a hand in acknowledgment and revved the tractor engine, but Adrienne realized their pace didn't accelerate at all. Obviously, Nick knew the speed that would be safest for his cargo. He also knew how to fool a little boy with a quick rev of an engine.

They reached the barn, and Adrienne and Sammy climbed out of the wagon. For the next fifteen minutes, Nick used a large hook tool to hook and carry bale after bale of hay from the barn and load them into the wagon.

Adrienne tried not to notice how his biceps and back muscles danced beneath his shirt as he carried the heavy bales.

Her head filled with the memory of the single kiss she'd shared with him, and the sun overhead suddenly felt hotter and more intense. She tried to ignore the flashes of heat that fired through her. Drat the man anyway, she thought. He looked hot no matter what he was doing.

When he was satisfied he'd loaded the wagon enough, he indicated for Sammy and Adrienne to follow him into the barn. Adrienne followed Sammy into the building. There was no sign of Nick, except his hat hanging from a wooden post.

"He's hiding," Sammy said with excitement.

Before them were stacks and stacks of hay bales, but they stood in front of a stall that held nothing but loose hay piled about three feet tall.

Nick jumped out at them and grabbed both her hand and Sammy's and pulled them into the thick bed of hay. Adrienne's laughter joined Sammy's as she landed on her back, cushioned by the fresh-smelling dried grass.

She sat up and watched as Nick picked Sammy up and tossed him in the air, Sammy giggling hysterically as he landed a couple of feet away.

"Hay fight," Sammy exclaimed and picked up handfuls of hay and threw them at Nick.

Adrienne did the same, laughing as Nick quickly started to look like a straw man with hay stuck in his hair and on his clothes.

The hay fight transformed into a wrestling match with Nick first taking Sammy down and then chasing after Adrienne. She ran from one corner to the other in an attempt to escape him, but he caught her and wrestled her down, his body half on top of hers.

Her breath whooshed out of her, not due to the soft fall, but due to his intimate closeness to her. His gaze held hers for a long moment, and in the depths of his dark blue eyes, she saw unbridled desire. She saw the kiss he wanted to give her in those eyes, and she yearned for it to happen.

He quickly rolled off her and once again went after Sammy.

She managed to get out of the stall before he could catch her again, and by that time, Sammy had thrown himself like a monkey onto Nick's back.

Adrienne watched from outside the stall as Nick and Sammy continued to wrestle. Nick seemed to know instinctively how to give Sammy a thrill yet be as gentle as possible so the six-year-old didn't get hurt.

He'd already given her a thrill. His body being so close to hers had fired up a desire for him that had been simmering for what felt like a lifetime.

Her heart also warmed as she saw how easily Nick interacted with the little boy. It was obvious Sammy adored Nick and that the feeling was mutual.

Nick would have made a terrific father, she thought once they were back in the wagon and headed to the stables while seated on bales of hay. He was patient and treated the boy with just the right amount of respect and authority.

Once they reached the stables, Adrienne sat on a bench just inside and watched while Nick unloaded the wagon, bale by bale. Nick hefted each one and allowed Sammy to hold the other end, giving the boy the belief that he was helping.

Adrienne had never thought about having children, but as she watched the two interact, she wondered what it would be like to have a little boy or girl of her own.

Wendy had come to be in her custody as an angry, grieving eleven-year-old who was mad at the world because her mother had been taken from her. Adrienne liked to think that if she had a baby to raise she wouldn't make the same mistakes she'd made with Wendy.

But there wouldn't be any babies for her, and from everything Nick had said, there wouldn't be babies for him, either. She thought there was something a little tragic about that.

Once they were finished stacking the hay, Nick lifted Sammy up on his shoulders as they walked back toward the house. Sammy rode those broad shoulders with a wide smile on his face and his hands resting comfortably on Nick's jaws.

It was at that moment that Adrienne realized she was more than just a little bit in love with Cowboy Nick.

With Nicolette and Cassie's help, Nick managed to keep Adrienne busy around the ranch for the next four days. One day, Nicolette took her to the house she and Lucas were renovating before moving in. Somehow, Nicolette managed to convince Adrienne to help her paint the master bedroom.

Cassie had kept her busy for an entire morning by asking Adrienne to show her what she did for a living. That afternoon, Cassie and Nicolette had planned a late-afternoon picnic and had insisted that Adrienne and Nick come along.

Nick had also done his job at keeping Adrienne busy. He told her he needed to check out some fencing at the back of the Holiday Ranch land. He'd invited her for the ride, and for two hours, they'd talked as they rode along the fencing that separated Holiday land from Breckenridge property.

As they rode back, they followed the fence line that separated the Holiday Ranch from the Humes Ranch, and he told her about the bad blood that had existed between Cass and Raymond Humes.

"It's kind of like the Hatfield and McCoy feud," he'd said. "Except nobody knows exactly how the fight started, and nobody seems willing to end it."

The day before, the bone lady had finally arrived driving a powerful white pickup and pulling a huge white trailer that Nick suspected held all kinds of special equipment. She hadn't come alone. She'd brought an assistant with her, a middle-aged man named Devon Lewison.

Cassie had made arrangements for Dr. Patience Forbes to stay in the bunk room that Lucas had used before falling in love with Nicolette and moving into the big house. The assistant apparently had a cot in the trailer that he would call home for the duration of their investigation.

It was at nine o'clock on the morning of the fifth day that Adrienne stood on the back porch waiting for Nick, and he could tell by her rigid stance and the nicer clothes she wore that there was probably no way he was going to keep her out of town any longer.

Nick slowed his footsteps as he approached her. There was no question that he felt a closeness to her that he'd never felt for any other woman. The time they had spent together the past four days had not just increased his lust for her, but had also yielded a healthy respect and the repeated surprise that he liked her…he liked her more than he should.

"Don't you dawdle, Nick Coleman," she said firmly when he was within hearing distance. "I've played it your way for four days now."

He stepped up on the porch with her. "My way? What are you talking about?" he asked, feigning innocence.

She narrowed her beautiful eyes, which were more blue than green today. "Don't you play dumb with me. I know you've gone out of your way to manufacture all kinds of things to keep me busy and on this ranch and out of town, but now it's time to get back to work. We have a killer to catch."

He leaned against the porch railing. "I was hoping we'd do a little fishing today," he replied. "The pond is full of bass and crappie, and if we'd catch enough, Cookie could do a big fish fry for everyone tonight. There's nothing more rewarding than landing a big fighting bass."

"I'm not spending the day fishing." She had that intractable tone in her voice.

"My friend Chad Bene called me last night and told me one of their ranch dogs gave birth to five puppies. Maybe you'd like to head over there and see the little critters?" He raised a dark brow quizzically.

She shook her head, her shoulder-length hair shining in the sunshine. She looked beautiful and sexy and on the verge of an imminent explosion. "Nick, you can't change my mind with warm and fuzzy puppies or the promise of a fish fry. There is absolutely nothing you can say to change my mind. It's time for me to get back to the reason I'm here in Bitterroot, and if you need to be here at the ranch, I understand. But with you or without you, I'm heading into town."

Nick shoved his hands in his pockets and rocked back on his heels. "Got yourself all worked up about it, don't you?" he said with a touch of amusement and then wondered when they had gotten close enough for him to feel comfortable to tease her.

Her cheeks grew pink. "I'm not worked up. I'm just ready to get on with things."

Before Nick could reply, Dillon Bowie's patrol car pulled around the house and parked. "Good morning," Dillon said as he got out of his car and approached them.

"You look a little more relaxed than the last time I saw you," Nick observed as Dillon joined them on the small porch.

The lawman pointed in the distance where the huge white van was parked next to the crime scene tent. "The arrival of Dr. Patience Forbes has put my mind at ease that at least we can begin the process of figuring out the mystery of all those skeletons."

"What's she like?" Adrienne asked.

Dillon frowned. "Petite, red hair, green eyes, definitely attractive, but she's also intense, very bossy and a little bit strange. I suppose I'll take strange if she can help us identify those skeletons, but I'm not here about her."

"Has something happened?" Adrienne asked eagerly. "Have you found out who killed my sister?"

"No, but I do have somebody who has moved up

on the suspect list since the last time we spoke. I've had an officer watching Wendy's grave since she was buried."

"Because sometimes the killer will visit the grave of the person he killed," Adrienne said, and then added, "I watch a lot of crime dramas."

Dillon nodded. "I figured it might be worth a shot. Last night at around midnight Wendy's grave had a visitor. Perry Wright showed up with a single red rose and spent fifteen minutes on his knees weeping in front of her headstone."

"Did you arrest him?" Adrienne practically vibrated with tension. Nick placed a hand on her shoulder, wanting to steady her for whatever was to come.

"It's not illegal to leave a rose on a grave and cry," Dillon replied with a frown. "So, no, he wasn't arrested. In fact, I told the officer not to interact with him at all. But it got me thinking about Wendy's car, which we know is probably still someplace in the area."

"Larry." Nick instantly knew where Dillon's thoughts had gone. Adrienne looked at him questioningly. "Larry is Perry's brother who owns the car lot," he explained.

"And a large garage for mechanic work plus at least a couple of acres of a variety of junked vehicles," Dillon said. "It's possible Wendy's car is out there now hidden in plain sight, and if we find it there, then we have a link to Perry that could lead to his arrest."

Dillon looked at his wristwatch and then gazed up at Adrienne. "I'm meeting a couple of my deputies at the car lot in about fifteen minutes. I just wanted to keep you up-to-date."

Nick groaned inwardly, wishing Dillon hadn't told them his plans. He knew exactly what would happen next.

"Thanks for the update," Adrienne said.

Dillon nodded. "I'll keep you posted." He walked back to his car and left.

"I'm going, too," Adrienne said.

It was exactly what Nick had expected, and he knew there was no way he or Dillon would be able to stop her short of hog-tying her to a wooden post.

Larry's car dealership was open to the public, and Dillon questioning the man wouldn't force Larry to shut down his business.

Nick tensed and touched the butt of his gun. If Larry Wright was complicit in his brother's murder of Wendy, then who knew what kind of danger they all might be walking into.

Chapter 10

"I should have known it was Perry," Adrienne said vehemently as she rolled down the Jeep's passenger window to allow in some air. "It's always the shy, quiet type who ends up being the crazy bad guy."

"We don't know for sure that Perry is the crazy bad guy," Nick replied. He followed some distance behind Dillon's car.

Adrienne wanted to tell him to speed up. Didn't he realize they were on the verge of solving everything? That this could be the end of the danger to him and to her?

She was certain Wendy's car was either at the car lot or in the junkyard. She felt it in her heart, in her very soul. She was positive the mystery was about to be solved and finally Wendy would rest at peace with her killer behind bars.

"We know he had a crush on Wendy. He must have told her about it, and when she told him she wasn't interested in him, he exploded. That's what the quiet loners do. They spend years stuffing down their feelings and then they just explode. Maybe he'd seen her with you and so after he stabbed her he drove to the ranch and buried her there, hoping that you'd be implicated in her death." It all made perfect sense in her mind. It had to be right because so far nothing else had made any sense.

"Adrienne, you're jumping to all kinds of conclusions," Nick said, a gentle warning in his voice. "It's possible we won't find Wendy's car there. It's possible Perry had nothing to do with Wendy's death."

"The car will be there," she replied firmly.

She closed her eyes and could see it all, Perry confronting Wendy and Wendy blowing him off. She could see Perry's pleasant features twisting with an explosion of suppressed rage as he withdrew a knife from his pocket and stabbed her. In the heart—the place where she'd hurt him.

Perry was slim built and it was possible he hadn't been strong enough to break through her motel room door. It had to be Perry. She was certain of it. His visit to the graveyard and his tears could have been the regret of a killer.

This was the beginning of the end. Justice for Wendy and a finality for her. She looked over at Nick and then back out the passenger window. The end was coming at just the right time—before she got any more involved with Nick.

Her heart thudded the uneasy rhythm of anxiety.

Would Larry stop them from searching his property? How fast could Dillon get a search warrant, if necessary? Was there even enough evidence against Perry for a judge to issue a search warrant?

As they reached the official city limits of the small town, her heartbeat accelerated. Although it would be difficult to say goodbye to Nick and all the other people at the ranch who had been so kind to her, she needed an end, especially after the past four days.

Spending time with Cassie, Nicolette, little Sammy and Lucas had given her a glimpse into what ordinary life in Bitterroot would be like. And she'd liked what she'd seen.

During those four days, she had learned the names of most of the cowboys who worked the ranch, had seen the bonds of caring and kindness. She'd also learned so much more about Nick.

He was fiercely loyal to his coworkers and devoted to the ranch. He might be damaged by the forces of fate that had blown him helter-skelter in his youth, but she sensed a wealth of untapped love trapped inside him, ready to spring free if he would just allow himself to trust again.

He had a fun sense of humor, a firm moral compass and the ability to put her in her place when she needed it. Yes, it would be hard to tell him goodbye, but it was an inevitable conclusion to this painful chapter of her life.

She didn't know what the next chapter might hold. She was going back to a small apartment with the knowledge that she would never look forward to a text or a phone call from Wendy again. It would be a lonely place, especially after her interaction with so many people here.

She sat up straighter in the seat as the car lot came into view. A small sales building with huge windows was topped by a sign that read Fair Larry's Car Lot. Beyond the sales building was a large tin shed that she assumed was used for the repair and servicing of vehicles. To the far side of the shed, a pasture appeared to grow old and wrecked cars, trucks, combines and tractors.

Nick parked next to one of the three patrol cars, and before she could unbuckle her seat belt and get out, he grabbed her arm. "Don't get involved with Larry. Don't interact with him at all. The best thing you and I can do right now is hang back and let Dillon do his job."

She nodded impatiently. Dillon and three of his officers were approaching the sales office. She just wanted to go and be in there to hear how Larry reacted to their presence and their desire to search his property. Was it possible he knew what his brother had done?

"I don't intend to interfere," she said and pulled her arm from his grasp. She quickly unbuckled her seat belt and left the Jeep, aware of Nick hurrying just behind her.

"What in the hell is this all about?" a man Adrienne presumed was Larry Wright asked Dillon. It was hard for Adrienne to believe that Larry and Perry shared the same parents.

Unlike Perry, who was thin and almost delicate looking, Larry was barrel chested, with blunt features and a booming voice that rattled the windows. He looked like a man who was used to getting his way, no matter the consequences or obstacles.

Dillon explained why they were there, and Larry looked at him incredulously. "You really think that punk brother of mine has the nerve to stab a woman to death? He's a wussy. He cries like a baby if he gets a damned paper cut. You're all out of your mind to even suspect him."

"Then, you won't have a problem with allowing us to search the property," Dillon said calmly.

"What in the hell does my property have to do with that woman's murder?"

"Wendy's car was seen in the area. If your brother had anything to do with her murder, then it's possible her car is here," Dillon said.

Larry frowned and raked a hand through his thin, sandy-colored hair. It was obvious he was unhappy and just wanted them all to go away.

"I can always have one of my officers get a search warrant if necessary," Dillon pressed. "Judge Harry Branson usually is a soft touch when it comes to search warrants and murder."

Larry threw his arms out to his sides, a pulse of irritation knotting his thick jaw. "Go ahead, do your search. I can assure you that there's no dead girl's car here."

Dillon instructed Officers Jeffries and Taylor to check the front lot while he and Officer Ramirez looked inside the mechanic shed. He instructed Larry to stay with him. After they'd checked those areas they would begin the search of the junkyard. Dillon ignored Nick and Adrienne, along with another customer who was present.

Adrienne turned to Nick. "You and I can start checking the junkyard," she said. She couldn't just stand around and do nothing. Nervous energy made it impossible for her to simply be a bystander.

Besides, despite Larry's claim to the contrary, her gut told her Wendy's car was here. It was possible Larry didn't even know that his brother had parked the car somewhere on the property, where he could easily access it whenever he wanted. There was no fence or barrier around the junkyard.

"Dillon didn't appear to be happy to see us here. We should just wait and let the officers do their job. We don't need to make trouble. We should just stay out of the way," Nick said.

"I'm not looking for trouble. I'm looking for my sister's car," she retorted.

"Can I talk you out of this?" Nick asked.

"No," she replied. "I'm not just going to stand around. I'm heading into the junkyard." She took off walking toward the entrance to the vehicle graveyard and Nick hurried after her.

Dillon exchanged a concerned glance with Nick. Nick took her hand and held tight. "Don't worry. I'll make sure she stays out of trouble."

"Larry, you come with us," Dillon said. Larry opened his mouth as if to protest, then slammed it shut and nodded.

The group broke up as they went to their designated areas to search. "Dillon probably didn't want Larry to have a chance to call one of his men and move the car before we can find it," Adrienne said as she and Nick waded through tall weeds and overgrown grass to reach the junkyard.

Her nervous energy rose as she viewed the sea of metal before them. There appeared to be no rhyme or reason for how the vehicles were parked. There were no neat rows to walk down, no pathways to easily access a full view of everything.

From their viewpoint at the beginning of the area, she couldn't even see the end. Still, her heart continued to tell her that this was the place Wendy's killer was hiding the car.

She pulled her hand from Nick's grasp. "We can cover the area a lot more quickly if we separate," she said.

Nick frowned and looked around. "Okay, but be careful. There are all kinds of rusty and sharp things out here. I don't want you getting hurt. And if you see another person anywhere in the area, you call to me."

Although Nick had agreed to separate, as Adrienne began to weave through the maze of dead machinery, she noticed that he remained only a few yards away from her. It was as if he was afraid to get too far from her.

It didn't take long for her to forget his presence as she moved deeper into the labyrinth of twisted steel, stacks of tires and equipment she couldn't even begin to identify.

Find her car...name the killer. Find her car...name the killer. It was a mantra that filled her head as she continued forward.

If the car was here, then she was positive that

Perry Wright was responsible for Wendy's murder. She knew even if the car was found here Dillon would still have to build a case against Perry, who could use the defense that anyone could have parked the car in this maze.

But she was confident that if Dillon knew Perry was guilty, then he would work to find the evidence he needed to put the man away for the rest of his life.

At least he'd have a life, even if it was behind bars, she thought bitterly. His brother could visit him. He'd be able to work and eat behind bars.

Wendy's life was forever gone. New emotion pressed tight against her chest. Anger and grief mingled with the tension, making her feel half sick to her stomach.

By the time she and Nick had searched half of the area, Dillon and his other officers joined them. Wendy's car hadn't been found on the main car lot or in the large mechanic shed.

Desperation clawed at her. It had to be here. Wendy's car had to be on the lot. This was the only real lead they might get. It would be the clue they needed to catch the killer.

Nick had moved closer to her as they worked their way toward the end of the vehicles and junk. *Please*, she prayed inwardly. *Please let it be here.*

She owed it to Wendy to make sure the killer was caught. She owed it to Wendy for every time she had grounded Wendy, for each time she had taken away her cell phone or refused to listen to Wendy's pleas to go somewhere, to do something, to have a normal teenage life.

When they reached the end where there was nothing left but pasture and open fields, Nick stood by her side. "It's not here, Adrienne," he said softly.

"It's here," she replied frantically. "We just somehow missed it. We need to go through it all again. We just missed it," she repeated. She took two steps forward, intent on searching the junkyard all over again, but halted as Nick grabbed her arm.

"Adrienne, you can search this place a hundred times, and the answer will still be the same. Wendy's car is not here," Nick said.

She stared up at him, and something broke inside her. "But this made sense." A swell of sobs rose to the back of her throat. "Perry killed her. I know he did, and he hid her car out here. This was supposed to be the end with the bad guy arrested."

To her horror, the swell of tears released, and she was drowning in an emotional breakdown she couldn't control. Nick pulled her into an embrace as she continued to weep.

Everything else melted away. She no longer smelled the odor of oil and grease. She didn't see Dillon and his men when they left. She was in a dark hole and the only thing that kept her from falling into the very depths of hell was Nick's strong arms around her.

Nick finally managed to get Adrienne back into the Jeep. She'd stopped crying but hadn't spoken a word. She appeared hollow, empty…a mere shell of the strong woman he'd come to know over the past two weeks.

She was broken, and he didn't know how to fix her,

and it shocked him to realize how badly he wanted to fix her. She'd been certain that they'd find Wendy's car and that Perry would be identified as Wendy's killer.

She'd expected closure and instead had gotten nothing. The bitter disappointment had undone her.

When he reached the ranch, he parked the Jeep in the garage. After they both got out, he grabbed her hand, and instead of walking her to the big house, he pulled her toward the bunkhouse.

She didn't question the direction, but went with him willingly like an obedient child. She didn't need the company of Cassie and Nicolette and Sammy right now, he thought. She wouldn't want them to see her the way she was. What she needed was some time to pull herself together.

When they reached his bunk, he unlocked the door and ushered her inside. The room was small, with a twin-size bed, a chest of drawers, a straight-backed chair and a minifridge he had bought for late-night snacking and drinks. There was a bathroom with a shower, no tub. It was just the basics for a working cowboy to have a little personal space of his own.

She sat on the edge of the bed and stared at the opposite wall as if in a deep trance. Nick opened the top dresser drawer, where a bottle of whiskey nestled next to a stack of small paper cups.

He poured a generous jigger in one cup and then sat down on the bed next to her. She didn't even appear to process his presence. He nudged the cup against her hand until she took it.

"Drink it," he said and hoped the liquor would pull her out of her zombielike state.

She dutifully took the cup and downed the contents in one large swallow. Instantly, she choked and coughed, her cheeks flushing with color as she looked at him in surprise.

"I didn't expect that," she choked out.

"You needed it," he replied, grateful to see that her focus was clear and her color had returned to something approaching normal. She held his gaze. "It was either that or a slap to pull you back into your mind, and I don't believe in slapping women for any reason."

"Thank goodness for that," she replied and looked into her empty cup. "I think I wouldn't mind another one of these."

Nick took the paper cup from her, splashed a bit of the whiskey into it and then returned it to her. "That's it. The last thing you want is to get drunk right now."

She released a sigh of hopelessness. "Maybe that's exactly what I want. I'd like to be so drunk I can't think about all of this."

"That was exactly the way I felt when you found me in the bar that first night we met. I was there to drink myself into oblivion so I wouldn't think about Wendy's murder," he replied.

She sighed again, a hollow sound he felt in his heart. "I was just so sure that we'd find the car there. I was so certain that finally Wendy's killer would be arrested."

"This isn't the end, Adrienne. Dillon and his men are still working the case. He has officers checking sheds and barns and garages to find the car," Nick said, forcing optimism into his voice. "He knows whoever shot at us used a rifle, and he has the ballistics for when that rifle is found."

She eyed him with despondency. "We both know Dillon has more on his hands right now than he can handle, and his police force is small. It could take months before they manage to search every place in town and the surrounding areas for the car, and I imagine most of the ranchers around here all own rifles."

Nick didn't attempt to deny her words. He knew she was right. She downed the sip of whiskey, crushed the cup, tossed it into a nearby trash can and then released yet another deep sigh. To Nick's surprise, she leaned into his side, and it was only natural that he placed his arm around her shoulders for support.

"Right now, I feel more beaten up than I ever have since hearing about Wendy's death and arriving in town." Her voice was as soft as the sweet scent of her that eddied in the air.

"You've been so strong for so long. It's okay to be weak right now. I'll be strong for you," he replied.

She raised her head and looked at him, her lower lip trembling slightly as her eyes filled with the shine of impending tears.

Nick did the only thing he knew to do in an effort to halt her from crying again. He kissed her. Someplace in the back of his mind he assumed that she would protest, that his action would stir some kind of an angry response from her. Now wasn't the time for kissing.

Instead, she turned toward him and opened her

mouth to allow him to deepen the kiss. She tasted of warm whiskey and hot desire, and any thought Nick had of stopping the kiss immediately vanished.

From that moment on, everything happened organically. He didn't ask permission to tangle his fingers in her soft, long hair. But was grateful when she didn't protest. He didn't ask permission to lay her back on the bed, and she encouraged him as if it were the most natural thing in the world.

He desperately wanted her physically, but he also wanted her emotional pain. He wanted to take it away from her and replace it with mindless pleasure.

They kissed and caressed each other until they were both breathless. Nick's brain stopped working as he fell into a sensual haze of want. He didn't think, he only felt and tasted and wanted more...more.

She broke the kiss and stood, and while he watched with a heated gaze, she slowly took off all her clothes. He rolled off the bed and did the same, fired hot by the sight of her beautiful nakedness. They got back into the small twin bed that enforced intimacy. Their bodies moved together, warm and as if starved for contact with each other.

He explored her soft curves with his hands while his mouth moved from her lips and down the length of her neck. Her hands caressed up and down his back, shooting flames of fire through him with each touch of her fingers.

Lost. He was lost in her with no thoughts of right or wrong, good or bad. They didn't speak a word, as if their hearts and bodies communicated anything the other one needed to know.

She gasped in delight as his tongue laved first one of her taut nipples and then the other. She tangled her hands in his hair, pulling him closer.

He was fully aroused, ready to take possession of her at any moment, and yet wasn't willing to indulge himself until she had reached the peak of her pleasure.

He moved a hand slowly across her stomach and then down to caress her upper thighs. She arched her hips up, as if to encourage him to touch her as intimately as a man could touch a woman.

Still he teased and denied her, stroking her inner thighs until she mewled with need. Only then did he give her what she wanted, using his fingers to glide across her sweet spot.

She moaned and he increased his pressure, moving his fingers faster as he sensed her imminent climax. Her gaze met his and in her eyes he saw the hazy, mindless pleasure that filled her. Blue…her eyes were blue, he thought, answering a question he'd wondered about.

With another gasp, she reached her peak, her body stiffening and trembling at the same time. Nick could stand it no longer. He moved on top of her and entered her, instantly surrounded by moist heat.

He stroked slowly at first, wanting the pleasure to last as long as possible, but as she grabbed his buttocks and pulled him into her with each thrust, he increased his pace.

All too quickly, control slipped away and they frantically moved together in a unison that carried him over the edge. For several long minutes, they remained in place, his elbows bearing the brunt of his weight as he stayed on top of her.

"Don't say that this shouldn't have happened," she said. "Right now I don't want to hear that. I don't even want to think about it. I'm still in the glow."

He couldn't help but smile. "I gave you a glow?"

"You could use me as a high-beam flashlight right now. As far as I'm concerned, this is the best thing that's happened to me in years."

"It's not what I intended when I brought you here," he said and finally rolled to one side of her, nearly falling off the edge of the small bed.

She placed a hand softly on his cheek and smiled. "I know that."

"I just thought you needed some time before heading back to the big house and the others," he said. Her hair was tousled and her lips looked slightly swollen, but she was right—she had a definite glow.

She shifted her position slightly and looked around the room. "So this is where you live."

They were face-to-face, so close that he felt the warmth of her breath. "This is it," he replied. "Cass had these bunks built the first year I came to work for her. We all had the choice of living here or someplace else if we wanted, but each of us chose to stay here at what we refer to as the cowboy motel."

"She must have been somebody special."

"She was one of a kind," Nick agreed. He still grieved her passing. "She wasn't just our boss. She was also mother, mentor and friend."

She touched his face again, running her fingertips lightly down his cheek. "I'm sorry for your loss.

I'm sorry for all the losses you've suffered in your lifetime."

His heart clenched. "I'd say we both got a pretty raw deal. I doubt that at eighteen your plans included raising Wendy." He reached out and moved a strand of her hair back from her face.

"They didn't, but I would make the same decision today that I did then. Wendy was my family. She was all I had, and I was all she had. It was important that we stayed together, and I promised our mother that I would always keep her safe."

"This ranch and the men who work it are my family. They're all I need." He got out of the bed. "I'll be right back."

He went into the bathroom, wondering if she'd caught the warning in his words. They might have just made wonderful love together, but that didn't change anything. He was still a man determined to go it alone through life.

He'd intended only a quick cleanup, but thinking of the walking they'd done through the junkyard earlier, he decided on a quick shower. He made it very quick, aware of Adrienne waiting for him. He hoped she'd gotten dressed, because seeing her naked in his bed would only make him want her again.

But when he left the bathroom minutes later, he found her wrapped up in his sheet and sound asleep. As quietly as possible, he dressed in clean boxers and jeans and pulled a clean T-shirt over his head, then sat in the chair near the bed and gazed at her.

Without the stress tightening her features, she was even more beautiful than he'd already thought. She looked right in his bed, even if the bed was really too small for two people to share.

When he thought of what they had just experienced together, he recognized that she was getting in far too deep, that she'd found a little crack in his heart and had begun to power through it.

He couldn't let that happen. He refused to allow it to happen. It scared him. She scared him. She hadn't given him any indication that she saw him as anything other than a partner. She hadn't told him that she was in love with him, although their mutual lust for each other had been undeniable.

But lust wasn't love, and he certainly wasn't in the market for love. So what came next? He feared she was still in danger, and he also feared that he wouldn't be able to keep her on the ranch any longer.

She was so hard-headed and so determined to find the killer, and each day they spent together she dug a little bit more under his skin. She needed to go home for her own physical safety and for his emotional safety.

He suspected the attempted break-in at the motel had been an effort to warn her off, but she'd refused to be cowed by the threat. His biggest fear was that she'd continue on a path that would put her directly in the hands of the killer, and this time it wouldn't be a threat… It would be another murder.

Chapter 11

Adrienne came awake slowly, subconsciously soothed by the whisper of Nick's scent that surrounded her. She had been dreaming, and in her dream she and Nick had made beautiful love. It had been pure and simple magic.

Wait…it hadn't been a dream. It had been real, and it had been wonderful. They'd made love as if they were meant to be a couple, instinctively knowing when and where to touch and how to move to create the most pleasure.

She opened her eyes to see Nick seated in the chair near the bed. She quickly sat up and shoved her hair away from her face. "Oh, my gosh, I'm so sorry," she said. "I didn't mean to fall asleep."

He smiled. "No need to apologize. It's been a roller-coaster kind of day, and you obviously needed to crash out."

She pulled the sheet up to cover her bare breasts, slightly embarrassed now that the heat of the moment was over and he was fully dressed. "What time is it?"

"Almost five," he replied.

She frowned and reached for her bra and T-shirt, which were on the floor next to the bed. "Another day of no answers." She would have heard if either of their cell phones had rung.

"I have an answer for you," he said, his eyes dark and unreadable. "Go home, Adrienne. Go back to Kansas City and get on with your life. Dillon will find the killer and let you know."

She stared at him, both stunned and oddly hurt that he'd encourage her to leave right now after what they'd just shared. "That's what the killer wants me to do—to stop asking questions, to tuck my tail between my legs and run for the hills."

"You've had two near misses that, but for luck, would have seen you dead. I'm not willing to give this creep a third opportunity to get to you," he replied.

"It's not your decision to make." Irritation overrode the embarrassment of nakedness. She dropped the sheet and put on her bra and then pulled her T-shirt over her head. She got out of the bed and stepped into her panties and then yanked up her jeans, aware of Nick's unwavering gaze on her.

"I don't run, Nick. When I'm faced with a challenge, I dig in my heels and deal with it." She thought of all the times when she'd thought life had finally beaten her, when she had been tempted to throw in the towel and allow the state to take care of Wendy.

But she hadn't and she wasn't willing to give in now. She was a fighter, not a quitter.

Nick sighed. "I had a feeling that's what you'd say."

"This has always been my problem, Nick. I appreciate everything you've done, but I understand if you're tired of babysitting me."

He stared at her for a long moment, his eyes a midnight blue that spoke of turbulent thoughts. "It's not that," he protested. "I'm afraid for you. And I'm afraid that I won't be able to stop something bad from happening to you."

He'd told her that night by the pond that he didn't feel fear, that he hadn't been afraid since he was eight and abandoned at a zoo by his mother. She saw the fear now, the painful burden he carried, and the caring in his eyes.

She knelt down in front of him and grabbed his hands in hers. "If anything happens to me, you'll know it was a risk I was willing to take. It would be my fault and my fault alone. You shouldn't have any guilt about anything that might happen to me."

She released his hands and stood. "Besides, I'm not anticipating anything bad happening to me. Even though we didn't find Wendy's car on the lot, I now believe that Perry killed my sister."

"What about Zeke Osmond?"

She frowned, thinking of the creepy cowboy. "He still could be guilty," she agreed reluctantly. "But in either case, I know what they look like. I know where they work, and if they come after me, I'll see them coming."

"Then, what is your plan?" he asked.

She sank back on the bed. "I don't know," she admitted. "Somehow, some way, I need to investigate everything I can about their lives. Maybe tomorrow I can do a little work on the computer and see what I can find out about the two." She offered him a smile. "That should make you happy. At least I'll be in the house and out of trouble."

"That does ease my mind…for tomorrow. But I doubt you find much of an internet presence for either of those men."

"You'd be surprised what I could potentially dig up. I'm a magician when it comes to the internet. I'm not so sure about Zeke, but Perry strikes me as the type who might have an online presence. I'll just take things day by day," she replied. "And now I'd better get out of here and to the big house if I want to eat dinner."

Nick stood. "I'll walk you to the house."

They left the bunk and began the long walk. "You know I'm not going to let you go off on your own," he said. "Whatever you decide to do, I'm at your side."

"I appreciate your continued support," she replied.

Her heart was a tangled mess. Her skin still retained the smell of him, the imprint of his heated caresses, and yet she knew her presence in his life was a burden he could do without.

Selfishly, she didn't want him to stop helping her. His name had been cleared. He had no more reason to continue to investigate, but she wanted him by her side.

She was in love with him. If she'd been on the verge before, then making love to him had shoved her over the cliff. She was hopelessly, crazy in love with him, and he just wanted her to go home.

"You know what happened between us earlier can't happen again," Nick said as they reached the back porch.

"I know," she replied.

It was simply confirmation of what she already knew—that he would never allow himself to love anyone again.

As much as she'd love to make love to him each and every night for the rest of her life, she knew that it would only complicate things and lead to an even more difficult goodbye when the time came for her to leave. And she knew that when she did leave, it would be with a broken heart.

"It just wouldn't be a good idea." His voice was low and heavy.

"I get it, Nick," she replied. "It would only complicate things between us, and we don't need any more complications."

"Exactly." He released what sounded like a sigh of relief. "I'll check in with you sometime around noon tomorrow." He stopped just short of stepping up on the porch. "Promise me you'll be here."

She smiled. "I promise."

He nodded, as if satisfied, and then turned and began the walk back to the "cowboy motel." She stood at the door and watched him go, her heart already aching with the goodbye that was yet to come.

Adrienne hit her computer the next morning after breakfast had been eaten and all the other occupants had not only dispersed from the room, but from the house, as well.

Nicolette, Lucas and Sammy had left to go to their house and do some more painting, and Cassie had left with foreman Adam to head into town.

The house was quiet, and Adrienne was determined to use the time to find out whatever she could about Zeke Osmond and Perry Wright. Before she could get started, a knock fell on the front door.

She got out of her chair and hurried to answer. Dillon stood on the porch and offered her a tentative smile. "How are you doing this morning?" he asked.

"I'm okay. Yesterday was a little rough. I thought sure we'd find Wendy's car, but it's a new day and I'm better now."

He held out a paper bag. "Maybe this will help even more."

She took the bag from him and opened it to see Wendy's glass bluebird. She looked at Dillon in surprise. "You don't need it anymore?"

"There's no reason for us to hang on to it. It belongs with you."

"Thank you," she said emotionally. The figurine brought with it both a bittersweet grief and a loving link to the sister she'd lost.

"We're still working on it, Adrienne. I won't rest until I have the man responsible for your sister's death behind bars."

Adrienne nodded. "I know, and I appreciate all your work."

Dillon left, and Adrienne carried the bag into the kitchen. She withdrew the bluebird and held it in her hands for several long moments. The glass was cool, but warmed quickly with her touch.

It had been Wendy's bluebird of happiness. Their mother had wanted Wendy to look at it and know that she was loved, that it symbolized their mother's wish for Wendy's happiness.

She finally set it next to her computer and threw the bag away. If anything would keep her focused, it was Wendy's keepsake. With renewed determination, she got to work.

She began to search for Zeke Osmond and was surprised when she was led to a webpage showcasing the Humes Ranch. It was meant to be an advertisement for selling cattle and horses, but there was an About Us page. She clicked on it, and it brought up a picture of owner Raymond Humes, an older man with silver hair and hawk-like features, and another photo of the ranch hands who worked the ranch.

She easily picked out Zeke from the group of fifteen men. Even in a photo, he appeared arrogant and slimy at the same time.

"Did you kill my sister?" she whispered aloud.

She reached a finger out and touched his face. She quickly pulled her hand away, sickened by the very sight of him.

There was no information about the men, only a list of their names. From there, she hit a dead end. She couldn't find any trace of Zeke Osmond anywhere else she searched.

She doubted that a cowboy on a ranch in Oklahoma had much interest in surfing the internet or creating a social network page. Zeke would much rather torment his women up close and in person.

When she typed in *Perry Wright*, she came up with dozens and dozens of results. She found a psychiatrist in Maine, a former marine in Washington. There were dentists and lawyers all around the country sharing the same name as the man she sought.

She checked out several sites that had no information other than the name, but each one listed the wrong man in the wrong place.

She lost track of time, occasionally stopping to stare at the bluebird next to her computer. Each time she did, her mind filled with memories. They weren't all bad ones; there were happy ones, as well.

She remembered a movie night when she had rented a horror film that Wendy had insisted she'd wanted to see. Adrienne had popped popcorn, and the two sisters had watched the movie, alternatingly screaming and cuddling together on the sofa.

She remembered Wendy's laughter when Adrienne's first attempt at a chocolate soufflé had resulted in a flat brown pancake. Wendy's first attempt at mascara, her first walk in high heels, a surprise loving hug when Adrienne comforted Wendy after a bad dream...

There had been laughter and love.

The bluebird reminded Adrienne that it hadn't been all bad, that there had been some good times along with the bad times.

She focused on the computer screen with renewed determination.

Her adrenaline shot up when she found a Perry

Wright on one of the popular social networking sites. She clicked on it and found herself staring at a picture of the Perry Wright she sought.

"Bingo," she whispered softly.

She leaned forward to read the personal profile he'd created for himself. According to the site, he lived in Bitterroot, Oklahoma, and worked as a medical biller. He was single and looking for friendship and love.

She started as the back door opened and Nick walked in, bringing with him the scent of fresh, clean air and his familiar, sexy cologne. She looked at the clock on the oven and realized it was already noon.

Nick lightly touched the back of her hair. "Are you lost in the maze of the internet?" he asked.

She smiled up at him. "Actually, I'm making progress. Unfortunately, I couldn't find much of anything on Zeke, but I've got a page pulled up on Perry. I was just about to check on what he listed as his interests. Pull up a chair."

Nick pulled a chair from the table next to hers and sat, his close presence instantly a slight distraction. "I see Dillon gave you Wendy's bird," he said.

She nodded. "He stopped by earlier and gave it to me." She focused on the computer screen and then got back down to business. "Perry belongs to a popular social networking site. His profile has his name, where he lives and the fact that he's single. There's also a place for him to list his interests."

She scanned down and read what he'd listed. "He likes reading, walks in the country and good conversation."

"All I've ever seen him do is stutter in shyness and cry," Nick said. "Can you just make up whatever you want on these places?"

"Basically, yes," she replied. "It also says he has a degree in medical billing, likes fast cars and enjoys rifle-shooting competitions." Her heart skipped a beat, and she looked at Nick, remembering the night they'd been shot at in the middle of Main Street. "Rifle-shooting competitions," she repeated.

"I didn't know that about him," Nick admitted. "I'll call Dillon, and he can check out what kind of rifle Perry owns and what kind of ammo he uses."

He pulled his cell phone from his pocket and made the call. "Dillon says he's on it," he said once he'd disconnected. He dropped his phone back into his pocket and stood. "How about lunch at the café? It doesn't look as though lunch is happening around here."

"That sounds good. I've worked up an appetite." She turned off her computer and stood with one lingering gaze at the blue figurine.

Soon, she thought with a new optimism. She could feel it—the noose slowly closing in around Perry Wright's neck.

Nick felt her new optimism fill the Jeep as they headed into town. It worried him. He feared another devastating letdown for her.

While he found the information about Perry apparently participating in shooting competitions interesting, he still had a hard time believing that Perry was their man. Like Larry, Nick wasn't sure he believed

Perry had the nerve to plunge a knife into a woman's chest. That was so up close and personal.

Hopefully, it wouldn't take Dillon long to get hold of Perry's rifle and ammo and do a ballistics test that would confirm whether he had been the shooter who had attacked them on Main Street. If it turned out he was, then Nick was sure Perry hadn't ever won a shooting contest. Whoever had shot at him had suffered from terrible aim.

"I can't decide what I want for lunch," she said, her tone light and as if she were at peace. "Maybe I'll try one of those monster bacon burgers you always get."

"Can't beat bacon and beef on a bun," he replied, trying to match his tone with hers even though what he wanted to do was warn her not to get her hopes up.

When they hadn't found Wendy's car on Larry's lot, Nick had begun to doubt Perry's guilt. When he tried to figure it all out, his head ached with confusion.

In fact, when he tried to sort out his feelings for Adrienne, his head hurt, as well. He tried not to examine all of the emotions she stirred inside him.

He'd initially wanted the killer caught as quickly as possible to clear him from any wrongdoing, but now he wanted the killer caught so that Adrienne would no longer be in danger or be a presence in his life.

And yet when he thought of her leaving, when he considered no longer seeing her again, his heart ached with a new pain that he refused to take out and examine.

"How long will it take for Dillon to find out if the

bullets that he retrieved from the night of the shooting match ones shot from Perry's rifle?" she asked.

"Not too long. Officer Juan Ramirez is trained in ballistics. I imagine we'll have an answer by sometime tomorrow." He parked down the street from the café because all of the parking places directly in front were taken up by other vehicles.

Lunchtime on Fridays was usually busier than on other weekdays. Daisy called it her preweekend rush. It was as if people just couldn't wait for Saturday to come.

They walked inside, and the first people Nick saw were a handful of cowboys from the Humes Ranch, including Zeke Osmond, seated at the counter.

Zeke made a big show of turning around and watching as Nick and Adrienne found an empty booth. Nick wanted to punch Zeke in the face when he saw him ogling Adrienne with a salacious grin.

Zeke turned back around and said something to his buddies, and they all laughed. Thankfully, Adrienne seemed unaware of Zeke's actions.

There was no question that Adrienne looked particularly hot today in a pair of white capris, orange sandals and an orange blouse that picked up the red strands in her hair. Nick wanted to cover her up with a blanket and make sure that no other man could admire her attractiveness except him.

As with most of their meals, Jenna approached their table with a bright smile and her order pad. "If it isn't my favorite couple," she said.

"We aren't a couple," Adrienne protested. "We're partners in crime fighting."

Jenna raised a blond eyebrow. "Sure look like a couple to me and most of the rest of the town. I've heard bets are being placed on if the grieving sister can capture the heart of the lonely cowboy."

Nick scowled. "Those people have too much time on their hands if they're indulging in such nonsense."

Jenna laughed. "Okay, then, I guess I won't get in on that bet. Now, what can I get for you two?"

They placed their orders, and while they waited, Adrienne chattered like a magpie about the weather, the food the café served and anything else that jumped into her mind. She seemed more than a little bit manic.

There was a new strength and assurance in her eyes, as if she believed that it was just a matter of hours and Perry Wright would be arrested.

"Adrienne, please don't get your hopes up too high," he said softly when she stopped talking to take a breath. "It's very possible that Perry isn't the man we're looking for."

The smile of pleasure that had lit her face wavered for just a moment. "If you're worried that I'll break down again, then don't. What happened after the car lot thing isn't going to happen again. But I can't help the hope that Perry Wright is our man and that it's only a matter of a day or two before he's arrested."

"And then you'll be back home to your life in Kansas City," he said.

The smile of pleasure completely disappeared. "Yes, back to a lonely, isolated life that doesn't sound too appealing right now."

"You'll build a new, better life when this is all over," he assured her.

Their conversation halted as Jenna served them their bacon cheeseburgers, fries and two root beers. "Is there anything else I can get you?"

"I think we're good," Nick replied.

"I'm not going home to fellow cowboys and people who care about me," Adrienne continued when Jenna had left their booth. "I've felt more alive here in Bitterroot than I've ever felt in my life."

"Maybe that's just because you've had a driving mission here." Nick hated the picture she'd just painted of her life. Now she wouldn't even be able to look forward to phone calls and texts from her sister.

"Maybe," she agreed and then eyed the burger in front of her. "This looks delicious."

"Let's dig in," Nick replied, grateful for anything that would take the vision of her alone and lonely out of his head.

While they ate, they talked about the progress Lucas and Nicolette were making on their house. "I wouldn't be surprised if they move in within the next week or so," Adrienne said. "I imagine Cassie will hate to see them go. She'll be left all alone in that big house."

"She'll have Adam to occupy as much time as she wants," Nick replied. "I think he has a thing for her."

Adrienne raised an eyebrow. "Do you think it's a mutual thing?"

"Hard to tell," Nick replied. "She seems to be somebody who holds her cards close to her chest. None of us men have really gotten a good feel for what she thinks about much of anything yet."

"Like what?" Adrienne slid a stray piece of bacon between her lips.

"About ranching, about Bitterroot in general and the new life she was handed when her aunt died. You know she's a New Yorker and owns a store there. None of us know for sure what her intentions are concerning the ranch."

"You mean you think she might sell?" He nodded. "She's certainly not going to do anything with the crime scene there," she replied. "And who knows how long it will take to clean that all up."

"True," he agreed. "What we're all hoping is that she'll stick around and forget about New York, but there are some women just not cut out for small-town ranch life."

Cassie might not end up being a small-town girl, but Nick knew that Adrienne could be. She fit in here, appeared comfortable in the small community. Nick shoved those thoughts away, telling himself that she didn't belong here.

For the next few minutes, they fell into a companionable silence as they focused on their meal. Nick thought of all the things Wendy had told him about Adrienne. Wendy had said she was tough, and she was. Wendy had called her stubborn and strong willed.

Adrienne was all those things, but so much more. She was tough, but she also had the softest heart. She was stubborn but only when something mattered to her. Nick was attracted to all those qualities, and as he sat across the table from her, he wondered what it would be like to sit across a table from her every evening for dinner, every morning for breakfast.

He woke up each morning with an eagerness to see her and went to bed and dreamed about her every night. He wanted her to get the hell out of town, but he wanted her to get the hell in his bed. He wanted her out of his life and yet was starting to dread the idea of life without her.

"How about a piece of pie to finish up?" Jenna's voice pulled Nick from his uncomfortable thoughts.

"Not for me," Adrienne said and looked down at her half-eaten burger. "I'm having enough trouble getting this down."

"I'm good, too," Nick said.

But he wasn't good. He needed to gain some distance from the beautiful woman seated across from him, a woman who made him wish for things he shouldn't, yearn for a life he refused to dream.

"You've gotten very quiet," she said as they drove back to the ranch. "Is anything wrong?"

"No, not at all," he replied. "I was just thinking that we've given Dillon everything we can to pursue the investigation of Perry, and maybe tomorrow you could stick around the house and I'd do some chores that I've neglected and left to the other cowboys."

He felt her gaze lingering on him. "I've taken up way too much of your time and put an additional burden on the men you work with."

She'd begun to take up too much of his heart, he thought. "I'm not complaining, and I'm not quitting on you. I just need a day or two to catch up on things around the ranch."

"I could definitely use a day to catch up on some of my work," she admitted.

"Then for the rest of this afternoon and tomorrow, we take another break, both from the case and from each other. You'll be fine with Nicolette and Cassie, and I'll reconnect with the cowboys to take up some of my normal chores."

He parked the Jeep at the back door of the house, where she got out of the vehicle. "You'll let me know if you hear something from Dillon?" she asked before closing the door.

"Of course, and you do the same. Let me know if he calls you with any information."

She nodded and closed the door. He watched her back as she walked up the stairs to enter the house. Her hips held a sexy sway, and her hair sparkled in the sunlight. She turned at the door and waved to him, her smile instantly making him regret his decision.

He put the Jeep back into gear and headed for the garage, his hands clenching the steering wheel a bit too tightly. This was a good decision. Even though it would last for only a day and a half, he had to distance himself from her. They had gotten far too close, and at the moment she felt as dangerous to him as he thought the killer was to her.

Chapter 12

The next morning, Adrienne stood at the kitchen window after breakfast and tried to pick out Nick from the number of men on horseback in the distance. Unfortunately, there were too many black hats and broad shoulders for her to be able to specifically identify him.

She'd had a nice afternoon and evening with Cassie, Nicolette, Lucas and Sammy the day before. Breakfast this morning had been pleasant as well, but there was no question that she'd missed seeing Nick before she went to bed.

She sighed and moved away from the window and to her computer. Hopefully sometime today they'd hear something from Dillon about Perry and his rifle. In the meantime, she did have business to attend to.

It didn't take her long to lose herself at her computer taking care of the details of the business she'd built for herself.

Two potential new clients had contacted her and sent their books by email for her perusal. One of the standards she had set for herself when she'd first started the publicity business was that she wouldn't represent just anyone who tapped on her shoulder. She picked and chose the authors she decided to work with based on both their talent and their drive to succeed.

She represented fifty-two writers who wrote romance, paranormal and other genres. They were all relatively prolific, which kept her busy doing her best to get the authors the publicity they deserved.

Time faded away as she worked. She'd print off the two new manuscripts sometime this afternoon and settle in to read them. As always, the potential of finding a new client was exciting, but she'd read a lot of bad books over the years.

It was eleven o'clock when Nicolette came into the kitchen. "Cassie and I are going out to lunch, and we'd love for you to join us."

"I don't think Nick would approve of me being at the café or in town," Adrienne replied.

"Lucas has already checked with Nick. He doesn't have a problem with it, and we aren't going to the café. We're going to Tammy's Tea House. It's a little restaurant that caters to women. Lucas will drop us off and pick us up, and we all think it's safe for you to go."

"Then, I'm in," Adrienne replied. Maybe it would take her mind off thoughts of Nick that had intruded throughout the morning.

"Perfect. We'll plan on leaving in about half an hour," Nicolette replied.

"I'll go freshen up." Adrienne closed down her computer and headed upstairs. She was looking forward to the girl time. It was just what she needed to stop obsessing about Nick Coleman and the fact that Dillon could call at any moment and tell her Perry Wright had been arrested.

It was exactly eleven-thirty when Lucas escorted the three women to his king cab pickup, where Adrienne and Cassie took the small backseat and Nicolette slid into the passenger side.

"Where's Sammy?" Adrienne asked curiously.

"Dusty is keeping him busy cleaning and oiling saddles and harnesses," Cassie said. "At noon, they'll head to the cowboy dining room, where Sammy will swagger and pretend that he's as old and as seasoned as the rest of the men."

"That son of mine would be happy if Cassie and I left him every day to eat in the cowboy dining room," Nicolette said with a smile.

The drive into town seemed to take no time at all, and once there, Lucas pulled up in front of a restaurant that had a light pink awning that announced it as Tammy's Tea House.

Lucas got out first, his hand on the butt of his gun and his eyes narrowed as he gazed around the area. He nodded to indicate that it was safe for the women to get out of the truck.

Cassie immediately hurried Adrienne into the establishment, and they were followed by Nicolette.

Adrienne felt bad that they had to go to so much trouble just for her to have lunch with them.

A tall, thin woman greeted Cassie and Nicolette by name and then introduced herself to Adrienne as Tammy Tyler, the owner. The interior of the restaurant was low lit, and the walls were painted a pale pink. Small round tables were covered with lacy white tablecloths and adorned with fresh-flower centerpieces in delicate glass bowls.

It was obvious this wasn't a place where men would feel comfortable, but rather dedicated to giving women a pleasant experience. Several tables were occupied by groups of women, and Tammy led them to a table toward the back of the room.

The menus were small and trimmed in lace, and after Tammy took their drink orders, Adrienne opened her menu with interest. The fare was light, interesting salads and sandwiches with delicious-sounding desserts.

"Do you eat here often?" Adrienne asked the other two.

"Not too often, but whenever I get the urge to get off the ranch and have a dainty, female kind of meal, Nicolette and I sneak away and eat here," Cassie said.

"And I highly recommend the strawberry-and-pecan spinach salad and any of the sandwiches," Nicolette added.

"And the fudge-brownie volcano is to die for," Cassie added. "You cut the brownie with a fork and all this lovely chocolate comes rushing out."

Tammy returned with their drinks and a basket of

freshly baked blueberry scones to start them off. She then took their orders and left the table.

Adrienne sipped her raspberry tea and they all helped themselves to the scones, which proved delicious. "What a fun place," Adrienne said. "I'll bet all the women in town like coming here."

"Tammy is only open for breakfast and lunch, and she definitely has a loyal following among the women in town," Cassie replied.

"I'd have Tammy cater my wedding reception if I didn't think Cookie might come after me with a butcher knife," Nicolette said in amusement.

"You're going to get married on the ranch?" Adrienne asked.

"No, we're getting married in church and then Cassie has insisted we have a reception dinner afterward in the cowboy dining room," Nicolette explained.

"And Cookie would kill you if you brought in an outside caterer," Cassie said. "And the last thing I want is for you to tick off Cookie. That man scares me more than a little bit."

Nicolette laughed. "According to Lucas, he scares all the cowboys more than a little bit."

Tammy arrived with their meals and Adrienne turned her attention to Cassie. "And what about you? Has a special cowboy captured your heart?"

"No way," she replied.

"I think she's secretly sweet on Adam, but just won't admit it," Nicolette said.

"He's my foreman, not my boyfriend," Cassie protested.

"Speaking of being sweet on somebody, you and Nick have grown very close," Nicolette said.

"It's so strange. I came here determined to have him arrested for murdering my sister, and now I trust him more than any man I've ever known," Adrienne replied.

"When I see the two of you together, it looks like more than just trust to me," Cassie observed with a sly smile.

Adrienne felt her cheeks grow warm. "He's a great guy, and I've grown to care about him a lot, but I'll probably be leaving here in just a matter of days."

"That's too bad. You've been good for Nick." Cassie paused to take a bite of her dainty cream-cheese-and-cucumber sandwich. She chased it with a sip of her tea and then continued, "Nick has always been kind of quiet and brooding, but when he's with you he looks happy and he talks more."

"Don't read anything into it," Adrienne replied. "Nick and I have a common interest in finding Wendy's killer, but he's made it clear to me in any number of ways that he's not looking for any kind of a romantic relationship."

Her heart filled with her love for the cowboy who had protected her, who had calmed her nerves and made exquisite love to her.

"You're in love with him," Cassie said softly. Her gaze was intent on Adrienne, as if she were looking into her soul.

Adrienne opened her mouth to protest, but the words of denial wouldn't come. Instead, she shrugged. "It really doesn't matter how I feel about Nick," she finally said. "I came here to find Wendy's killer, and when that's done, I'll head back to Kansas City."

"You should tell him how you feel," Nicolette said. "Cowboys are some of the most stubborn men on the face of the earth, and sometimes they just need a little prodding in the right direction. Trust me, I know."

Adrienne was grateful when the talk turned to ranch business. Cassie talked about a wild horse Adam was encouraging her to buy from the Swenson ranch and then changed the subject to Dr. Patience Forbes.

"Adam told me that Dillon told him the woman is as cold as ice and is definitely the person in charge. She won't let Dillon or any of his men inside the tent, and apparently Dillon is frustrated because she hasn't even begun to remove the bones from their resting places," Cassie said.

"Just think of all the families who don't know what happened to their loved ones," Adrienne said. "At least I had some closure in that Wendy's body was found and I was able to give her a proper burial. There are a lot of people out there wondering what happened to their loved ones. Maybe finally they'll get closure, too."

For the rest of the meal the conversation turned more pleasant. Nicolette talked about a housewarming she was planning at the new house, and Cassie mentioned a barn dance that Abe Breckenridge had planned on his ranch at the end of July.

While the two women talked about town happenings, Adrienne couldn't keep her thoughts from drifting to Nick. What was he doing right now? Eating lunch in the cowboy dining room with his "brothers"? Or had they finished lunch and he was now on the back of his horse, or fixing fencing, or moving hay?

Was he even thinking about her? Wondering what she might be doing right now? Or was he grateful for a day of not seeing her, not having to think about her at all?

How could she miss seeing him in less than a day's time? How could she feel bereft by a day of his absence? She was being foolish, daydreaming about a man who was in her life only temporarily.

On the drive home, she couldn't help but think of Cassie's words about her being good for Nick. She hoped she'd brought something positive to his life aside from the burden of him protecting her.

He'd had enough bad in his life. She desperately hoped he didn't look back on this time they'd shared and consider it a negative thing. Despite everything they had gone through together, she wanted him to think back on his time with her and smile.

What would happen if she did as Nicolette had suggested? What would happen if she told Nick that she was in love with him? Would it change anything?

The very idea both thrilled her and scared her. The last thing she wanted to do was alienate him in the time she had left here, but it grew more and more difficult for her to be around him and not share with him what was in her heart.

Nick sat in the cowboy dining room for the evening meal, not paying attention to the conversations that swirled around him.

Instead, his head was filled with thoughts of Adrienne, as it had been throughout the entire day. As he'd ridden the fence line, he'd wondered what she was doing. When he'd stopped to repair a piece of fence, he'd wondered if she was smiling or laughing and what she might be thinking.

When he was eating lunch, he'd wondered if she was enjoying hers at Tammy's Tea House. How she was getting along with Cassie and Nicolette?

He'd desperately wanted to distance himself from her by taking a day away, yet his brain refused to cooperate. She might have been away from him all day, but thoughts of her had intruded upon his mind almost every minute of the day.

He told himself it was just because he'd grown accustomed to her being around him. Thinking about her had become a habit he had to break. He shoved his plate aside and forced himself to focus on the conversation between Adam and Forest.

"Is Cassie going to buy that horse from the Breckenridge place?" Forest asked.

"I'm trying to talk her into it. She's a gorgeous three-year-old filly, but has had no training and not much human contact at all," Adam replied. "She's spirited and mistrustful and the perfect candidate for a Forest intervention."

Forest smiled. "I could use a new challenge in my life."

A challenge. That was what Adrienne had become in Nick's life. He wanted to help her, he needed to protect her, but he also had to guard his own heart at the same time.

He'd never believed a time would come that he'd be threatened by his own emotions, but something about Adrienne Bailey made him feel slightly vulnerable, and he didn't like the feeling at all.

After dinner, he remained in the dining room, shooting the bull with the other cowboys and listening to Mac strum his guitar. Dusty challenged the others to arm-wrestling contests, and just for grins, Nick agreed to the challenge.

He easily put Dusty down and laughed as Dusty blustered that he had pulled a muscle and had a headache and that was the only reason Nick had won.

It was just after eight, and twilight was falling when Nick got a call from Dillon. He listened to what the lawman had to say, and after he hung up, he knew he needed to share the information with Adrienne.

It can wait until morning, a little voice whispered in his head. *There's no reason to upset her tonight.* Time enough to share what Dillon had told him in the morning.

Even as these thoughts drifted through his head, he found himself walking in the near darkness toward the big house. He hated the way his heart beat just a little faster in anticipation of seeing her despite the fact that he was carrying bad news.

When he reached the back door of the house, he could see her seated at the desk in the kitchen. She was alone in the room and focused on her computer screen.

Clad in jeans and a pink T-shirt, with her hair flowing in soft waves down to her shoulders, she looked both beautiful and completely relaxed.

He considered backing away, returning to the bunkhouse and not bothering her for the night, but they had each promised one another that if one of them heard anything from Dillon they would tell the other person.

Stepping closer to the door, he knocked softly. She turned, and when she saw him, her face lit with the beautiful smile that warmed him inside and out.

She jumped up out of the chair and unlocked the door to allow him inside, but he remained on the porch. "Nick, I didn't expect to see you tonight."

"Why don't you come out here and sit on the porch with me," he replied.

She didn't hesitate. They sat down on the top step, and he took his hat off and placed it next to him. "Did you get a lot of work done today?" she asked.

She sat so close to him he could feel her body heat radiating to him. He could smell the scent that he would forever be able to identify as hers alone. It would haunt him long after she was gone.

"I spent most of the day out in the pasture dealing with breaks in the fence line," he replied.

"Do breaks happen often?" she asked.

"More often than they should. We suspect that some of the ranch hands from the Humes place are responsible for a lot of them. What about you? Did you enjoy your lunch out at the girlie place?"

She laughed. "The girlie place?"

"That's how the men refer to it." He knew he was small talking, putting off the inevitable moment when he'd steal away her laughter and take away her smile.

"It was wonderful. The food was delicious, the

atmosphere held just the right amount of frills and Cassie and Nicolette are terrific and I enjoy their company."

"Nobody gave you any problems?"

She shook her head. "Not at all. It was a perfect lunch, and I've spent most of the rest of the day catching up on my business work. The good news is I got a new client, and I'm really excited about representing her. She writes really edgy suspense novels."

She had good news and he had bad, and more than anything, he hated to share what he had learned from Dillon. He stared up at the darkening sky. "Right before I came up here, I got a phone call from Dillon," he said, deciding the faster he bit the bullet the more quickly he could escape. He immediately felt the tension that filled her body and sat her up straighter. He lowered his gaze to look at her.

"He had news?" she asked eagerly.

"Yeah, but unfortunately not the kind of news we were hoping for. Dillon retrieved two rifles and a box of ammo from Perry Wright's apartment. While the ammo was the same, the ballistics tests didn't match up to the bullets that were shot at us."

She slumped forward and lowered her face to her hands. Nick feared she might start crying again, but she raised her head and a deep sigh escaped her. "Nothing seems to be going our way. We just can't get a break."

He didn't reply. He had nothing to say, and he certainly couldn't disagree with her. They couldn't seem to get a break in this case. Even Dillon and his officers hadn't been able to move the investigation forward in any meaningful way.

"I thought about waiting until morning to tell you," he finally said.

"No, I'm glad you told me now. Does Dillon have plans to test Zeke Osmond's rifle, as well?"

"I'm not sure. I'll mention it to him when I speak to him again." It wasn't much, but it was all he could offer her. If Zeke Osmond had been behind that rifle and had wanted Nick dead, then he'd be dead. Zeke was a crack shot.

He was surprised when she reached for his hand, as if needing it as an anchor for her emotions. He liked the feel of her smaller hand in his. It surged up all the protective instincts he had inside him.

"What kind of a teenager were you?" he asked, wanting to end the night on a lighter note. "Were you wild and willful like Wendy?"

He was pleased to hear a small laugh escape her. "Not at all," she replied. "Our mother got sick with serious heart issues when I was fifteen. Between care-taking for her and keeping things running at home, I didn't have time to be anything except grown-up and responsible." She turned to look at him. "What about you? What kind of teenager were you?"

"During the time that I was out on the streets, I was definitely a loner. There were lots of street kids, but I kept my head down and stayed to myself. Survival was the name of the game. Once I got here, thanks to Cass, I realized I had an opportunity to make something of my life. She had plenty of rules and regulations, but I hungered for them and I needed them. Like you, I didn't have much time to be a wild teenager."

"I think teenage years are vastly overrated," she replied.

"I definitely agree." He was glad to see some of the defeat had left her eyes. "I got lucky when Francine Rogers decided to give me a second chance at life and brought me here."

"Francine Rogers is the social worker?"

"Yeah. She and Cass were good friends, and she brought all of us here. She visited the ranch at least once a month throughout the years. She hasn't been out here since Cass's funeral."

"She must be a special woman, too."

Nick nodded, remembering the tall, thin woman with coffee-colored skin, dark eyes and short salt-and-pepper hair. "She was brave to drive around at night alone and look under overpasses and in alleys for kids she thought she might be able to help in some way or another."

"She must have seen something special in you to bring you here to her friend's ranch."

"I don't know what she saw. My mother certainly didn't see it. Michelle didn't see anything special, either." His heart clenched tight.

"Michelle... Was she a local?"

"Yes, but she was a small-town girl with big-city dreams. We dated for a couple of months before she told me that her dreams were bigger than hanging out here and dating a cowboy. She left town soon after that."

"So she broke your heart," Adrienne said softly.

Nick frowned thoughtfully. "Not really. My heart wasn't fully involved with her. She was just another reminder that I was meant to be alone."

She squeezed his hand. "I don't believe that's true," she replied. "I see the love you have for all the other cowboys. I've watched you interact lovingly with Sammy. I believe there's a wealth of love in you that you're just holding back, Nick." Her eyes held a warm glow that threatened to pull him in.

He pulled his hand free from hers. "If it's there, it's nothing I intend to tap into." He mentally reinforced the walls around his heart. He wasn't willing to take any more chances on loving anyone. So far, the experience of love had been fairly devastating for him.

They were silent for a while, the only noise the click of crickets and the buzz of nocturnal bugs. Nick knew he should get up and return to his bunk, but for the moment, he was content with the heady scent of her surrounding him and the familiar sounds of the ranch at rest.

"I don't know where we go from here," she finally said. "We've talked to almost everyone in town and given Dillon all the names of potential suspects. I guess now it's just a waiting game for us."

He turned and looked at her. "You told me before that you were willing to wait as long as it took, but you know cold cases can last for years. How long are you really willing to put your real life on hold?"

Once again, she looked up to the night sky and was quiet for several long moments. "I don't have an answer to that yet. To be honest, I didn't have much of a real life in Kansas City. I work, I go to the grocery store, I pay my bills and that's my life. I've felt more connection to this place than where I've lived for years."

She gazed back at him. "Cassie and Nicolette have become friends. Daisy and Jenna at the café also feel like potential friendships just waiting to happen. And then there's the fact that I've fallen in love with you."

He stared at her, wanting to believe he'd somehow misunderstood her words, yet knowing he hadn't by the emotion he saw shining in her eyes, the love that seeped out of her pores.

"That's not… I never…" he stuttered in an effort to find a rational response.

She held up a hand to quiet him. "You don't have to say anything. You've made it very clear where you stand. I just needed to tell you what was in my heart. I couldn't hold it in any longer."

She looked up into the night sky and then back at him. "I can't take away the wounds you've suffered in your past. I can't imagine how the rejection from a mother would scar a little boy. All I can tell you is that I love you with all my heart and soul, and if you could just tap into that guarded place in your heart, I believe you love me, too."

She stood abruptly and looked down at him, her eyes filled with a profound sadness. "If you could just trust in my love, then I think we could have something magical that could last a lifetime." She didn't wait for him to reply. She turned and went back into the house.

He didn't move. He was still stunned. He heard the lock on the door click into place and knew that if he turned around and looked she wouldn't be in the kitchen.

Once again, he looked up at the night sky. What usually looked beautiful and star studded appeared only as dark emptiness.

She loved him. Her words echoed in his ears. She loved him, and that love ached inside him. He wished she hadn't said anything, wished she had kept her feelings to herself.

He finally grabbed his hat and placed it on his head, but remained seated, still shocked by her words. Surely she was mistaken in what she thought she felt toward him.

She was a grieving woman, and he'd been her rock while she'd been here. She'd been through several traumas, and he'd been there to pick up the pieces and put her back together again.

She was a lonely woman going back to a lonely life. Was it any wonder her feelings toward him had gotten all tangled up?

She couldn't love him. It was impossible. She might admire him, feel gratitude toward him, but she was mistaking all that for love.

He finally stood and started the long walk back to the bunkhouse. He should have never made love to her. Even now, just thinking about it, he wanted to repeat the experience. But making love to her had been a big mistake.

The real problem wasn't that she thought herself to be in love with him. It was that he had fallen in love with her, and he intended to do nothing about it.

Chapter 13

Adrienne stood at the kitchen window and watched the sun slowly rise in the sky. The house was quiet; everyone else was still sleeping. She couldn't believe she'd told Nick she loved him last night. She just couldn't believe that the words had fallen out of her mouth. She should have never spoken from her heart.

The stunned look that had been on his face was now burned forever into her memory. She wasn't sure what she had been expecting, but it wasn't that.

She should have known that he wasn't in love with her. She'd been prickly and stubborn while in Bitterroot. Heck, she'd even given him a black eye the first time she'd met him.

Why would any man love a woman like her? Wendy had said it all. She was too mean, too controlling and too intractable to be in a relationship. She should have never spoken her feelings for him aloud. She'd been a stupid fool.

She remembered what Nicolette had said about stubborn cowboys just needing a nudge in the right direction. Nick was so much more than just a stubborn cowboy, and the bottom line was that he just wasn't willing to—or didn't—love her back.

Maybe it was time to go home. She had done everything she could think of to help find Wendy's killer and had come up with nothing. She wasn't a detective. She wasn't a professional investigator.

It was time for her to leave things to the real professionals and to distance herself from Nick, although she imagined he would be eager to keep his distance from her after she'd bared her heart to him.

She'd remain here another day and then leave first thing in the morning.

Today was Sunday, and while the traffic would be light, she couldn't quite force herself into working up the energy to pack up and take off today. She felt lethargic and utterly brokenhearted.

She'd been a fool in all ways. She'd been a fool to believe she could solve Wendy's murder, and she'd been equally foolish to believe that Nick might love her. Definitely time for the fool to go home.

She moved away from the window at the same time she heard cheerful voices heading toward the kitchen.

"Good morning." She forced a happy face as Nicolette, Cassie and Sammy entered the room.

"Good morning to you," they all chimed back.

"You're in for a real treat this morning. Sammy is going to make his famous pancakes," Nicolette said.

"All by myself," Sammy said with obvious pride.

"Pancakes are one of my favorite breakfast meals," Adrienne said. She poured herself a cup of coffee and joined the other two women at the table.

"Cowboy Lucas showed me how to make them just perfect," Sammy replied. He went to the cabinets and gathered bowls and the ingredients he needed and got to work.

"Be prepared to be amazed," Cassie said with a wink.

Adrienne smiled and then took a sip of her coffee, warmed despite her heartache by the easy friendship she'd built with the two women and the young boy. It would be hard to tell them all goodbye.

She decided to wait until after breakfast to tell them that she was taking off to go home to Kansas City the next morning. There was too much laughter, too much fun happening at the moment with Sammy displaying his pancake-flipping skills.

He served Adrienne first and waited for her to take her first bite of the two stacked cakes. She buttered and poured syrup, took a big bite and closed her eyes while making yummy sounds.

Satisfied that he'd accomplished what he wanted, he served Cassie next and then Nicolette and then joined them at the table with his own plate.

Breakfast conversation was light and easy but did nothing to change Adrienne's plans for departing the next morning. It wasn't until Sammy had left the kitchen and it was just the three women relaxing and sipping the last of their coffee that she told them her plans to leave the next day.

"You can't go yet," Nicolette protested. "Next Saturday Lucas and I are officially moving into the house and we've decided to have a little housewarming party and you have to come. You helped paint our master bedroom. You have to stay and see the whole thing put together."

"We insist," Cassie said. "Nicolette and Lucas are furnishing the house this week and then having the party. Please stay to be a part of their celebration."

"Besides, maybe with another week of working the case, Dillon will have the answers you need to go home with true peace in your heart," Nicolette added.

There was no true peace in a broken, shattered heart, Adrienne thought. Still, maybe Nicolette was right. Maybe within another week Dillon could find some answers. Besides, it felt boorish and ungrateful to tell them no. Against her better judgment, she found herself agreeing to stay until the following Sunday.

Seven more days. Surely she could keep away from Nick for seven more days and then leave and never look back. She'd refuse to look back on the moments she'd spent with the cowboy who had won her heart.

It was after lunch and she was seated at her computer when she realized Nick was at the back door. A wave of pain and faint embarrassment swept through her.

Reluctantly, she got up from the desk and let him in. He stood just inside the door, worrying his hat between his hands, obviously ill at ease.

"I was just wondering where we were in our investigation," he said.

"We're nowhere," she replied and refused to meet his eyes. "I'm done. I'm finished with playing amateur sleuth. I'm ready to leave it all to Dillon and his men. You can go back to being a cowboy again without worrying about me getting myself in trouble."

"Adrienne…about last night…"

Her gaze shot up to his, and she thought she spied a touch of pity in the blue depths of his eyes. The last thing she wanted to see from him was any pity.

"What about it?" she asked.

"I'm just sorry…"

"No reason to be," she interrupted him. She looked at the wall just behind him, finding it easier to look at than the face she'd come to love. "You gave me plenty of warning. It's obvious we aren't on the same page. I'd planned on heading back to Kansas City tomorrow, but Cassie and Nicolette have insisted I stay until next Sunday so that I can be there at her and Lucas's housewarming party on Saturday. So I'll be around here this week and then I'll be gone."

"Is there anything I can do? Anything you need?" he asked. His voice was as soft as a caress, and only made her heart ache more.

"No." *Love me*, her heart begged. "Just go back to doing—to being—whatever it was you were before I ever came to Bitterroot," she replied. "I have plenty of things to occupy me here in the house until I leave."

"Things won't be the same without you around."

He was torturing her with kindness. "Things will be a lot less complicated without me around."

"I hate that it has to end like this." His voice held a depth of emotion that only made her hurt more. He was killing her.

She managed to look at him again. "It's funny. I just realized that deep in my heart I thought maybe the universe had conspired to bring us together. I believed that perhaps there was some cosmic reason why your mother abandoned you and you eventually wound up here, that my mother died and I raised Wendy and she was murdered so that I wound up here, too."

A slightly bitter laugh escaped her. "I started to believe that all the bad things had happened to create something wonderful and you were my wonderful." She shrugged. "I guess sometimes bad things happen, and only bad things come out of them."

"I never meant to hurt you, Adrienne."

She forced a smile. "I know that, and I'll be just fine. Don't worry about me, Nick. I'll go home and make new friends. I'll build a new life for myself that includes other people. I'm a survivor, and loving you and you not loving me back isn't going to break me."

Something sparked in his eyes, something that looked a lot like love to her, but it was there only a moment and then gone and his eyes went flat and fathomless.

"Then, I guess I'll just see you around the ranch," he said and backed toward the door as if ready to escape. She nodded, and after he stepped outside, she watched him walk away.

She raised a hand and placed it against the warm window glass, and remembered touching his cheek.

She was certain she had seen love in his eyes, had heard it in the deep caress of his voice. But it wasn't enough to allow him to overcome whatever forces kept him alone.

It wasn't enough to make him believe that he deserved love and a happily-ever-after.

On Wednesday, Nick was in the same foul mood he'd been in since his last interaction with Adrienne on Sunday. Thank God she hadn't cried, for her tears would have destroyed him. It was bad enough that he'd seen the wealth of pain shining from her eyes even as she'd told him she'd be just fine without him.

There had been nothing new in Wendy's case, although he knew that Dillon had appointed a couple of officers to continue to chase down leads and check out buildings for Wendy's car. Dillon had been attempting to work with Dr. Patience Forbes, whom he called Dr. Dreadful under his breath.

"She's a fire-breathing dragon who is moving at a snail's pace and making me insane," Dillon had confessed to Nick the day before.

Nick didn't care what was happening with the skeletal remains or how difficult Dr. Forbes was to work with. He cared about the fact that he had broken Adrienne's heart.

It would be easier if she still believed him to be a person of interest in her sister's murderer. It would be so much easier if she still wanted to punch and kick him instead of loving him.

After a quick shower, he pulled on his jeans and a white T-shirt and headed for the stable. Dawn was just beginning to break, and he hoped a ride on his horse, Raven, would drive out both his foul mood and any thoughts of what might have been—could be—if he just let go of all control.

The loneliness that had been torched into his soul for nearly a lifetime had been eased by Wendy's presence and banished by Adrienne's in the time he'd spent with her. Now it was back, gnawing like a hunger that couldn't be sated no matter how much he ate.

When he got to the stables, Forest was there, saddling up his own mount. Forest was one of the few of them who had known the love of two parents, but when he was fifteen, they'd died in a car accident. Forest had gone immediately to the streets and had easily survived due to his intimidating size until the time that Francine had brought him here to Cass.

"Good morning," Forest greeted him.

Nick grunted.

Forest eyed him curiously. "You're wearing your attitude a little crooked lately, buddy," he said. "Got something you need to talk about?"

"Nothing worthwhile," Nick replied. He walked Raven out of the stall and put on the bridle. Raven stood patiently, accustomed to the routine of being saddled and ready to ride.

"I'm thinking 'nothing worthwhile' has pretty chestnut hair and gave you a black eye the first time she met you," Forest said. Nick frowned as Raven danced away from him and gave a low whinny. "Even Raven is feeling your bad mood," Forest observed.

"I'm not in a bad mood," Nick replied. Forest raised a dark brow. "Okay, maybe I'm in a little bit of a bad mood." Nick drew in a lungful of the familiar scents of horse and hay and leather and felt some of the tension leave his body.

"I'll be my old self within a week or two," he said and stroked Raven's nose.

"I think most of us are a little on edge and will be until those skeletal remains are removed and things get back to normal around here."

Nick gazed at the big man. "I've noticed that you've been hanging close to the tent since Dr. Forbes arrived."

"Just curious, that's all," Forest replied, but Nick could have sworn the man blushed. "Get saddled and get out of here. Maybe the morning breeze will set your head on straighter."

Nick did just that, and within minutes, he and Raven were dashing across the pasture at an exhilarating pace. There was nothing Raven liked better than when Nick allowed her to run full-out. And this morning, Nick felt as if he needed the rush of the air in his face and the powerful animal beneath him.

He wanted the breeze to blow every nuance of Adrienne out of his head. He wanted to gallop away from the visions of her head thrown back in laughter, the stubborn straightening of her shoulders and her passion-glazed eyes as he took possession of her.

He needed to forget it all. He needed to forget her. She was just a passing ship in the ocean of his life…like his mother…like Michelle…and like Cass and Wendy.

Adrienne would come to her senses and realize she'd mistaken gratitude for love. Hell, it had probably happened already. She'd leave town and not look back. He was accustomed to seeing the backs of women who had left him. He refused to allow Adrienne to hold any more importance than the others.

He finally slowed Raven to a cool-down pace. He raised a hand in greeting to Clay Madison, who was on horseback in the middle of the cattle herd, checking the welfare of the stock.

He also saw Jerod Steen and Tony Nakni, fellow cowboys, riding the fence lines. For all intents and purposes, it was business as usual on the ranch if they didn't count the crime scene tent, the six skeletons and his tangled, torn heart.

He rode around the pond and tried to forget the night he'd told her about his past and she'd wept tears of pain for the little boy he had once been.

An hour later when he returned to the stable, he told himself he felt better. Nothing had really changed since Adrienne had first come to town. He was back working with the men he respected, the men who were his family. It was all he needed. Since the time Francine Rogers had brought him here, this was all he'd ever needed.

Adrienne worked to fill every hour of the day after her last talk with Nick. She worked at her computer, and one entire afternoon helped Cassie rearrange the furniture in her bedroom.

Lucas, Nicolette and Sammy were gone most of the time, busy working to prepare their new home and finish preparations for the party on Saturday. Monday and Tuesday evening with just Cassie and

Adrienne at home for dinner, Adrienne had treated Cassie to some of her culinary talent.

Monday had been beef Wellington and Tuesday had been chicken cordon bleu. Cassie had been delighted at what she called real citified food and confessed to Adrienne how much she missed the city.

She intentionally stayed away from any window with a view of the pastures and the cowboys. She tried to keep thoughts of Nick Coleman from intruding into her mind, but it was impossible.

It would have been easier not to think about him if she was back in Kansas City, but she had promised Nicolette she'd stick around for the housewarming party.

By Thursday evening every nerve in her body was on edge. She and Cassie were alone in the house, as the others hadn't come back from their work at their new home yet.

Darkness had fallen outside, and Cassie excused herself to head upstairs for a shower while Adrienne sat at the desk in the kitchen and tried to focus on anything but Nick.

She'd caught up with all the work that needed to be done for her business during the past couple of days and found herself staring at the computer screen and fighting off the wave of tears that threatened each night when her heartbreak seemed to magnify and consume her.

Each morning she awoke with the stupid hope that Nick would come to the big house, pull her into his arms and tell her that he'd been the fool. She fantasized about him professing his love for her and his desire to be with her for the rest of their lives.

And each day that didn't happen, and that was when the pain resonated through her. She could fantasize all she wanted, but the truth was the next time she saw Nick would be at the housewarming party, where they would probably exchange uncomfortable forced pleasantries, and Sunday morning she'd be gone.

She was vaguely aware of the sound of swooshing water through pipes and knew that Cassie had started her shower. Cassie had looked tired at dinner, and Adrienne suspected she intended an early night. Maybe that was what Adrienne needed, too. An early night of sleep that didn't include visions of Nick.

A faint knock sounded on the back door, and her heart leaped into her throat. She turned in her chair, and instead of seeing Nick, Jenna stood on the porch.

Tentative happiness transformed to confusion. What was Jenna doing here? She unlocked the door and opened it to allow the waitress inside.

"Jenna, what's going on?"

"I need you to come with me." There was an intensity in Jenna's blue eyes. She reached out and grabbed Adrienne firmly by the arm. "I have something to show you. Trust me, you're going to want to see it."

Adrienne yanked her arm from Jenna's grasp. "What do you have to show me?"

"Something important." Jenna grabbed her again.

This time, Adrienne couldn't pull her arm from Jenna's strong grasp, and her heart began to beat an uneven rhythm. Something was off. Something wasn't right with the whole situation or with Jenna.

The woman was clad in her uniform from the café. She'd obviously just gotten off her shift, but she didn't belong here, and there was something dark in her eyes that frightened Adrienne.

Fear turned to terror as Jenna pulled a syringe from her pocket. "Don't make this difficult," she warned, her voice a low whisper.

Adrienne had no idea what was happening, but the last thing she wanted was whatever was in that syringe. She grappled with Jenna to keep the syringe from touching her.

She fought as she had with Nick on the first night she'd seen him. She got free from Jenna's hold and swung her arms, kicked her feet to keep the woman at bay.

Jenna managed to grab her again, and Adrienne felt the sting of the needle in her back. Almost instantly Adrienne went woozy, falling into Jenna's body as she still tried to fight.

As her knees buckled and she slid down the length of Jenna's body, she grabbed at the woman's T-shirt in an effort to somehow save herself.

Unconsciousness claimed her before she hit the floor.

Chapter 14

The big bell that hung from the porch at the big house rang frantically. It pealed through the air and Nick jumped up from his bed. He quickly strapped on his holster, his heart banging with adrenaline.

The bell was used only for emergencies. It had always been a way to signal to the cowboys that there was some sort of emergency and Cass wanted all hands on deck.

As he opened the door to his bunk, half a dozen of his fellow cowboys were doing the same, all of them armed and running toward the house in the distance.

There had been only three times in the past that Nick could remember that bell being rung. The first had been years ago when Cass had fallen down the stairs and broken her leg. She'd managed to drag herself outside and somehow grab the rope to ring the bell.

The second time had been a little over a month ago when Nicolette had seen a masked man at Sammy's upstairs bedroom window. Now as he raced toward the house all he could think about was Adrienne.

Half of the men headed for the back door while Nick and several others ran around the house and entered through the front door. Within seconds the men who had gone around back returned and said that the back door was locked.

Cassie stood in the living room, clad in a dark blue robe and with a look of deep concern on her pretty features. "I can't find Adrienne," she said.

"What do you mean you can't find her?" Nick asked, his heartbeat accelerating.

"I went upstairs to take a shower, and she was working on her computer. When I came back down to tell her good-night, she wasn't there. I assumed maybe she went to her room, so I checked there. I've checked the whole house. She's not anywhere inside."

"Let's not panic," Forest said. "Maybe she just stepped outside to take a walk."

"I'm calling Dillon," Nick replied tersely. "Why don't the rest of you check out the ranch? Maybe she went to the stables." Even as he said the words, he didn't believe them. There was no way she'd go outside and wander around alone. He pulled out his cell phone and made the call to Dillon, then looked at Cassie. "Let's check the house again."

The men headed for the doors as Nick followed Cassie upstairs. Somehow Cassie had just missed seeing her, he told himself. She was probably taking a shower or hadn't heard Cassie call for her.

She had to be here, he thought with desperation, because if she wasn't then he feared the unthinkable had happened and that Wendy's killer had somehow gotten to her.

He and Cassie went upstairs and searched every room, every closet while they called for her. There was no answer, and Nick's heart knotted into a ball of despair.

They continued the search on the lower level, checking the parlor and the coat closet and then the kitchen and pantry. Nick's heart beat faster when he saw her purse next to the computer. He opened it and saw the little Colt Mustang next to her cell phone. Wherever she was, she didn't even have her gun or her phone with her.

By the time Dillon and two of his men arrived, Nick was beside himself. "You need to check out Perry and Zeke and anyone else you might suspect in Wendy's murder," he said desperately to Dillon.

"I'm already on it," Dillon replied. He turned to Cassie to get the details that Nick already knew. "No sign of a struggle anywhere?" he asked when Cassie had finished.

"None that I saw," she replied. "Nick and I both looked around the desk in the kitchen and the back door and didn't see anything disturbed."

"Her car is still here, so she didn't just drive off anywhere." Nick's heart felt as if it might explode at any moment. "I've got the men checking the ranch, but I can't imagine her just wandering off in the dark alone. She's smarter than that."

There was no way he believed that she would do

anything so foolish as to take a stroll in the dark. She hadn't left the house at all except in the company of Lucas and Nicolette during the past few days.

"Would she have gone out with somebody?" Dillon asked. "Has she made friends with somebody who might have stopped by to take her out to the bar or for something to eat?"

"Not without her purse, and it's next to her computer in the kitchen." Nick felt as if his heart had been ripped out of his body and there was nothing left inside except a simmering terror.

"You said she was at her computer the last time you saw her?" Dillon asked Cassie. Cassie nodded. "And you didn't hear anything?"

"Nothing, but I was in the shower for a while. I'm not sure even if she screamed I would have heard her." Cassie's face was pale. "What could have happened to her? We always keep the back door locked."

Dillon left the great room and went into the kitchen with Nick and Cassie following behind him. "The door is locked now. It doesn't look as though any attempt at a break-in happened."

"We've got to do something," Nick said in desperation. Unfortunately, he had no idea what to do, where to go. He only knew that Adrienne was in trouble.

The ranch hands started to check in, letting Dillon and Nick know that there was no sign of Adrienne anywhere on the ranch.

"He has her," Nick said, surprised at the emotional tremble in his voice. "Whoever killed Wendy now has Adrienne, and we don't know where in the hell to look. We have no idea who might have taken her.

I'm telling you she didn't leave this house willingly. She was taken."

"I should be hearing back anytime from the men I sent to the Humes Ranch and the officers checking out Perry Wright," Dillon said as if his words might ease some of Nick's fear.

Nothing could ease his fear. He was drowning in it, suffocating from it. The fact that he didn't know what to do or where to look for her only made his panic worse.

He needed action. He was desperate for answers, but none were forthcoming. He couldn't make sense of anything. Why would Wendy's killer want to kill her sister? Whom had Adrienne gotten too close to? Whom had she threatened? He racked his brain but came up empty.

Dillon's phone rang, and by the look on his face the news wasn't good. He hung up and looked at Nick. "She's not with Zeke Osmond, and she isn't with Perry Wright."

Nick stared at him. If not them, then who?

Adrienne came to with her head feeling as if it was stuffed with cotton. She looked around dully. She was seated in a straight-backed wooden chair, and wherever she was, it was dark. Only the moonlight drifted through slats of wood and a hole in the roof of whatever building she was in. In the dimness she could make out stacks of baled hay near where she was seated, but there was also the scent of gasoline and grease and rubber tires.

She frowned and shook her head, trying to make

sense of things. Had she gone to the stables and somehow passed out? Was she in the barn at the ranch? Was Nick here, as well?

No, that couldn't be right. The barn didn't have a hole in the roof and broken slats of siding. The Holiday barn hadn't smelled of oil and grease.

It was only when she tried to raise her hand to her aching head that she realized her wrists were tied to the chair, as were her ankles.

That was when it all slammed home. Jenna at the back door. Jenna fighting with her. Darkness caused by whatever Jenna had given her.

Jenna? Why had the waitress done this? What on earth did she want from Adrienne? Nothing made sense.

She tried to work her wrists free, but the rope was tied too tight. She also attempted to free her feet, but again found herself firmly bound. It was so dark she didn't know if scooting the chair would help her evade danger or move closer to it.

Her brain spun in an effort to make sense of everything at the same time a shiver of fear shot up her spine. Disoriented and confused, she knew that she was in trouble.

Her heart beat fast and furious as her mind continued to grow clearer. There was no way Jenna had brought her here for anything but harm. Why would Jenna hate her? She'd always been so friendly, so supportive. Maybe Jenna had a crazy twin sister nobody knew about. The ridiculous idea almost made Adrienne laugh out loud, and she knew she was becoming more than a little hysterical.

Minutes ticked by—agonizing, long minutes. She tried again to free her wrists and ankles, but only managed to make her skin raw and painful.

Something was going to happen. Eventually, Jenna would come back. It was just a matter of time before Adrienne had the answers to what was happening—answers she was sure she wasn't going to like.

Her mind raced, seeking to make sense of what Jenna had done and why, but nothing made sense. Or maybe Jenna just intended to keep her tied up until she died of thirst. Her throat immediately went dry at the thought.

Nick had told her that Jenna lived alone on her family ranch on the outskirts of town. If she screamed, the only person who would hear her was Jenna.

Jenna.

She hadn't been on anybody's radar. Everyone had been looking for a man. Adrienne now understood how she'd managed to keep the motel room door closed. It had been woman against woman, not a woman against a man's strength.

Had she intended to kidnap Adrienne that night? To take her and throw her into Wendy's car and drive off in the night? Tears filled her eyes. Nobody was going to look for her here. Nobody was going to find her.

The last thing Adrienne remembered before passing out was the cold look of hate in Jenna's eyes. She and Jenna had struggled by the back door, but Adrienne didn't remember the crash of anything falling and breaking, and she didn't remember bumping into any furniture—nothing that might indicate a struggle had taken place.

Nick, her heart cried out in agony. She wouldn't get one last chance to see him again, to gaze into his beautiful, midnight-blue eyes. It didn't matter that he didn't love her. She'd just wanted a final moment to tell him goodbye.

The terror inside her was a palpable thing, beating her heart in an impossible rhythm as dreadful anticipation filled her.

What happened next? She didn't want to consider the answer.

A light turned on, and she winced against the sudden brightness. Nobody came in, but she gasped when she saw Wendy's car parked inside what appeared to be an old barn.

Shock momentarily stole her breath.

Jenna had killed Wendy.

The waitress had stabbed Wendy twice, buried her body on the Holiday Ranch, packed up her belongings and parked her car here. If she'd killed once, there was no reason to believe she wouldn't kill again.

Why? The question still begged to be answered. Why on earth would Jenna do such a thing to Wendy? A coworker, a woman she professed to have liked? And why had she marked Adrienne for the same kind of end?

Jenna stepped into the barn. "Hello, Adrienne."

Adrienne drew in a deep breath in an effort to stay calm. "Jenna, what's going on?"

The woman had changed out of her work clothes and into an old pair of jeans and a black T-shirt. Her blond hair was loose instead of pulled into a neat ponytail as it usually was when she was at work at the café.

She walked to a bale of hay and sat. "What's going on? I'm taking out the trash."

"Taking out the trash?" Adrienne looked at her in confusion.

Jenna nodded. "Your sister was trash. She blew into town and set her sights on Nick. Nick was just about to make a move on me. I felt it in my heart that it was just a matter of time until he and I were happily together, but then your stupid sister showed up and ruined things."

Adrienne stared at the pretty waitress. Nick? This was all about Nick? Adrienne's head reeled in stunned surprise.

"Wendy was just friends with Nick," she protested.

"That's what she said, but I knew better." Jenna's voice was filled with hateful scorn. "She spent all of her free time with him. It didn't matter that she was too young for him, that she was an outsider and had no right to him. She just pushed herself on him, taking away any time I was meant to have with him. So I took out the trash."

Tears filled Adrienne's eyes once again. "She was just friends with Nick," she repeated in a mere whisper.

"Whatever." Jenna waved her hand in dismissal. "At first I wasn't too worried about her because I didn't figure she'd stick in town for long. Then she started to talk about staying, maybe making Bitterroot her permanent home, and that's when I knew I had to do something about her."

"And so you killed her?"

Jenna grinned, a look of pure evil. "It was so easy. She was so gullible and so trusting. She was eager to make new friends, and she played right into my plan. I watched her leave the Holiday Ranch on that Friday night, and I texted her to see if she wanted to meet up with me at her motel and go to the Watering Hole for a couple of drinks."

"And she said yes."

Oh, Wendy, Adrienne thought, *if only you'd said no. If only you'd said it was too late or that you were too tired, then maybe you'd still be alive today.*

"I picked her up at her motel and drove her to a field not far from here and pretended to have car trouble. She got out of the car to help me open the hood and then I stabbed her."

Adrienne winced at Jenna's matter-of-fact tone. She could have been describing a trip to the grocery store to pick up fresh fruit.

"I wrapped her in a tarp I had in the trunk so that she wouldn't bleed in the backseat of my car and then I drove to the Holiday Ranch and parked out on the street. I carried and dragged her to that shed."

"Why? Why there?"

Jenna shrugged. "She liked being close to Nick, so I figured I'd put her close to him. I didn't know anything about those other skeletons being there. I just found some loose floorboards and dumped her in. I really never expected her body to be found. The last thing I wanted was a murder investigation, but that damned tornado screwed up my plans."

"And your plan was to make everyone believe she'd just left town." A dullness of defeat took hold of Adrienne. Jenna had been so cunning. There was no way she'd be caught.

She nodded, her blond hair shining under the overhead light. "I drove back to the motel and parked next door in the dry-cleaning parking lot, and then I used her key to get into her room, packed her things and drove her car here."

She frowned in obvious irritation. "The hardest part of the whole plan was getting back to my car. I got a ride to the Watering Hole from one of the other waitresses and told her I'd find my own way back home and then I left the Watering Hole and got my car and came back here. The trash had been taken care of, and it was time for me to start making progress with Nick."

"And then I showed up," Adrienne replied.

"It didn't take me long after seeing you and Nick together to realize there was one more piece of trash that needed to be taken care of."

"But Nick isn't in love with me," Adrienne exclaimed fervently.

"Don't lie to me," Jenna said, her voice rough with anger. "I see the way he looks at you, and I see the way you look at him. I'm not a stupid fool."

Adrienne wanted to laugh hysterically. She was going to be punished for a love that didn't exist, just like her sister before her.

"But you're no good for him. Your sister told me

all about you, that you were a mean witch and totally hateful, and Nick deserves much better than you."

Her words stabbed into the center of Adrienne's heart. She tried to remember what Nick had said about the way Wendy had felt about her. Wendy had loved her.

Jenna spoke lies. *Evil always speaks lies*, she told herself.

"You'll never get away with this," Adrienne said frantically.

"I already have," Jenna replied confidently. "I've thought of everything. I got you out of that kitchen without any sign of a struggle, then relocked the door behind me so that nobody would suspect anyone had come inside. I'm not a suspect in Wendy's death and I won't be a suspect in your disappearance."

Everything she said was true, Adrienne thought in despair.

Jenna stood and dusted her hands together, as if ready to get to work. "I'm going to find a better place to bury you so that nobody will ever find your body. Your disappearance will just be a mystery that eventually everyone will forget. Life will go on, and I'll get Nick. We'll eventually get married and live happily ever after."

Adrienne's heart beat with terror. Jenna picked up a long length of rope and twisted it around her wrists. "I don't want you bleeding in my barn, so I think the easiest way of getting this done is to strangle you."

She smiled as if she'd just offered Adrienne a cup of coffee. "Don't worry, I've heard it only hurts for a minute or two. If you don't fight it, it will be over before you know it."

As she advanced, Adrienne looked around desperately, trying to find help from somewhere from something. There was nothing but death coming closer.

Chapter 15

Nick paced the great room like a caged tiger. Cassie sat on the sofa with Lucas while Nicolette had taken Sammy upstairs to play video games with him. She didn't want her son in the midst of all the tension and a potential crime scene.

Dillon was on his cell phone, ordering officers helter-skelter around town in an effort to find Adrienne. Nick wanted to be somewhere, actively participating in the search, but he didn't know where to go.

The other cowboys had left, also to check out what they could find about Adrienne's disappearance. In truth, although Nick wanted action, he was reluctant to leave Dillon's side. The chief of police would be the first person to learn of any developments from all the people who were out searching.

Helpless and impotent, Nick continued to pace, his

thoughts filled with every moment he'd spent with Adrienne. She'd made him mad and she'd made him laugh. She'd pried secrets from him and then had soothed the wounds exposed. She'd gotten in deeper than he'd ever allowed another person.

She'd been a fighter and his lover, and he couldn't abide the idea of her being gone forever from the earth. He wanted her to have a happy life in Kansas City. He didn't want her joined with her sister in the afterlife.

Dammit, it wasn't her time to die.

He left the great room and went into the kitchen and sat at the desk where she had been working before whatever happened had happened.

Rubbing his hand across his forehead, he wondered what they had missed. How had two women been kidnapped and one murdered without a single clue, without any lead at all?

He thought back since the time that Wendy's body had been found, searching his memory for any nuance that had been missed, any person who had been overlooked, but there was nothing and nobody he could think of.

Broken. He felt broken inside, and the only way he could be fixed was for Adrienne to be found alive and well. Dillon walked into the room and Nick stood. "No news?" he asked, even though he knew the answer by the expression on Dillon's face.

"I've got the whole team looking everywhere. I've questioned most of the cowboys here, and nobody saw anything unusual. Nobody has seen her since Cassie went up to take a shower." Dillon released a sigh of frustration. "Honest to God, Nick. For the first time in my career, I don't know what to do."

Nick clapped him on the back. "I know you're doing everything you can." His voice sounded as hollow as Dillon's eyes looked. "I just keep wondering why Wendy was killed. And now why somebody would take Adrienne. I kept getting hung up on the why of it all."

Dillon motioned him to the table, where they both sat. Cassie came in and poured them each a cup of coffee. She'd had the coffee flowing since Dillon and his men had first arrived.

"Should I make sandwiches? Have Cookie prepare something to feed everyone?" Her blue eyes simmered with the same need that Nick felt inside—the need to do something, anything constructive.

"It might be good if Cookie laid out some food for everyone involved in the search," Nick said.

She nodded. "I'll grab one of the cowboys and have them get Cookie." She looked at Dillon. "You might let all your officers know that within thirty minutes or so they can fuel up at the cowboys' dining room behind the bunkhouse."

"Thanks, Cassie," Dillon replied. "They'll appreciate it."

She drifted out of the kitchen. Neither man touched the coffee she'd poured them. Nick stared at the back door, trying to figure out whom Adrienne would have trusted, whom she might have let in.

She wasn't a fool, and she knew there had already been two attempts to hurt her. She'd have been wary and wouldn't have opened the door to just anyone.

Unable to sit still, Nick got up from the table, and as he stood, something hard crunched under his foot. He frowned and bent down to see two small pieces of plastic. Apparently, his foot had broken whatever it was in half.

He picked up both the pieces and set them on the table. Dillon leaned forward with interest. It was obviously some sort of a name tag with a safety pin on the back to attach it to clothing.

NA JEN.

His heart leaped to life as he switched the pieces around.

JENNA.

He looked at Dillon. "Why would Jenna's name tag be in this kitchen?"

"I have no clue. Has she visited here recently?" Dillon asked, a new tension in his voice.

Nick shook his head. "The last time she was on the ranch was the day of Wendy's funeral, and she never came inside the house, but went to the cowboy dining room."

Jenna? He thought of the pretty blond waitress and tried to make sense of the name tag in front of him. "It's got to be her."

"But why would Jenna want to kidnap Adrienne?" Dillon asked.

Nick's adrenaline pumped through him. Dillon stood from the table. "I don't know why," Nick said. "All I know is that if her name tag is here, then she must have been here, as well. Here, in the kitchen where Adrienne was the last time anyone saw her.

Adrienne probably wouldn't have thought twice about opening the door to her."

"I'll check it out. I'll drive out to her farm," Dillon said.

"I'm coming with you," Nick replied in a tone that allowed no argument.

Dillon hesitated only a moment and then nodded. He instructed two officers to follow them, and within minutes, Nick was riding shotgun in the patrol car as Dillon sped toward the old farm where Jenna lived.

Nick's insides twisted in knots even as his brain worked to make sense of everything that had happened. Had it been Jenna wielding the rifle that had shot at them that night on Main Street?

Had the waitress been at the motel room door, trying to break in to get to Adrienne? That would mean that Jenna had killed Wendy. Why? What could her motive possibly be?

And if Jenna had murdered Wendy, then she probably planned to do the same to Adrienne. His blood iced, and he willed Dillon to drive faster.

His greatest fear was that it was already too late. Nobody knew exactly what time Adrienne had disappeared, but it had been at least two or two and a half hours that she had been gone.

It took only a second to plunge a knife into a person. Jenna's farm was isolated enough that she could shoot a gun and the odds of anyone hearing it were minimal.

Maybe Jenna had stopped by for some reason and she wasn't responsible for Adrienne's disappearance, he told himself. But he didn't believe it.

Adrienne and Jenna hadn't been friends, although if Jenna had appeared at the back door, Adrienne probably wouldn't have thought twice about allowing her inside. They had been friendly, but definitely not friends.

"We never thought about it being a woman," Dillon said, breaking into Nick's thoughts.

"Adrienne was certain it was Perry, and I placed my odds on Zeke. Jenna would have been the last person on earth I'd have thought of as a murderer. What I can't understand is why."

"Hopefully we're just minutes from answering that question," Dillon replied. He turned on the county road that would take them to Jenna's farm.

Nick leaned forward in desperate anticipation, his seat belt pulling taut against him.

Please let her be there. Please let her still be alive.

He prayed to the entire universe, to every superior entity he could think of.

By the time Jenna's ranch house came into view, he vibrated with energy, felt slightly nauseous from the adrenaline spike that soared through him.

"Her car is here," Dillon said as he pulled into the long lane that led to the house. Lights drifted out of the windows, beacons in the otherwise dark night. "It looks as though she's home."

Was Adrienne inside? Or had Jenna already accomplished what she'd set out to do? Dillon had scarcely pulled the car to a halt before Nick had unbuckled his seat belt and was out of the passenger door.

Jenna's ranch home showed the signs of neglect in

the faded red shutters at the windows and the white paint that had grayed in the elements. The grass was overgrown and a flower bed held nothing but dead plants. An old riding lawn mower that looked as if it belonged in Larry's junkyard stood in the middle of a growth of weeds.

By the time Nick pounded on the door, Dillon was at his side, and officers Ramirez and Goodall had gone around to the back of the house to make sure Jenna didn't try to escape out a window or a door.

Dillon knocked again at the door. "Jenna, it's Dillon. Open up."

There was no reply and no sound coming from inside.

Nick reached out and tried to turn the doorknob. It was locked.

"Break down the door," Nick said, the urgency inside him reaching mammoth proportions. "You have reasonable cause."

Dillon nodded, and on the count of three both of the men hit the door with their shoulders. Dillon and Nick both pulled their guns as the door sprung open.

Dillon went in first, his gun leading the way. Nick was like a shadow just behind him, his weapon also ready and in his hand. The living room was neat and held the usual furnishings.

There wasn't a sound except the soft footfalls of the men as they first cleared the kitchen and then headed down the hallway that led to three bedrooms and a bath.

She has to be here.

Nick's heart cried with pain as each room was

cleared. Finally, there was only one room left, the master bedroom with a closed door.

The faint click of the air-conditioning coming on nearly shot Nick out of his shoes. He'd never been on edge like this in his entire life.

He grabbed the doorknob of the last bedroom, and when he opened it, Dillon rushed in. Almost immediately Dillon's gun pointed downward, indicating to Nick that the room was empty.

"You'd better take a look in here," Dillon said somberly.

Nick stepped into the bedroom and was shocked to see photos of him in frames on the dresser and on the nightstand. They had obviously been taken when Nick was unaware.

"I'd say we just found our motive," Dillon said. "Nothing more deadly than a jealous female."

Nick stared at the pictures. Wendy had been killed because of him? Adrienne was missing because of some insane crush Jenna had on him? It all was because of him?

Jenna was just a pleasant, attractive waitress at the café where Nick often took his meals, but he'd never flirted with her, had never given her any indication that he had any interest in her.

Crazy. She had to be crazy. And her car was here, so she had to be on the property somewhere.

"We've got to find her. If she killed Wendy because Wendy and I were spending time together, then she intends to do the same to Adrienne." A new urgency filled Nick as he looked at Dillon. "They're here somewhere."

"We'll find them," Dillon said as the two left the bedroom and headed for the back door, where the other two officers were waiting.

In the distance there were two outbuildings, a shed and the barn. A faint light spilled from the cracks in the barn wall. "You two check out the shed," Dillon said to his men. "Nick and I are headed for the barn."

They took off at a run, and all Nick could think about was that fate had not been kind to him in the past and he had no reason to believe things might change now.

He couldn't help but expect the worst—that they were too late and Adrienne was already dead.

As Jenna approached with the rope in her hands, Adrienne fought in an all-out attempt to free herself. When she realized it was not possible, she used her foot against the floor to topple her chair sideways.

She cried out as her body made contact with the ground. She didn't expect to escape, but she was determined not to make it easy for Jenna.

Jenna laughed. "You stupid woman. I can strangle you no matter what position you're in."

"You're crazy," Adrienne cried. "Nick is never going to be with you. It doesn't matter how many women you kill. He'll never want you."

"Shut up. Just shut up!" Jenna screamed. She kicked at Adrienne, thankfully connecting with the back of the chair instead of with Adrienne's vulnerable body.

As she moved around to get to Adrienne's head, Adrienne used her feet to spin the chair away from

Jenna. Unfortunately, with her feet bound she could only move an inch or two.

Jenna managed to stop her and get the rope around Adrienne's neck. Jenna crouched down and pulled the rope just tight enough to hurt, but not cut off air.

"I liked Wendy, but she got in my way. I liked you, too, Adrienne. I really did. I tried to warn you twice, but you refused to stay away from Nick. I left you that note and then I shot off those bullets on Main Street. I could have easily hit Nick, but I didn't want to. I just wanted to scare you. If you'd just left town and gone back to Kansas City, it wouldn't have had to come to this."

Adrienne tried to talk, but the rope pulled tighter. She wanted to tell Jenna that it didn't have to come to this, that Nick didn't love her and she planned to leave town on Sunday morning.

Still, deep in her heart she knew that Jenna wouldn't believe anything she said. Jenna was past rational talk, beyond being human. She was a killing machine without remorse, determined to "take out the trash" and in her twisted mind keep Nick to herself.

The rope twisted tighter, and Adrienne struggled to breathe. She closed her eyes, not wanting Jenna's malevolent glare to be the last thing she saw.

Instead, as she felt the air being cut off from her lungs, she filled her head with visions of Wendy, whom she hoped to meet again soon, and then of Nick, whom she would love through eternity.

Then there was no air at all, and she felt herself floating into the darkness that awaited her.

* * *

Nick and Dillon burst through the barn door and into a nightmare scene that Nick knew he would never forget for the rest of his life. Rope ties held Adrienne to a chair lying on its side. Jenna was crouched over her, pulling on a rope wrapped around Adrienne's neck.

"Jenna, stand up or I'll shoot," Dillon yelled, his voice echoing in the cavernous barn.

Nick dropped his gun and ran to Jenna. With the roar of an enraged bull, he shoved her aside. He fell to his knees, his eyes misting with tears as he frantically unwrapped the rope from around Adrienne's neck.

"Breathe, baby," he said in desperation. "Come on, Adrienne, take a breath for me." She was too still, her face an unnatural color. Pale, her entire face was too pale. Her slack mouth gave her the look of death.

He pulled her chair to an upright position.

"Adrienne, dammit, take a breath." He placed his lips against hers, wanting to breathe for her. At the same time, he was vaguely aware of Officer Michael Goodall using a knife to cut through the binds that held her to the chair.

Once she was free of the chair Nick laid her flat on the floor.

He blew into her and waited.

Nothing.

He placed his mouth against hers once again and blew a little harder. She gasped and coughed and breathed.

Nick nearly fell to the floor in sweet relief. She gasped again and then hungrily drew in a deep breath.

She opened her eyes and stared at him and then began to cry.

"It's okay," he murmured as she continued to cry. "Everything is okay now."

She reached up and clung to him, as if afraid that he was a mirage that might disappear at any moment.

Dillon handcuffed Jenna, who looked defiant and angry. "It had to be done," she said. Her expression softened as she met Nick's gaze. "If she and Wendy hadn't come to town, then you would have been mine. We would have been so happy together."

Nick helped Adrienne to her feet and held her tight against him. "Never," Nick replied in open disgust as his hand caressed up and down Adrienne's back. "Get her out of here. Looking at her makes me sick to my stomach."

Dillon handed Jenna over to Ramirez. "Take her to the station and book her on murder and kidnapping charges. That will just be the beginning."

Adrienne's crying had turned into hiccupping sobs, and still she clung to Nick. Dillon walked around Wendy's car, shaking his head as if he couldn't believe how this had all gone down.

Hell, Nick was having trouble processing it all. The most important thing of all was that Adrienne was alive and in his arms.

Dillon and his men could sort out everything else. The danger was passed and the mystery had been solved. Dillon would have no problems building a case that would keep Jenna behind bars for the rest of her life.

Adrienne finally took a step back from Nick.

"How…how did you find me?" Her voice sounded scratchy and raw, and her throat was bright red where the rope had twisted against her vulnerable skin.

"We found Jenna's name tag by the kitchen table," Dillon replied.

"It was the only clue we had." Nick wanted her back in his arms, feeling her heart beat against his own once again.

"She knocked on the back door…wanted me to come with her, but something wasn't right. She grabbed me and I fought her," she said. "I must have somehow pulled the name tag off her in the struggle."

She leaned weakly against Nick's side. "I think I was dead." She looked up at him. "I think I died and you breathed life back into me." She winced and raised a hand to her throat.

"No more talking," Nick said firmly. "You need to rest your throat."

"I just want to get out of here," she whispered. "I need to get away from here."

Nick looked at Dillon, who nodded and held out the keys to his patrol car. "Take her back to the ranch. I can get a statement from her tomorrow. I imagine my team and I will be busy here tonight collecting evidence, and I can catch a ride with one of them when we're done. I'll also get a ride to the ranch tomorrow to pick up my car and take an official statement."

"Then, we'll see you tomorrow," Nick replied, and together, he and Adrienne left the barn and headed back to the house in the distance.

"Should we have a doctor look at your throat?" he asked.

"I'm sure it will be fine," she rasped.

That was the last thing Nick said to her. He didn't want to force her to use her bruised and raw throat to reply.

They also didn't talk as they got into the patrol car and headed toward the Holiday Ranch. In the illumination from the dashboard, he could see that she was still pale, obviously still shaken up by what had occurred.

She needed time to distance herself from the horror and healing sleep that hopefully wouldn't contain any nightmares from the terrifying events.

He wanted to go inside the house with her, crawl into bed with her and hold her while she slept. He wanted to be her nightmare slayer and her wound healer, but he knew that wasn't possible—at least not long term.

While tonight had shown him an insight as to just how much he loved her, he still wasn't willing to take his heart out and give it to her. He loved her, but she would never know how he felt about her. There was no point because in his mind nothing had changed.

She was better off without him. He wasn't good enough for her. He wasn't good enough for anyone.

Despite everything Cass had done for him, he was still that little boy abandoned by his mother, he was still that young man who had watched Michelle walk away.

When they reached the Holiday Ranch, Lucas was at the back door awaiting them. Nick led Adrienne from the car and up the stairs to the bedroom where she'd slept since moving into the house.

"Do you need help getting ready for bed?" he asked.

She shook her head, her eyes holding gratitude that let him know she was glad he'd come inside with her. She grabbed a nightgown from a drawer and then disappeared into the bathroom.

Nick pulled down the spread on her bed and turned on the lamp on the nightstand. Just because he didn't intend to have a future with her didn't mean he would completely abandon her tonight.

She'd been through a trauma few people experienced. She needed support and caring, and he planned to be by her side until she fell asleep.

She came back into the bedroom, her face scrubbed clean and shiny and clad in a green nightgown.

He gestured her into the bed and she slid beneath the sheet like a dutiful child. He pulled up a nearby chair next to her bed and sat.

"Thank God we found you," he said and tried to keep the depth of his emotion out of his voice. "Thank God it's over now and you're safe."

She nodded and raised a hand to touch her red neck.

"How about I get a cool cloth for you to put on your throat?" he asked.

She nodded again and he went into the bathroom and ran cold water over a clean washcloth. When it was soaking wet he wrung it out and then took it back into the bedroom.

Gently he laid it over her wounded throat and fought against the desire to press his lips to hers. He quickly sat in the chair once again.

"You have all the answers you need now to go home to Kansas City and build a happy life," he said.

Her gaze held his for a heart-stopping moment, and then she sighed wearily and closed her eyes.

Nick remained seated next to the bed long after he realized she'd fallen asleep. She had to know that he'd just basically told her goodbye.

The danger was over and the mystery solved. She was strong and independent and would be fine.

He just wondered how long it would take him to forget the woman who had blackened his eye and dented a heart he'd forgotten he owned.

Chapter 16

The next morning had been almost comical as Cassie, Nicolette and Sammy all tried to meet Adrienne's each and every need without making her say a word.

It was just after noon when Chief Bowie arrived to question her and fill in the details of what had happened the night before.

When she answered his questions, she realized her throat was still a little sore and raspy, but the interview didn't take long, and after Dillon left Cassie insisted Adrienne not talk anymore.

It was hard to understand that kind of obsession, that kind of jealousy that would drive a woman to kill. Jenna had to have suffered some other form of mental illness in order to be so coldly capable of doing what she'd done.

Cassie fixed her a hot cup of tea and Adrienne sat at the table and stared out the window. Nick hadn't come to the house to check in on her, although the last thing she remembered before falling asleep the night before was him telling her she could return home and live a happy life.

Those words had made it clear to her that he was already distancing himself from her.

Nick. She had a feeling he'd haunt her far longer than she wanted him to. He would be a discordant chord in her heart, an unsung song in her soul for a very long time to come.

She turned away from the window with a sigh. All she had to do was get through the next couple of days, attend Nicolette's housewarming, and then she'd leave here and go back to Kansas City to rebuild her life.

The next couple of days were as long and as hard as she thought they would be. Nick kept his distance and she began a new grieving process—the grief over unrequited love.

Daisy stopped by to visit her on Friday, appalled at what Jenna had done. "I would have never guessed her to be so crazy, so wicked," she exclaimed. "I guess that just goes to show you that you can never tell about folks. I think maybe she went crazy after her parents died and she spent so much of her time alone in that house."

Adrienne didn't care what event had driven Jenna over the edge. She was only grateful Jenna was behind bars and wished that she'd been caught before she'd murdered Wendy.

By Saturday morning, Adrienne dreaded the housewarming party that afternoon. She knew Nick would be there. She'd see him and probably have to make small talk with him, and it would be another study in torture for her.

She was seated at the kitchen table nursing a cup of coffee when Cassie came into the room. She poured herself a cup of the brew and then joined Adrienne at the table.

"I have to admit, it's going to be darned lonely around here with Lucas, Nicolette and Sammy moved into their new house and now you leaving, as well. Are you sure you don't want to stick around here a little longer?"

"I can't." She cast her gaze out the window where she could see the men on horseback, but they were too far away for her to pick out the one who had stolen her heart.

"You fit here," Cassie said. "Your sister is buried here. From what I understand, you can work from anywhere. Why not stick around and be my friend?" Cassie grinned.

Adrienne tried to smile back, but it crumpled before it fully formed on her lips. "I can't stay here because I'm in love with Nick." The confession tumbled out of her mouth unbidden. "And he doesn't love me back. He told me so."

"Oh, Adrienne, I'm so sorry."

Tears formed in Adrienne's eyes, and she quickly raised her coffee cup to her lips. She took a drink, and by that time, she'd managed to stanch her tears. "You don't always pick the person you fall in love with. It just happens. It happened for me, but it didn't happen for Nick." She shrugged. "That's just reality."

"I've never been in love," Cassie said. "I've always been so obsessed with my shop in New York and my artwork that romance had no place in my life. It still doesn't."

"Apparently it isn't anything for me, either," Adrienne replied. "I have no desire to seek any kind of a relationship with anyone else ever again."

"You can't let Nick determine what your future might hold. There might be a Prince Charming just waiting around the next corner," Cassie said optimistically.

Adrienne managed a wry smile. "And I'm sure at the corner I'll turn the wrong way and miss him." She took another sip of her coffee. "I'm fine, really. I just feel sorry for Nick. I think he truly cares about me, but he's just too damaged, too afraid to trust."

"That's the thing about all the cowboys who work here. They've all been damaged by their childhoods and time spent on the streets. My aunt Cass made them into good men, but she couldn't heal the old wounds that linger inside each one of them."

"It's just sad that so many good men will never know the joy of loving and being loved."

"Love is overrated," Cassie said. "As long as you have passion in your life, then you can be just fine by yourself. I have passion for my paintings and for owning a successful shop."

"What about this ranch?"

Cassie frowned. "Since you're leaving town, I'll tell you a little secret. My plan is to sell the ranch and get back to my life in New York City. None of the men know that, and I would prefer they don't until I tell them. I thought I was going to be able to get out of here when we finished putting up a new shed."

"And then the bodies were found," Adrienne said.

Cassie nodded. "And now this place is a crime scene, and I don't know how long it's going to take to resolve things so that I can finally get back to where I belong."

"Since I've known you, it has always looked as though you belonged here," Adrienne observed.

"I'm doing the best I can for the ranch and men while I'm here, but sooner or later I'll be back in the city," she replied firmly. She checked the clock. "I think I'll head upstairs and start getting ready for the housewarming party. You can ride with me, and I'm planning on leaving around quarter till two."

"I'll be ready," Adrienne assured her. After Cassie left the kitchen, Adrienne finished her coffee, rinsed her cup and put it into the dishwasher and then headed upstairs to change her clothes.

Today she would see Nick. She hadn't seen him since the night he had breathed life into her body, held her as if she was his entire world. That moment when she'd taken a breath and opened her eyes, she'd seen love pouring out of him. In her heart she believed he loved her, but that didn't make the way things were ending any different.

He'd cared for her that night when Jenna had tried to kill her. There had been love in his touch, in his eyes, but his words had reiterated to her that there was no future with him. She knew he'd asked about her welfare over the past week. Lucas had told her, but he hadn't attempted to try to see or speak with her.

Today she would see him, and it would be the last time she'd ever see him again.

She dressed in an emerald-green-and-white sundress, knowing that the cinched waist complemented her figure. If this was going to be the last time Nick saw her, then she wanted to give him a final vision to remember.

She went a little heavy on the mascara, lengthening her already long lashes. A faint wisp of eye shadow, a bit of blush and light glossy lipstick finished her cosmetic application.

White sandals with a small heel and green-and-white earrings finished the look she wanted to achieve. She knew she looked feminine and pretty and she also knew it wouldn't make a difference to Nick, but it was her armor against him, and hopefully a taunting last look at what he was willfully rejecting.

"Nice," Cassie said as she came down the stairs and into the living room, where Cassie was dressed and ready to go.

"Back at you," Adrienne replied. Cassie also wore a sundress, a deep blue that enhanced the color of her eyes. "Shall we?" She stood and grabbed her purse. "I had Sawyer bring the car around to the back door. He'll ride with some of the other cowboys to the party."

Adrienne smiled and shook her head. "I think if I was here for months I still wouldn't know which name went with what cowboy."

Cassie laughed. "It took me about a month of

daily interaction to finally get them straight." The two walked out the back door and got into the sedan that had once belonged to Cassie's aunt Cass.

"I can't believe Nicolette and Lucas won't be around anymore, but I've never seen the two of them so happy. And Sammy is over the moon at the idea of Lucas becoming his new dad," Cassie said, and turned onto the road just outside the ranch entrance.

"I can't wait to see how the house has all come together. The last time I saw it I was painting a bedroom wall, but there were still lots of things to get done. Have you seen the place they bought?"

"I've been over there several times since they bought it. It's a nice spread with plenty of land for Lucas to ranch. Knowing Nicolette, everything will be beautiful today. She has great taste and will have filled the house to exude warmth and love."

Warmth and love. Adrienne wondered what that would feel like. She'd come to Bitterroot looking for a murderer, and while she'd accomplished what she'd come here for, falling in love with Nick certainly hadn't been in her plans.

When they reached the attractive ranch house, the driveway was already filled with vehicles, including a familiar gray Jeep. Adrienne steeled herself for an encounter with Nick, and her stomach tied into a knot as Cassie parked along the side of the road.

Just get through the afternoon.

That was her only thought as she and Cassie left the car and approached the house. All she had to do was stay pleasant and not show anyone, especially Nick, her broken heart.

Tomorrow morning she'd be gone, making the long drive back to Kansas City with only memories of her sister and the cowboy of interest who had stolen her heart along with the dream of a happily-ever-after she'd never known she'd possessed.

Nick knew the moment she entered the house, although he initially didn't see her. It was like a sixth sense that fired off in his head, a sudden shift in the energy that set him on edge.

Nick and a couple of the other cowboys were in the open, airy kitchen, where a spread of food had been laid out on the big wooden table.

Lucas and Nicolette were busy being door greeters to the variety of people they had invited to share in their happiness. Nicolette had done an amazing job decorating the house with furnishings that were warm and welcoming.

Sammy had excitedly shown Nick his room, complete with bunk beds, cowboy-patterned curtains and matching bedspreads. Built-in bookshelves held a variety of toys, books and figurines of cowboys.

At the moment the last thing on his mind was the cute little-boy bedroom. All of his senses were filled with Adrienne. He heard both her and Cassie's voices and knew that Sammy was probably giving them the tour of the bedrooms. It wouldn't be long before Sammy would bring them into the kitchen.

He didn't want to see Adrienne again.

He was desperate to see her again.

He'd consciously kept away from her all week long, and it had been the longest week of his entire life.

He'd wondered how she was dealing with the aftermath of nearly being strangled to death. Had she finally gotten the peace she needed where her sister's murder was concerned?

Each meal he took in the cowboy dining room had felt strange. He should have been seated across from Adrienne, watching those eyes of hers changing colors with her mood and her clothing choice, waiting for the gift of one of her gorgeous smiles.

Each night as he sat alone in his bunk, he thought of the nights he'd sat in the moonlight with her, talking about ridiculous things like aliens and what life might be on other planets. The sound of her laughter rang in his ears when he least expected it, making him feel as if he was going slowly insane.

He'd asked Lucas every day how she was doing and had even found himself doing chores that kept him close to the house on the chance he might get a glimpse of her.

"Earth to Nick." Dusty's voice pulled him out of his thoughts. "I said you should try these little bacon-wrapped cheesy things. They're so good."

Dusty picked up another of the appetizers speared with the colored toothpicks and popped it into his mouth and then threw the toothpick in a nearby trash can. "We've got to get this recipe for Cookie."

"Nicolette will skin you alive if you stand there and eat the whole tray before the rest of the guests arrive," Nick replied. "And I have a feeling taking a recipe to Cookie would be like asking for a meat cleaver in the back of your head."

Dusty laughed.

And then she was there, standing hesitantly in the kitchen doorway. She was a vision in green and white, and Nick's heart slammed hard against his ribs at the sight of her. Her hair hung in soft waves, and her glossy lips begged for a kiss.

"Hi, Forest, Dusty and Nick." She spoke first, and Nick was glad because, for a moment just looking at her, he'd completely lost his ability to speak.

"Hey, Adrienne," Dusty replied. "You've got to try these bacon-cheesy things, they're awesome."

"Actually, Nicolette said something about punch."

Forest pointed to a large cut-glass punch bowl and matching dainty cups on the nearby counter. "It's pink. I'm always leery of drinking anything pink," he said.

Adrienne's small laugh sounded forced, and she didn't look at Nick as she headed for the counter, although he was acutely aware of her. She ladled herself a cup of the pink punch, close enough to him that he could smell her familiar scent. She quickly left the room without Nick saying a word to her.

He cursed himself for his silence. He'd felt the tension emanating from her, and he could have at least broken that tension by uttering a simple pleasantry.

He grabbed one of the little bites that Dusty had talked about, pulled it off the toothpick and popped it into his mouth. He chewed without tasting and wondered why the mere sight of her had set off an ache deep in his heart.

The scent of her lingered in the room, like a haunting refrain of a song he couldn't quite get out of his head. She'd told him she loved him, and he'd rejected that love. He'd not only rejected her, but also his own feelings for her.

Tomorrow she would be home, and the time she'd spent in Bitterroot would eventually fade. The feelings she thought she'd had for him would also fade until he was just a distant memory of a cowboy who had helped her out in her time of need.

In the next hour, more of the cowboys from the ranch arrived and found their way to the kitchen, where they ate the goodies and shot the bull. Several of the waitresses from the café joined the party, and Nicolette appeared to refill the food trays.

Finally, Nick could stand it no longer. He had to find Adrienne. He needed to talk to her. He wanted one last conversation with her before she left in the morning.

He found her in the living room seated on the plush brown leather sofa and chatting with Daisy. "Excuse me," he said, interrupting their conversation. "Adrienne, I was wondering if I could talk to you for a minute."

Her eyes narrowed slightly…wary yet curious. "Okay," she replied and got up from her seat.

He looked around the crowded room. "How about the back porch?"

"Go on, honey," Daisy said. "I see a lot of people I can be a nuisance to." She got up and patted Adrienne on the shoulder and shoved her closer to Nick.

Nick led Adrienne to the back porch, where a cushioned two-seater glider invited them to sit. They each sat on opposite ends, the space between them indicative of the state of their relationship.

"I…uh…I just wanted to know if you were okay," he said. "I mean, after everything that happened to you. How are you doing?"

She stared straight ahead, not looking at him. "I'm fine. I finally have peace where Wendy is concerned, and tonight I'll be packing up the car to leave in the morning." She could have been talking to a stranger, her tone was so stilted and formal.

"I'll bet you'll be glad to get away from the red dust of Oklahoma and all of us cowboys," he said, hoping to see just a hint of a smile curve her lips.

"Actually, I love it here, red dust and cowboys included. It would be easy for me to call Bitterroot my home, but I can't stay here." She turned to look at him, and her eyes were a dark storm of swirling greens and blues. "I can't stay here because of you."

This time it was Nick who broke eye contact with her and gazed straight ahead, his heart twisted and tight in his chest. "I'm sorry I can't give you what you need."

"And I'm sorry you won't take what *you* need," she replied. "I love you, Nick, and I believe if you could just let go of your past, look forward instead of backward, you'd realize you love me, too."

She stood abruptly, causing the glider to swing beneath him, and he looked up at her. "You were my demon slayer when you rescued me from Jenna. I could be your demon slayer if only you'd allow me in. I love you like nobody else ever has, like nobody else ever will."

Her eyes swam with unshed tears, with an emotion so intense he felt it inside his heart, straight to his very soul. "From everything I've heard about Cass Holiday, she took in a dozen broken boys and turned them into upstanding, strong men. I think that someplace inside of you there's still an eight-year-old little boy watching his mother walk away from him. Until you make peace with that inner child, you'll never really know real happiness, true love."

She spun around and disappeared back into the house, leaving Nick alone and recognizing that he was a fool, but unwilling to change the inevitable absence of Adrienne from his life.

Chapter 17

Adrienne sat on the edge of the bed as early-morning sunshine danced through the windows. She felt empty. Yesterday she'd spoken all the words she'd had in her heart to Nick, and nothing had changed. She hadn't really expected things to change, but she'd hoped, and now that last modicum of hope was gone. Today, she'd leave the Holiday Ranch and never return to Bitterroot.

Even though Wendy rested here, Adrienne would probably never return to visit her gravesite. She had the precious bluebird that would serve as her memory of the precocious child she had raised into a beautiful, kind young woman.

She'd return home and try to find a new normal for her life, a life that might include making new friends and stepping out of her comfort zone. She'd certainly done that here. From the moment she had punched Nick in his eye to her heartfelt words the day before, she'd been out of her comfort zone.

Looking at the clock on the nightstand, she saw that it was just after seven. Cassie had promised that she'd eat breakfast with her around eight before she left for the long drive home.

She stood and stripped the bed, feeling guilty that she would be leaving Cassie sheets that needed to be washed and put back on the bed, but Cassie had insisted she'd take care of the bedding. After that, Adrienne headed for the shower.

She stood beneath the spray of water and found herself suddenly crying. Weakly, she leaned against the side of the glass enclosure and wept for Nick, and wept for herself and the love she had found but had never truly possessed.

Her body ached for his arms around her. Her arms hurt with the need to embrace him and hold him tight. She wanted to watch his eyes go from light to dark blue depending on his mood, see that sexy lip slide that made up his smile.

But it wasn't to be. And that was why she cried. For the first time since realizing the depth of her love for Nick, she now felt the depth of the pain of her heartbreak.

She finally managed to pull herself together and get out of the shower and dress for the day of driving in a comfy pair of jeans and a sky-blue T-shirt. All she had to carry downstairs was a small overnight bag.

She dropped the bag at the bottom of the staircase and followed the scent of coffee into the kitchen.

Cassie stood at the stove, clad in a blue robe and flipping strips of bacon in a skillet.

"Good morning," Adrienne said.

Cassie jumped and whirled around, a fork held in her hand. "You scared me! And it's not a good morning. My best friend in the whole world has left me to live with her man and now my new best friend is going away, as well."

"And you'll be just fine." Adrienne walked to the counter and poured herself a cup of coffee.

"Of course I'll be fine, but that doesn't mean I won't be lonely."

Adrienne laughed. "Anytime you get lonely, just step outside your back door and holler for a cowboy. I know Adam would be here in a flash for whatever you might need."

Cassie's cheeks grew pink, and she turned back to face the stove. "Adam is a nice man, and I know he's here for me. I like him a lot, but I don't feel any real spark with him." She forked the bacon out of the skillet and onto a paper towel on a plate. "Of course, I'm not looking for sparks with anyone. Eggs scrambled or over easy?"

"Whatever is easiest for you." Adrienne sat at the table and watched the woman who had become her friend. "I don't know how I'll ever be able to thank you for everything you've done for me since I've been here."

"It was my pleasure," Cassie replied. "I've loved having you here."

Minutes later they sat together to eat, and Cassie told her about the shop she owned in New York and the painting that was her passion.

"Once the ranch is sold, I'll have the money to get a bigger storefront and really make my passion a success," she said.

"And what happens to everyone here when you sell?" Adrienne asked, thinking of all the wonderful men she'd met who worked on the ranch.

Cassie frowned. "I'm hoping to find a buyer who would be willing to keep the men here working. They're all good men, and they've worked together for a long time. They'd be a real asset to anyone who buys the ranch."

"That would be nice." Adrienne thought of how Nick thought of his fellow cowboys as brothers. It would be tragic if he lost the only family he'd known since first arriving at the ranch when he'd been a teenager.

All too quickly breakfast was over and the dishes were put away, and it was time for Adrienne to say goodbye. She was grateful when she walked outside to her car that there was no sign of Nick. Her heart couldn't stand seeing him one last time. She didn't need an official goodbye from him.

She placed her overnight bag in the trunk, closed it and then turned to hug Cassie. "We won't lose touch. We can call or email each other," Adrienne said.

The two women broke apart and Adrienne got into her car and rolled down the driver's window.

"And we will stay in touch," Cassie promised. "Drive carefully, Adrienne."

Adrienne nodded, and with a wave, she started down the long lane that would take her off Holiday property and onto the road that headed home.

As she turned onto the main road, she glanced in

her rearview mirror, and her heart stuttered as her foot fell off the gas petal.

Behind her, riding hell-bent for leather, was a familiar cowboy on a big black horse and wearing his black cowboy hat. He looked like a villain in a Western movie, but he was the man who owned her heart, and he was waving at her to pull over.

Her initial thought was to step on the gas and leave him behind, but her foot didn't listen to her brain. Heart pounding, she pulled to the side of the road and rolled to a stop.

What on earth was he doing? Did he just want to give her a final goodbye? Did he just want to torture her one last time before she got away?

He pulled his horse up behind the car and then dismounted and approached her door. She rolled down her window and gazed up at him, wary of what to expect.

"You had your say yesterday and now I want to have my say," he said. "Will you please get out of the car and talk to me?"

She stared down at the center of her steering wheel, unsure if she wanted to hear anything more that he had to say. If this was just an effort on his part to explain that he didn't love her or why he couldn't love her, she didn't want to hear it anymore. Even as she thought this, her hand went to the door handle and she opened her door.

She stepped out of the car and looked at him, finding it impossible to read his midnight eyes. "What is it, Nick? I think we've both said everything that needs to be said between us."

He tipped his hat back so that she could better see

his eyes, but still she couldn't read what was behind them, what he was thinking.

"I thought a lot about what you said to me yesterday at Nicolette's house," he said. "When I was eight years old and my mother walked away from me, I was helpless to stop her. When I was twenty-one and Michelle walked away from me, I didn't want to stop her because I knew she didn't love me."

He shifted from one foot to the other, looking suddenly vulnerable. "I woke up this morning and realized that this time I had the power to stop a woman from walking away from me, a woman who I love, a woman who I want and need in my life. That's why I stopped you, Adrienne. I'm not that little boy anymore. I'm a man ready to give my love to you, if you'll still have me. I love you, Adrienne."

She stood motionless and closed her eyes. "Say it again," she whispered.

"I love you, Adrienne, and I want you in my life forever."

She opened her eyes, and tears began to fall.

He looked utterly sick. "I'm too late, aren't I? I waited too long to tell you my true feelings," he said with a heaviness to his voice. "Please don't cry."

She half laughed, half sobbed. "You silly cowboy, these aren't tears because you're too late. They're tears of happiness," she exclaimed. "I love you, Nick Coleman."

His eyes shone with a light that came from within, the light of real happiness, of demons slain and a promise for the future. She gasped as he grabbed her and pulled her into an embrace that nearly took her breath away.

His lips took hers in a kiss that tasted of love found, of love cherished and a fire of passion that filled her soul. When the kiss finally ended, he gazed at her and stroked a finger down her cheek.

"How about I go to Kansas City with you and help you load up everything you own, and then we come back here?" he said. "I don't know what the immediate future looks like. We'll need to find a place to live, and I know I'd like to keep my job at the ranch."

She placed a finger over his lips. "We'll make it work. Whatever needs to be done, we'll figure it all out together."

His eyes were lighter blue and held a happiness she'd never seen there before. "Your sister tried to matchmake for me the whole time that I knew her." He stroked a hand down the length of her hair. "I think right now she's probably smiling down at us, pleased that in her death we found each other."

His words brought a new sense of peace to her heart. Yes, she thought, Wendy would be thrilled that the two people she loved had found love with each other.

Nick's lips claimed hers once again, and when they finally stopped kissing, he touched the tip of her nose in a loving gesture. "I don't know about you, but I'm ready to get this future started."

He released his hold on her and stepped to the back of the car, where his horse stood. "Raven, home." He hit the horse on its hindquarters, and the horse took off toward the ranch.

"Will she get back safely?" Adrienne asked worriedly.

"She's well trained. She'll go right back to the

stables, where Forest is waiting to unsaddle and take care of her," he replied.

She looked at him in surprise. "So you were that sure of what was going to happen between us before you came after me?"

His eyes darkened slightly. "I hoped...I prayed, and Forest knew that if Raven appeared at the stables riderless then I'd gotten my wish. He also knew if I was on Raven's back when I returned then my heart had been destroyed."

"Love never destroys hearts," she replied.

He nodded, his eyes bright again. "Now let's get going so we can get back here and really begin to build our lives together."

He got into the passenger side of her car, and she slid in behind the wheel, unable to believe the way things had turned out.

The love that filled her heart for him consumed her. The wounded little boy was gone, and next to her was the man she knew would be at her side through a lifetime. The person of interest in her sister's murder had become the cowboy of her heart.

Cassie sat on the back porch at twilight and watched as Dillon approached from the distance. He'd arrived only a few minutes earlier and had headed to the crime scene, she presumed to check in with Dr. Patience Forbes.

She could tell by the handsome lawman's walk that he was ticked off. She didn't know Dillon Bowie very well. Most of their interaction had been because of bad things happening on her ranch. But she did know him well enough to recognize that he was irritated.

He stepped up on the porch and sank down in the chair across from hers. "That woman is going to give me gray hair."

"I assume you're speaking of the illustrious doctor," she replied. "I haven't had any interaction with her yet."

"Be grateful. She's like a pit bull guarding a piece of fresh meat. She doesn't want me or anyone else anywhere near those bones. She needs a T-shirt that reads Does Not Play Well With Others, and she hasn't even moved one single bone from the hole in the ground where they were thrown."

Cassie sat up straighter in her chair in surprise. "Then, what has she been doing since she got here?"

"Taking pictures and working on her computer, diagramming the position of each and every bone. At this rate, we won't have any answers about the skeletons for a year."

"Don't even say that," Cassie exclaimed. The last thing she wanted was to be stuck here any longer than necessary. "At least the mystery of Wendy's murder was solved."

"And thankfully we figured it out before Adrienne became another victim," he replied. "Now all I have to do is solve six more murders and hope that in the meantime nothing else pops up to further complicate my life."

"I just want my ranch back," Cassie said.

"You do realize that every man on this ranch is a suspect in whatever happened to those people under the shed."

Cassie frowned. "My aunt Cass wouldn't have a man here who could be responsible for that."

Dillon stood, his gray eyes the color of steel. "It's my belief that somebody on this ranch or very near here is a serial killer. Time will tell who that might be. Good night, Cassie."

He left the porch and headed to his patrol car. Cassie shivered as she thought of his words. Was one of her men, the men she'd come to like and respect, really a serial killer?

She looked in the direction of the Humes Ranch. The bones were old, although she didn't know how old. Everyone knew that Raymond Humes and her aunt Cass had hated each other, but nobody seemed to know why.

Something evil had happened here on this land, and she could only hope that Dillon and Dr. Patience Forbes would be able to find the answers.

* * * * *

MILLS & BOON®

The Thirty List

At thirty, Rachel has slid down every ladder she has
ever climbed. Jobless, broke and ditched by her
husband, she has to move in with grumpy
Patrick and his four-year-old son.

Patrick is also getting divorced, so to cheer themselves up the two decide to draw up bucket lists.
Soon they are learning to tango, abseiling, trying
stand-up comedy and more. But, as she gets
closer to Patrick, Rachel wonders if their
relationship is too good to be true…

**Order yours today at
www.millsandboon.co.uk/Thethirtylist**

MILLS & BOON®
INTRIGUE
Romantic Suspense

A SEDUCTIVE COMBINATION OF DANGER AND DESIRE

A sneak peek at next month's titles…

In stores from 19th June 2015:

- **Surrendering to the Sheriff** – Delores Fossen *and*
  The Detective – Adrienne Giordano

- **Under Fire** – Carol Ericson *and*
  Leverage – Janie Crouch

- **Sheltered** – HelenKay Dimon *and*
  Lawman Protection – Cindi Myers

Romantic Suspense

- **How to Seduce a Cavanaugh** – Marie Ferrarella
- **Colton's Cowboy Code** – Melissa Cutler

Available at WHSmith, Tesco, Asda, Eason, Amazon and Apple

Just can't wait?
Buy our books online a month before they hit the shops!
visit www.millsandboon.co.uk

These books are also available in eBook format!